THE THINGS WE CHERISHED

BOV

Please return/renew this item
by the last date shown.
Books may also be renewed by
phone or the Internet.

Tel: 01253 478070
www.blackpool.gov.uk

3411400555528 8

THE THINGS WE CHERISHED

Roger Dykmans, a young university student, is living with his brother Hans, an international emissary who's secretly working against the Nazis. As time goes by, Roger finds himself increasingly drawn to Magda, Hans' Jewish wife. But their secret world is turned upside down when Magda and her young daughter, Anna, are arrested by the Nazis. The Gestapo make a deal with Roger and he is faced with an impossible decision – should he betray his brother to save the woman they both love?

THE THINGS WE CHERISHED

by

Pam Jenoff

Magna Large Print Books
Long Preston, North Yorkshire,
BD23 4ND, England.

British Library Cataloguing in Publication Data.

Jenoff, Pam
    The things we cherished.

    A catalogue record of this book is
    available from the British Library

    ISBN   978-0-7505-3628-8

First published in Great Britain by Sphere in 2011

Copyright © 2011 by Pam Jenoff

Cover illustration © Yolande de Kort by arrangement with
Arcangel Images

Published in Large Print 2012 by arrangement with
Little, Brown Book Group

Magna Large Print is an imprint of Library Magna Books Ltd.

Printed and bound in Great Britain by
T.J. (International) Ltd., Cornwall, PL28 8RW

0555528

For my girls,
Charlotte & Elizabeth

One

PHILADELPHIA, 2009

'You know, don't you, that you're looking at twenty-five to life?' Charlotte peered over the top of the file at the seventeen-year-old with the rows of tiny braids who slouched in the chair on the other side of the graffiti-covered table, staring intently at his sneakers.

The preliminary hearing had not gone well. Charlotte had hoped that the judge would take one look at Marquan's baby face, with its wide smooth cheeks and the unblinking almond-shaped eyes, and know that he was not a danger to anyone, that he did not belong here. She thought that Judge Annette D'Amici, who herself had once been a public defender, might have a soft spot for a teenager with no record of prior violence who was about the same age as her grandchildren. But in a streak of phenomenally bad luck, Judge D'Amici had called in sick, replaced for the day by Paul Rodgers. Rodgers, a political wannabe who viewed the bench as a stepping-stone to a higher state office, had earned a reputation as a hanging judge during his first term. He barely glanced at Marquan before banging his gavel and remanding him to the juvenile wing of the city prison.

Normally, Charlotte would have chalked the hearing up as a loss and gone on to her next file

11

and courtroom, dispensing with the morning's caseload. But Marquan was different. They had met almost two years earlier when he'd been a scared fifteen-year-old brought in on a petty drug charge. There was a sparkle that told her he had intelligence, a quiet dignity in his perfect posture and the way he looked at her with those somber brown eyes, seeming to see right through. He had promise. She'd done all the things she usually didn't get to do with a docket of thousands of cases per year: getting Marquan into a first-time offenders' track that left him with no permanent record, as well as an after-school mentoring program in his neighborhood. So why was he sitting here now, dull-eyed and hardened, facing a murder charge for a carjacking gone wrong?

Because it simply wasn't enough. The after-school programs amounted to only a few hours per week, a drop in an ocean of poverty and drugs and violence and boredom in which these kids had to swim every night on the streets. There had been a police chase that ended with an SUV crushed against the pavement steps of a row house, two small children pinned fatally beneath its wheels. Marquan hadn't meant to hurt anyone; of that she was certain. He had a little brother the same age as those kids, whom he walked to school every day, escorted home again each evening. No, he had simply been along for the ride when the stupid plan was hatched and he didn't have the strength or good sense to say no.

Charlotte drummed the edge of the table, running her fingers along a heart that someone had carved into the wood with a knife. 'If you would testify,' she began. There had been three boys in the car, but Marquan was the only one who had not fled the scene. 'I mean, if you're willing to say who was there with you...'

She did not finish the sentence, knowing the proposal was futile. No one talked where Marquan came from. *DON'T SNITCH!* screamed the brazen T-shirts of the kids she passed in the Gallery food court at lunch, kids ditching school and hanging out, waiting for trouble to find them. Snitching meant never going home again, never closing your eyes and knowing if you or your loved ones would be safe. Marquan would sooner take the sentence.

She exhaled sharply, glancing up at the water-stained ceiling. 'Anything you want to tell me?' she asked, closing the file, watching for the imperceptible shake of his head. 'If you change your mind, or if you need something, have your case officer call me.' She pushed back from the table and stood, knocking on the door to be let out.

A few minutes later, Charlotte stepped from the elevator and made her way across the lobby of the Criminal Justice Center, thronged with prospective jurors and families of the victims and the accused who pushed past the metal detector toward the security desk for information. On the street, she swam through a cloud of cigarette smoke left by courthouse clerks lingering before the start of their day, then paused, her eyes traveling left toward the hulking Reading Terminal Market. A walk through the open stalls, a gastronomic world's fair touting everything from Amish delicacies to lo mein and cheesesteaks, would have been

13

just the thing to clear her head, but there wasn't time.

As she reached the busy intersection beneath the shadow of City Hall, William Penn peering down piously from his perch atop the tower, Charlotte paused, inhaling the crisp late-September air. There were only a few days like this each fall in Philadelphia, before the persistent humidity of summer gave way to the cold rainy winter.

Still thinking of Marquan, Charlotte entered the office building. On the sixth floor, she stepped out of the elevator and proceeded down the drab corridor. The voice of section chief Mitch Ramirez, arguing with a prosecutor, bellowed through an open doorway. 'Are you going to fucking tell me...?' Charlotte smiled as she passed. Mitch was a legend among the defenders, a seventy-two-year-old dinosaur who had marched in the civil rights protests of the sixties and could still go toe to toe with the best of them when he thought his client was getting a raw deal.

She stopped before the door to her office, indiscernible from the others she had just passed. It wasn't much; a glorified closet, really, with a small desk and two chairs wedged close together – a far cry from the marble and mahogany suite she'd had when she was a summer associate at a large New York firm. But it was all hers. It had taken two years just to get it, to fight her way out of the pit of rookie defenders who shared the sea of cubicles one floor below and have a door that closed so she could hear herself think.

Charlotte reached for the handle, then stopped, studying it. The door was ajar. She was certain

14

that she had closed it when she left for court that morning, but perhaps one of the other attorneys had dropped off a file. As she stepped inside, her breath caught.

There, in the narrow chair across from her desk, sat her ex-boyfriend.

'Brian?' she asked, as though unsure of his name. The word came out in a croak.

He stood, unfolding from the chair. Brian had the tall, broad-shouldered frame that fashion houses paid good money for, brown hair that flopped improbably to his forehead no matter how many times he got it cut to a shorter, more professional length. Despite the muscular arms that suggested a threat on the basketball court, he conveyed an air of vulnerability that implied he might cry at a chick flick and made women want to take care of him.

Looking at him now, it was almost possible to forget that he had broken her heart.

'Hello, Charlotte,' he said, his use of her full name a reminder of the years that had come and gone since their last meeting. He bent to kiss her and a hint of his familiar Burberry cologne tickled her nose, sending her places she had hoped never to go again. 'You're looking well.' He brushed off his legs, his expensive suit woefully out of place in her tiny drab office. She was suddenly self-conscious about her black knit pantsuit, practical and unflattering. His Chanel-and-heels wife would not have been caught dead in it.

He waited for her to speak, then filled the silence when she did not. 'I didn't mean to startle you. Your secretary let me in.'

She did not, Charlotte reminded herself, have a secretary. He must have been referring to Doreen, the office admin. Doreen was usually too busy updating her Facebook page to help visitors, but it was easy to see how Brian might have charmed her into unlocking the office and letting him wait. She studied him again. There was a paunch that bespoke too many overpriced steakhouse dinners, missed visits to the racquet club he once frequented daily. But he still had that appeal that had sucked her in almost a decade ago – that had gotten her in trouble in the first place.

She took a deep breath, centered herself. 'What are you doing here?'

His expression changed as he processed the new rules of the game: pleasantries were to be dispensed with, business stated. 'I'm in town for work and I was hoping to talk to you about something.'

You've left Danielle, she thought suddenly. Realized after all these years that you made a fatal mistake, that I was the one. The scenario rushed through her head: his profuse apologies and tears, her eventual gracious acceptance and forgiveness. It would be messy, of course. There was the divorce, the question of whether to reside here or in New York. 'About a case I'm working on,' he added.

The vision evaporated, a raindrop on a warm, humid day, so quickly gone she might have imagined it. So this isn't about us after all, she thought, feeling very foolish. Brian wanted something, but it wasn't her.

'Let me buy you lunch?' he asked.

She shook her head. Thirty seconds around

16

Brian and he was already toying with her mind. She needed to get as far away from him as possible. 'I can't. I'm due back in court in half an hour.'

'Of course. Dinner then. Does six work?' She could see him calculating the time that the meal might take, whether he could make the nine o'clock train back to Manhattan. Back to Danielle. Her stomach twisted, the bile undiluted by the years.

For a second she considered taking back an ounce of the control that had been stolen from her all those years ago and declining his last-minute invitation. She might have plans after all. Usually they consisted of nothing more than Thai takeout in front of the television, a hot night of *CSI* reruns with her cat, Mitzi, but he didn't have to know that. Her curiosity was piqued, though. Did Brian really have business in Philadelphia or had he come all this way just to see her? And what on earth could it be about?

'All right,' she replied, trying to sound casual.

'Buddakan?' The choice was an obvious out-of-towner selection, one of the pricey Stephen Starr restaurants that received national attention and spawned a clone of the venue in New York. The furthest thing possible from the quiet BYOBs she loved, like the Northern Italian one in Greenwich Village they had frequented as students, its name faded with the years.

She considered suggesting an alternative venue like Santori's, a Greek trattoria in her neighborhood, with its gorgeous hummus plate and complimentary ouzo shot at the end of the meal. But

17

this was not a social call and she didn't need Brian invading that part of her world. 'Fine.'

'I'll let you work then,' he said, walking from the office, not looking back. That was Brian. He treated life like a movie set – when he left a scene, the lights went out and it simply ceased to exist.

It was not until the door closed behind him that she sank to the chair, trying not to shake.

They had met during law school while interning with the war crimes tribunal at The Hague, assisting with the prosecution of genocide in the former Yugoslavia. She could still remember walking into the tiny Dutch bar, and seeing Brian for the first time. He was holding court amidst a semicircle of other interns, mostly female. She'd stood there for several seconds, staring at him in spite of herself. Though she could not hear what he was saying, there was something in the way he spoke that captivated her, a confident manner that seemed larger than life. His head turned in her direction. Embarrassed, she started to look away, but then his gaze caught hers and she was paralyzed, unable to move.

A minute later, he broke from his minions and made his way to Charlotte, holding out a second beer as though he'd been waiting for her. 'Brian Warrington.'

'Charlotte Gold,' she managed, trying not to stammer.

'I know. You're the Root Tilden from NYU, right?' She hesitated, taken aback. She had not expected him to know who she was or that she'd received the prestigious public-interest fellowship. 'I'm at Columbia. I think we're both ass-

18

igned to the Dukovic case. Your memo ⌐
evidentiary issue was very impressive.' She †
the urge to swoon. 'I'd like to get your take ᴏ.. ᴠ..ᴇ
of my witnesses.' Just then, the jazz band that had
been setting up in the corner started to play and
the voices around them were raised to a din.
'There's a little bistro just down the street that's
quieter. Want to go get something to eat?' Too surprised to answer, Charlotte nodded and followed
him from the bar, feeling the stares of the other
interns behind her.

After that, they were inseparable. They fell in
love over Belgian beer and heated debates about
the efficacy of the proposed International Criminal Court. When they returned to Manhattan that
fall, she abandoned her Greenwich Village dorm
room, accepting his invitation to move into his
Upper West Side apartment.

Though it had not been obvious from their egali-
tarian Dutch housing, she quickly realized once
back home that Brian was wealthy. She found
herself swept along to warm fall weekends in the
Hamptons, holidays at his parents' estate in Chap-
paqua. She spent less time at school, traveling
downtown only for classes. They made plans for
after graduation, fellowships with the UN, a short
engagement.

Her idyllic world came crashing to a halt in
December when she traveled to Philadelphia for
what was supposed to be a brief holiday visit with
her mother, Winnie, a retired math teacher. The
first morning over breakfast, her mother broke
the news that she had been keeping until after
Charlotte finished final exams: small-cell lung

cancer brought on, she suspected, by a smoking habit abandoned years earlier. By the time the persistent cough she'd taken to be allergies had sent her for a chest X-ray it was too late – she was stage four and had just months to live.

Winnie refused to let her take the semester off, so Charlotte commuted back and forth every weekend on Amtrak, watching with disbelief the speed with which her once-strong mother deteriorated. Brian offered to come along, of course, but she always declined, embarrassed to have him see the tiny suburban condo with its dilapidated furniture and yellowed walls. He didn't fight her on it but retreated gracefully, glad to be excused from the messiness of a life not his own. The time apart and her constant worry began to take its toll on their relationship and by March, when her mother had been discharged a final time to hospice care, Charlotte returned to New York to find a strange tube of lipstick beneath the vanity in the bathroom. Later she would wonder if perhaps he left it there purposely, a final act of passive-aggressiveness designed to hasten things to their inevitable conclusion.

She had confronted him that gray afternoon, hoping for denial or at least an explanation, ready to forgive. It was a day still damp and chilly enough to be called winter, their breath foggy in front of them as they clutched Styrofoam cups of coffee that neither actually drank. He looked down at the bench in the southeast corner of Washington Square Park that they had shared in happier times, now defiled because it would always be remembered for this. His face seemed a caricature of itself, drawn and weak. As he started to talk, she braced herself for the platitudes, that they had grown apart, it was just one of those things.

'I've met someone,' he said bluntly.

A rock slammed into her stomach. 'Her name's Danielle,' he continued. 'She went to Harvard, two years ahead of us.' Of course. Because she couldn't have been someone vacuous and trite. An image flashed through her mind of the holiday party at the firm where Brian was clerking this year. Through the haze of worry and despair over her mother, Charlotte recalled a sleek blond junior associate, a conversation about summer houses to which she could not at all relate.

'I'm sorry,' he finished. There were a thousand questions she wanted to ask about why and when and how. But he was already throwing his cup in the trash and straightening his coat, eager to move on to this new chapter of his life.

Three weeks later, she would learn the rest of the story. She opened the Sunday *Times* over breakfast and saw the engagement announcement, the happy couple staring back at her, Danielle's smile wider and more perfect than she remembered. She was flooded with disbelief. In the weeks since Brian told her about his new relationship, Charlotte had consoled herself over pints of Häagen-Dazs and bottles of wine, telling herself that it was nothing serious. Danielle was just the rebound until he figured things out. But in that moment, the truth came home to roost: Brian and Danielle were engaged. How long had they been seeing each other behind her back?

Unable to look away, she forced herself to continue reading. And somewhere between learning that Brian's grandfather had been CEO of a Fortune 250 company and that the bride would be keeping her name, she felt a sudden sense of release, like the air being let out of a balloon. She was relieved to have been excused from a world where she did not belong, a student given permission to change majors or drop a class that was too hard.

Giving up the rest was easy after that, and she turned down the fellowship to The Hague that she had been scheduled to start after graduation. Instead, she applied for and got the public defender position, returning to Philadelphia and slipping into the city like a pair of comfy old shoes.

That night at five minutes to six, Charlotte stepped out of a cab at Third and Chestnut and glanced down the street in both directions. Old City, once the province of Ben Franklin and the Founding Fathers, was now Philadelphia's version of trendy and she seldom ventured down to the endless rows of hip bars and restaurants that maligned the Federalist architecture of the neighborhood. Two blocks west, laughter spilled over from the throngs of tourists departing Independence Hall and the Liberty Bell as they boarded their motor coaches for home. A swath of parkland across the street sat in improbable late-day stillness, sunlight slatting through the crisp leaves.

Charlotte paused, wishing she'd been able to override her normal tendencies and arrive casually late. For a minute she considered circling the block, stalling for time to compose herself. But there was no point in delaying the inevitable – the sooner she met with Brian, the sooner she could put him and his devilish green eyes back on that train to New York.

As she approached the restaurant, she studied her reflection in the glass window of an adjacent store, smoothing her shoulder-length brown hair. There hadn't been time to go home – the modest Queen Village townhouse she'd bought before the neighborhood had become fashionable was a thirty-five-minute walk from the office, pleasant enough on a nice day, but too far in the wrong direction to make it before dinner. So after work she had stopped in Macy's, the city's one surviving department store. Resisting the urge to buy a new outfit entirely, she settled instead for a crème silk blouse to replace the knit top she'd worn previously under her suit and some make-up and perfume from samples at the Clinique counter.

Inside, Charlotte lingered uncertainly by the reservation desk, adjusting her eyes to the dimmer lighting. The Asian fusion restaurant was a cavernous sea of tables, walls draped in red silk, a massive gold Buddha statue dominating one side of the room. A dozen or more chefs bustled behind clouds of steam in the open kitchen to the rear. At the bar to the left, young twenty-somethings tried to impress one another over brightly colored ten-dollar cocktails.

'Can I help you?' the hostess asked without interest. Charlotte did not answer but scanned the room, spotting Brian at a table to the rear. That was unexpected; early was not his style, the notion of waiting for others unpalatable to him. As she approached, he stood, hurriedly tucking a Black-Berry into his jacket pocket.

'Thanks for joining me,' he said, sounding like he meant it.

She studied the menu the waitress handed her as she sat, grateful for the reprieve. 'Grey Goose martini, up, extra olives,' she said. She did not usually drink hard liquor on a work night, but the circumstances called for an exception.

'Same,' he said, surprising her again. Brian was strictly a beer drinker, or had been anyway.

'So you're in town for a case?' she asked when the waitress had returned with their drinks and taken their dinner order, a lobster pad thai for her, sesame tuna for him. He did not, she noticed, order an appetizer, further evidence of his hurry to get back to New York and Danielle. Pain stabbed at her stomach as she relived the rejection of a decade ago all over again. But she had not asked for this meeting, she reminded herself; he wanted to see her. 'Depositions?' She was suddenly aware of her own Philadelphia accent, the way she seemed to have gone vocally native again in the years since she had returned.

'Just passing through,' he replied, his own pro-nunciation devoid of geographical markings. 'I had a meeting in Washington this morning.' He was usually so precise, but there was a vagueness now to his words that made her wonder if he was telling the truth. Had he come down from New York just to speak with her?

'How have you been?' he asked, and if the question was just a pleasantry, a necessary step to

24

get where he wanted to go, he gave no indication – his face and voice conveyed genuine curiosity. He had always had the ability to make anyone think he was on their side, sincerely concerned with their best interests – which was exactly what made him so dangerous. She had not suspected anything was wrong, until the very moment he told her he was leaving for someone else.

'Great,' she replied, a beat too quickly. She suddenly felt naked, exposed. 'I'm working with juveniles...' She almost tuned herself out as she rattled on, wearing her job like a cloak. But the work, about which she was usually so passionate, sounded provincial, unsophisticated. 'And you?'

'Fine. I just came off a two-month securities trial and we, that is, Dani...' He hesitated, as though for a moment he had forgotten the impropriety of speaking about his wife to the woman he had left for her. As though Charlotte were anyone. 'Anyway, a vacation would be nice. Maybe Aspen.'

Charlotte imagined the two of them swooshing through the powder in perfect unison. She had always been a train wreck on skis, a menace to herself and those around her. 'But then this new matter came up,' he added, as she took a large swallow of her drink, steeling herself. 'That's why I wanted to see you.'

'Me?' she blurted out, louder than intended, nearly choking on the liquid. Brian was a securities litigator, defending lawsuits for the biggest brokerage houses in the country. What kind of matter could he possibly want to discuss with her?

He took a sip of martini, grimacing. 'It's a pro bono matter.'

Charlotte faltered, caught off guard. Pro bono work had never been Brian's thing – he had empathy for the less fortunate on an abstract, policy level, a sort of noblesse oblige inherent in his liberal, upper-class background. But he couldn't deal with the messiness that surrounded the actual clientele, the ambiguity of the individual cases. What had he gotten himself into now? It must be something high profile, she decided, a death penalty case, perhaps. Her annoyance rose. Firms were taking those on with increasing frequency because of the good press that usually ensued. But despite their resources, they were ill equipped to handle matters requiring such specialized expertise. And now he was here asking her for free advice.

The waitress returned to the table and set a plate in front of Brian. The food was served family-style, Charlotte recalled from her one previous visit, which seemed code for we-bring-out-whatever-we-want-whenever-we-feel-like-it. She shook her head as he gestured toward the plate, offering her some. 'Go ahead and eat.'

She expected him to reach for his fork and tear into the meal with the gusto she remembered, but he did not. 'Have you ever heard of Roger Dykmans?' he asked instead.

She repeated the name inwardly. 'I don't know. The last name, maybe.'

'Roger is a securities client of mine. His brother was Hans Dykmans.'

Hans Dykmans. The full name sparked immediate recognition. 'The diplomat?' Hans Dykmans, like Swedish diplomat Raoul Wallenberg and German industrialist Oskar Schindler, had been credited with saving thousands of Jews during the Holocaust. Like Wallenberg, he was arrested and disappeared mysteriously toward the end of the war.

'Yes. Roger is Hans's younger brother and the head of a major international brokerage house. Only now he's been arrested and charged as a war criminal for allegedly helping the Germans.' Brian paused, watching Charlotte's face for a reaction to the possibility that the brother of a war hero might have been a Nazi collaborator. But she was not as surprised as he might have expected. She had learned years ago that the extreme circumstances of the war provoked a wide spectrum of reactions, even in the closest of families.

Brian waited until the server put Charlotte's plate down in front of her before continuing. 'Recently, historians uncovered some papers that seem to implicate Roger. They claim he sold out his brother during the war, and that as a result, Hans was arrested and several hundred Jewish children he was trying to save were killed.'

Staring down at the scarlet tablecloth, Charlotte recoiled. She herself was the descendant of Holocaust survivors, or more accurately, one survivor. Her mother had escaped Hungary as a child, sent on a *kindertransport* to London and later to relatives in America. But the rest of her mother's family, her parents and brothers, had all perished in the camps. Many times in Winnie's lonely final days, Charlotte had wondered how different her life might have been had her mother grown up

27

surrounded by a loving family, rather than distant cousins who took her in out of obligation. Their coolness, Charlotte suspected, was what had sent her mother flying into the arms of the first man who ever glanced her way, and who would quickly break her heart, leaving her pregnant and alone.

She looked up at Brian, who was watching her expectantly, waiting for some kind of response. 'So Dykmans is a Nazi collaborator,' she said finally. 'And you're trying to defend him.'

'Accused collaborator.' He shrugged, taking a bite of his tuna. 'He's my client. I was asked by the partnership to take on the matter.'

'And you're here for my help,' she concluded, irritated. Did Brian not remember her family history or simply not care what the nature of his request would mean to her? 'Why me?'

Brian blinked several times, as though not accustomed to such bluntness. Of course not. He had spent the intervening years traveling in the social circles of the eternally polite, practicing the formalities of large-firm conference rooms and cocktail parties that made Charlotte want to scream and crawl out of her skin. He had not lived in the rough-and-tumble inner-city court system, where no one had time for niceties or the inclination to be circumspect. 'Well,' he began slowly. 'Because of your background, for one thing.'

She nodded, then looked over her shoulder, as though someone might overhear. The fact that she'd been a doctoral student in history before turning to the law, though not exactly a secret, was not something she had shared with anyone in Philadelphia. She had spent three years in Eastern

Europe on a Fulbright and other fellowships, researching the Holocaust. Her work, focusing on issues that had arisen after the war, like restitution of Jewish property and preservation of the concentration camps, was groundbreaking at the time, and she'd published some articles that had garnered a small amount of notoriety – not to mention a circle of valuable contacts. Originally, she had gone to law school planning to combine her interest in foreign affairs with a legal career, but then Winnie's death and Brian's betrayal came crashing down on her. So she'd applied for the position with the defender's office in Philadelphia, omitting any mention of her Holocaust work because no one here would have cared, much less believed she was seriously interested in a low-paying, public-interest job with those credentials.

'But it's more than that really,' Brian hastened to add. 'I mean, I've got the firm's resources. I can hire the world's top experts, get anyone I need on the phone. We have two former cabinet members who are of counsel, for Christ's sake.' He lowered his head and laced his hands behind it, then leaned back. 'But your forensic skills are so goddamned good, always were.'

She had forgotten his propensity to swear nonstop when making a point. He thought it gave him a certain machismo, made him seem tough, one of the boys. But to her it always felt forced and indicative of a certain lack of creativity. 'Remember the Dukovic case?' he asked.

She nodded. Dukovic had been a Bosnian war criminal, accused of the murder of dozens of Croats. At the last minute, the lone witness against

29

him, a twelve-year-old girl who had managed to survive months of imprisonment, torture, and rape, became too afraid to testify. It looked like Dukovic would walk for lack of evidence. But Charlotte had spent days poring over the documents, piecing together a way to link him to the atrocities through circumstantial evidence – and she finally persuaded the girl to testify. Dukovic was sentenced to a lifetime in prison.

'And you care,' he added. 'I mean, look where you are.' He gestured around the restaurant, but she knew he did not mean Buddakan literally. He was talking about the grittiness of her job, the fact that she was down in the trenches fighting for people who had little. 'You care that people get a good defense, that innocents are not wrongfully convicted.'

But Dykmans is nothing like my clients, she thought. He's a wealthy man with resources. 'Where's he being held?'

'Germany.'

'I didn't think the Germans were pursuing their war crimes cases.'

'They weren't, until about a year ago. But the Wiesenthal Center and the Department of Justice called them out on it until the pressure became too much.'

'I wish I could help you–' she said, starting to demur.

But Brian raised his hand, interrupting. 'An old man is going to jail for the rest of his life,' he said, eyes wide. 'He deserves a fair trial.'

Charlotte's exasperation bubbled over to anger. Did Brian think it was that easy, that if he played on her sense of justice she would simply capitulate to his will? It was as if he viewed her compassion as a weakness to be exploited. Brian's words echoed back at her: a fair trial. I've got a dozen kids sitting in jail across town who won't get that much, she wanted to say. But he wouldn't understand.

'What is it that you want me to do?' she asked instead. 'I mean, I'm hardly qualified to try the case in Germany.'

'Of course not. We've got the best firm in Europe handling that.' An expression that Charlotte could not decipher passed across Brian's face, then disappeared. 'No, what I'm looking for are your forensic skills. We need help figuring out what we're missing, what Dykmans isn't telling us.'

'I don't understand.'

'He won't talk to us.'

'You mean he won't cooperate in his own defense?' Brian nodded. 'So he admits to doing it?'

'No, he just won't say that he didn't, or help us find any evidence to prove that.'

Because he doesn't want to incriminate himself, Charlotte thought. She started to ask whether Brian thought Dykmans was innocent. Then, her defender's instincts returning, she decided against it.

'Why do you care so much anyway?' she asked instead, raising her hand as Brian opened his mouth. 'And don't give me another truth-and-justice speech. I want the real story.'

An indignant look crossed his face and she expected him to protest that this was all for the greater good. Then his expression seemed to

31

crumble. She had always been able to break through his veneer in a way that no one else (not even his wife, she suspected) could. 'It's about the partnership,' he said finally in a low voice.

Of course, she thought, as the pieces of the puzzle began to fall into place. Brian was almost nine years into practice, right about the time when he would be considered for partner. 'Dykmans is a major client,' he continued. 'I've basically been told that if I can get him acquitted, I'll make it. And if not...'

He did not have to finish the sentence. Associates who did not make partner at the big firms had a limited shelf life of a year, maybe two. Then they were expected to go in-house to a company or find something else to do, all less promising options that were surely unthinkable to Brian.

She scooped up some of the pad thai with her chopsticks and popped it in her mouth, chewing as she considered. The whole scenario was utterly surreal. Brian needed her help defending a Nazi collaborator. Accused Nazi collaborator. Not that there was anything personal or particularly flattering about it. He had come to her because she was, quite simply, the person who had what he needed, like a plumber when the toilet was stopped up or a mechanic for a broken-down car.

But the real question still lay unasked and unanswered. Why should she do it? Brian had broken her heart, taken everything from her. She owed him nothing.

Yet even as she prepared to deny his request, something in her stirred. She remembered her days in the dusty European archives, trying to piece together what had happened, bring some justice to those who could no longer speak for themselves. She'd loved the subject matter, but had been frustrated by its remote, abstract nature. Working on the Dykmans matter might finally be the chance to bring together her international and legal interests, in the way she'd hoped a decade earlier. Her interest was piqued. 'I have some vacation coming up,' she said finally. 'I can schedule it next month and then–'

'That won't work,' he interjected, cutting her off in a manner just short of rude. 'Roger's trial is in four weeks. We need to find the evidence to clear him and we need to do it now.'

Her chopsticks clattered to the plate. 'Four weeks?' Four weeks out they should be polishing their witnesses, practicing arguments in a mock trial – not searching for evidence.

'I know. It's far from ideal.' She watched him, waiting for an explanation as to the last-minute nature of his request, but he looked back, un-blinking and silent.

So he expected her to drop everything in her life and come running. 'I can't.'

'Dykmans is a wealthy man. You can name your price.'

Charlotte hesitated. It had not occurred to her to ask for money. 'I want Kate Dolgenos.'

'Excuse me?' It was clearly not the response he'd anticipated.

'She's the best criminal defense attorney in your firm, right?' And in the country, she thought, as Brian nodded. 'I want her to come down and handle the preliminary hearing for one of my clients next week. It's a juvenile felony case.' It was the only way she could bring herself to leave Marquan – to place him in the hands of someone better.

'But Dolgenos handles white-collar crime. She won't–'

'And I want her well prepared,' Charlotte persisted. 'Not just zooming in at the eleventh hour. She needs to meet my client first.'

He opened his mouth to protest, then closed it again. 'Fine.'

Charlotte bit her lip uncertainly. She had asked for the moon, not expecting him to call her bluff and actually agree to her terms. Her thoughts turned to her caseload back at the office. 'I can give you a week,' she said. In reality, she could get more. She hadn't taken a vacation in almost two years, a fact that was a source of ribbing around the office. Despite their workload, her boss would give her the time willingly and her colleagues could cover anything that came up. But she needed to preserve an emergency escape, a way out in case working with Brian proved to be too much. And a week was all, maybe more than, he deserved.

He exhaled, the relief visible on his face. 'Great.' He waved the waitress over, signaling for the check. 'Meet me at Newark Airport tomorrow night. The flight leaves at eight-fifteen.'

She brushed aside her annoyance at his presumption that she would say yes, the fact that undoubtedly he had already booked the tickets. 'Where are we going?' she asked as he handed a platinum credit card to the waitress without

34

looking at the check.

He pulled a business card from inside his jacket and handed it to her. 'Germany. We need to go to Munich to talk to Dykmans's attorneys.'

'Fine.' She drained her drink and stood, leaving the pad thai almost untouched before her. 'See you tomorrow,' she mumbled, then started for the door. She could not bear to be the one who remained behind, watching him leave again.

Two

BAVARIA, 1903

Johann had worked on the clock for nearly a year. Each night after Rebecca fell asleep beside him, breathing her shallow, even breaths that deepened and slowed as she dreamt, he crept from the house and returned to the small room at the back of the barn that served as his workshop. There he labored until the stub of candle he had taken from the kitchen was gone, or sometimes when the candle was a bit longer and more resilient, until the first starlings began to call to each other over the hills, signaling daybreak. Then he would return to the cottage and slip beneath the sheets, pressing himself against Rebecca's warmth and wrapping his hands around the growing roundness of her belly for an hour before rising again to tend to the livestock.

He had toiled all through the long bitter winter, his breath nearly freezing in the night air before him as he trudged to the barn through the hardened snow that covered the ground from October to April. As the spring rains came, turning the earth to a thick mud, he hastened his pace, trying to work longer, faster. The clock needed to be finished before planting season came and pulled him from his workshop for good.

Then the previous evening, Johann suddenly

tightened the final screw and knew that he was done. So he stowed the clock beneath the floorboards and returned to the house. He crawled into bed, trying not to disturb Rebecca, but she reached for him sleepily, urging him to make love to her in the gentle way he had learned since her stomach had grown.

Afterward, as her body rose and fell beneath his embrace, he lay awake, envisioning his masterpiece. Set on a brass plate beneath a dome of thick lead glass, the clock was just twelve inches high. It had a hand-painted face, black numbers on ivory, which offered modest cover to the bare mechanism behind. Suspended below were four curved prongs, a rounded ball on the end of each. They rotated slowly 180 degrees to the right and then, seemingly moved by an invisible hand, stopped and spun slowly in the opposite direction. Every minute, the clock let out an obliging tick, an almost-sigh, as though pushing the long hand with great effort.

It would be sold to Augustus Hoffel, the richest man in town, to sit on the mantelpiece of the elegant *Gasthaus* he ran. Or so Johann hoped. He had shown Herr Hoffel the photograph nearly a year ago and the man had seemed enthusiastic about the prospect of the clock, offered to buy it then and there. Of course he hadn't paid a deposit, nor given Johann the money he needed for the fine metal and other parts, and Johann had not dared to ask. Herr Hoffel was known as a man of repute, doing business on credit with merchants as far away as Regensburg. Who was Johann, a humble farmer, to ask for a down payment up front? So

Johann had to wait two months to barter and scrape together the materials he needed before beginning. But the clock was finer than anything he had ever made or even seen, and he felt certain that Herr Hoffel would buy it on sight, giving him without negotiation his full price, the sum he needed to buy passage to America for himself and Rebecca.

Rebecca. He stroked her raven hair, splayed across the pillow, smiling to himself as he always did when thinking of his wife, even when she was lying just inches away. Rebecca was the daughter of a wealthy merchant, and when they met, she had the eye of the rabbi's son. Were it not for Johann, she would be living in a grand house with running water, a toilet inside. But against all odds and her parents' virulent protestations, she had chosen him, the farmer who turned up each week at the kindergarten where she worked because she loved the children and not because she needed to, with his jokes and stories and whatever simple gift he could scrape together for a few pennies. He could not believe it when she accepted the proposal he had hardly dared to make. Rebecca's parents, who had stopped somewhere just short of disowning her, reluctantly agreed to host the marriage ceremony in their home, but had been too embarrassed to invite their friends.

He reached down, touching her hand, feeling the calluses that had not been there when they met. Rebecca had proven to be stronger than her sheltered upbringing might have suggested. She had taken gamely to his simple life, moving into the cottage with the crude planked floors left to him by his deceased parents. Under her care, the two-room shelter became homier than it had ever been; flowered curtains now adorned the windows, and handmade pillows softened the wooden chairs. She took on without complaint, too, the tasks that filled the day of a farmer's wife, learning to spin wool and clean and mend clothes until they were more thread than fabric, to churn butter and make meals with whatever was available, canning and storing what she could for the long winter months. She even worked beside him in the field, laughing and singing, until he insisted she stop out of fear for her condition.

Two years had passed since they stood beneath the canopy. Two years later and Johann still could not believe his good fortune that Rebecca had chosen him as her own. As he watched her sit before the cracked mirror each evening, combing her dark tresses in preparation for bed, he sometimes wondered if it was a dream, whether if he blinked he might wake up to find it all gone.

The minutes seemed to stretch endlessly as he lay awake. Finally, he dozed off. He slept fitfully, dreaming that he went to retrieve the clock the next morning and it had disappeared, the space beneath the floorboards empty. The vision faded, replaced by another, equally disturbing, of the clock falling from his hands and shattering into a thousand pieces on the ground.

He awakened, restless and drained, to the sound of the roosters crowing to a yet-unseen dawn. After washing at the basin with greater care than he otherwise would, he put on the clean brown work shirt and trousers that Rebecca had laid out.

'I'm going, *Liebchen*,' he whispered to Rebecca, breathing in the powdery scent where her neck met her ear.

'Did you eat?' she mumbled.

'Yes,' he lied, tightening his suspenders. In truth, he had been so anxious he'd forgotten about the piece of *Butterbrot* she left for him each evening.

'Check the calf.' She was referring to the two-week-old that had struggled to learn to suckle. Rebecca had spent hours each day feeding the animal from a bottle with a gentleness and patience that made Johann's heart swell.

At the doorway, he took one last look back at his wife and was flooded with longing. A twinge of anxiety rose in him unexpectedly and he fought the urge to return and kiss her good-bye once more.

Turning away reluctantly, he walked to the door, donning his boots with the cracked soles, the brimmed hat that had been his father's. The smell of manure grew stronger as he made his way to the barn. There he noted that the calf slept soundly, nestled at its mother's breast.

Then he walked to the clock shop at the back of the barn. It was nothing more than a large closet, a bench with some tools, a crude furnace for warmth. Johann's father had started working there as a hobby, making clocks as a way to earn extra money in the harsh winter months. He taught Johann to help from the earliest years, first handing him bits of wood or letting him hold a piece in place while he fastened it. Later, Johann would make his first clumsy attempt at building his own clock, his skills growing over the years under his father's wordless tutelage. And after his father died from an unfortunate kick by a horse, Johann continued to build clocks, the smell of the oil beneath the flickering lamplight a kind of mourning and tribute all at once. He sometimes imagined he heard his father working beside him still.

Then one day last summer when he was in town he met the American who showed him the drawing of the clock. He had gone to Teitelbaum's, the lone mercantile shop in town, to see if the proprietor had any work for him, as he sometimes did when he had a clock that required a particularly difficult repair. Herr Teitelbaum did not pay him in cash; rather Johann bartered his skills for the coffee and other practical items they needed, and sometimes when the job was a bit more involved, some white sugar to satisfy Rebecca's sweet tooth. There was a young man at the counter soliciting orders for various clocks and watches and other gift items from abroad that he hoped the shop might consider stocking.

'I'm afraid these are too dear for my customers,' Johann overheard Herr Teitelbaum say.

Dejected, the salesman started to put away the papers containing images of his wares and it was then that Johann had glimpsed the anniversary clock for the first time. 'May I?' he asked. The salesman shrugged and slid the paper down the counter in his direction. As he studied the intricate mechanisms and fine glass dome, Johann was instantly captivated. He asked the man dozens of questions about the timepiece, memorizing his answers, before the man seemed to grow weary of

41

the conversation and left.

For weeks afterward, the image of the clock stayed with him. Could he replicate it? It would be extremely difficult and time-consuming, but if it was possible, it would bring in the money they needed to leave. He summoned up his courage and approached Herr Hoffel, one of the few men in town with the resources to purchase the clock, and price was discussed and agreed upon. And so he had begun to work.

Johann pulled the clock from beneath the floorboards and set it on the workbench, appraising it anew. His hand traced the shape of the dome, hovering just above the glass as he resisted the urge to touch it and leave the smudge marks that would necessitate polishing it once more. He had built the clock from memory, adding his own modest touches where he dared to try and improve the end result. This was not the simple cuckoo clock that had been made in the region for centuries, with its basic wood design and crude mechanics. The anniversary clock, as the peddler called it, was a torsion model, intricately made and designed to run for more than a year before needing to be wound. Johann could not believe he'd actually been able to make it work.

He covered the clock with a small blanket and set out walking from the barn. The journey into town was not insignificant and any other day he might have taken the wagon, but he did not want to risk jostling the clock, trying to hold it steady as he drove. Anyway, it was a fine morning in the no-man's-land between winter and spring, with the still-damp earth giving off a sweet smell and

42

a gentle breeze clearing the fog.

As he ascended the hill, his eyes traveled across the rolling green earth, broken only by a stone monastery perched high in the distance. Then he looked back at the fields that fanned out below. The small but fertile plot of land, a few hectares in the lush valley nourished by the nearby river Main, had been owned by his family for generations. It would soon be time to till the soil. He would plant despite the fact that they would not be here for the harvest, hoping the promise of a late-summer bounty would raise the sale price of the land.

He shifted the clock to his other arm and looked down, concentrating on his footsteps and taking care not to stumble as the path that dropped into the forest narrowed and grew uneven. Sunlight crept through the pines, drying the needles on the ground to a brittle carpet that crackled beneath his feet.

His thoughts returned to Rebecca. The pregnancy had not come easily. Each month since their wedding there had been a hushed expectation, hope followed by disappointment. There were conversations, held only late at night in low voices though they lived alone, for who really spoke of such things at all, much less in the light of day? Whispers about what might be wrong, certain foods a woman might eat or salves she could apply that were rumored to help. But after the first year they had stopped hoping and accepted without recrimination that if God had not seen fit to bless them with a child, then the love they had for each other would be enough.

Then one morning when he least expected it, Rebecca rushed into the barn as he milked the cows and wordlessly took his hand and pressed it to her midsection, smiling broadly. He thought that his heart would burst. They had about five months, Rebecca said, and so he redoubled his efforts on the clock. He wanted them to go before it became too difficult or unsafe for her to travel, so their child could be born in America, in the comfort and safety his precious wife deserved.

The decision to leave had not been a simple one. It was more than just the farm: Johann generally felt as though he belonged here, considered himself first and foremost German – felt that way, at least, until the outside world reminded him otherwise every so often. The latest incident had come last winter, word of a Jewish merchant in a village to the east murdered by neighbors he had lived among all of his life who were convinced he was hoarding wheat in order to drive up prices. The man was shot, his house burned with his family still inside.

Things were worse in the countries around them. He'd seen it in the eyes of the poor haunted immigrants from the Pale who passed through town on their way to the cities looking for work, heard the whispered stories of pogroms that had decimated their lives in an instant. The violence wasn't just limited to the east – in Paris, a Jewish military officer was hung not a decade earlier, despite evidence of his innocence. And as much as Johann hated to admit it, Bavaria, stubbornly provincial and still steeped in its Catholic traditions decades after unification, was fertile ground

44

for Jew hating. No, something told him that the time to get out was now. His son (he did not know why he always pictured the child as a boy) would not be raised with the shadow that caused Johann to wake with every scratch in the night, reaching for the knife that he hid under the mattress. And in America, Rebecca would be safe.

So he had planned their route – a train to one of the North Sea ports, then a ship to America. Going by wagon to the coast would have been cheaper, but Rebecca's belly was growing every day. Time was of the essence.

He had of course told Rebecca immediately of his plan. She was bright and strong-willed and would not have permitted him to do otherwise, even if he had been that sort of husband. He had discussed it only in the most hypothetical of terms, not wanting to get her hopes up in case something went wrong. He had worried that she would object to leaving her parents before their only grandchild was born. But she simply smiled. 'Whither thou goest, I will go,' she said, quoting the Book of Ruth, eyes shining as she reaffirmed the promise she made on their wedding day to cast her lot in with his. She cleverly pointed out that they should sail to Baltimore, where the entry requirements were reputed to be less stringent than the busier New York port. She had a cousin there who might be willing to help. They agreed to tell no one of their plan, knowing that her parents would be enraged, and that their need to depart would signal desperation to sell and bring a lower price for the land.

He reached the end of the forest about twenty

minutes later, and the thinning trees gave way to a wide, rising plateau. In the distance to the south, Johann glimpsed the alpine peaks, snowcapped and breathtaking, ringed by a wreath of clouds. Though he had seen the view his whole life, it still filled him with awe. He had never been as far as the mountains, of course. He'd had romantic notions of taking Rebecca there for a weekend after their wedding, but there had always been fields to be planted, clocks to be made. Now he felt a sense of tugging sadness that he would never go. He would travel many times farther, but in the opposite direction, and the mountains would always remain just out of reach in his mind.

A few minutes later the land dropped off again, sloping gently downward. Below sat a sea of clustered red rooftops, a lone gray steeple rising from their midst. A wide plume of smoke, yet to be blown away by the fresh spring winds, seemed to hover over the town like a flock of birds.

Johann navigated the descent carefully, relaxing slightly as the road grew broader, turning from dirt to cobblestone. He crossed the wooden bridge over the small stream by the mill that signaled the edge of the town. Then he paused, studying the two- and three-story buildings that lined the street, their whitewashed fronts stained with the winter coal dust. He shook his head. It was considered a sign of prestige to live in the wood-latticed houses, but the idea of having neighbors so close on all sides made it hard for him to breathe.

The town had done better than its tiny size might have predicted, the beneficiary of geography that made it the last outpost after leaving Munich before heading over the border for points south in Austria. It was a place visited out of necessity rather than choice, frequented by merchants making their way to and from Vienna, wealthy holidaygoers pressing onward to hike and breathe the restorative alpine air. This weekday morning, the streets were crowded with wagons and men on foot, loading supplies.

The *Gasthaus* sat just east of the square, set back from the shops on either side, the centerpiece of the nicest street in town. Laborers stayed at the dingy boardinghouse by the depot, but the wealthiest visitors all made their way to Hoffel's, with its dozen or so bedrooms and stately garden beneath.

Johann walked up the steps, taking care to kick the dried mud from his boots before entering. *'Entschuldigen Sie bitte,'* he managed, excusing himself to the young woman in the vestibule, whom he recognized as one of the Hoffel daughters. She looked up from the register she'd been studying with annoyance. She was clad in a yellow silk dress he dearly wished he could afford for Rebecca, but she had a hawkish nose and harsh chin that no amount of money could soften. *'Ist hier Herr Hoffel?'* The girl eyed him incredulously, as though the notion he might have business with her father was unfathomable, then disappeared without speaking.

He peered around the dining room at the cloth-covered tables, not daring to sit on the finely upholstered chairs. The mantelpiece above the stone fireplace was crowded with porcelain figurines clad in the traditional Bavarian dirndl and leder-hosen. A savory smell, fresh roast and *Kartoffeln* cooking for the midday meal, tickled his nose and caused his stomach to rumble. It would be nearly lunchtime when he returned home and he hoped Rebecca might have warmed some of the dumplings from last night's supper for him.

A moment later Herr Hoffel burst into the dining room. 'Johann!'

'*Guten Morgen,* Herr Hoffel,' he managed as the older man wiped his hands on his pants, not daring to reciprocate with the same familiarity. Johann set the clock on the table where Herr Hoffel indicated, then stood motionless as the portly innkeeper studied the clock, trying not to cringe as he ran his fat fingers across the glass, smudging the pristine surface.

Herr Hoffel pulled at his graying beard, not speaking for several minutes. 'Hmm,' he said finally, equal parts murmur and snort. Johann held his breath. 'It is nice.'

Johann bristled inwardly at the word. *Nice* described the cheaply made clocks that sat in the department store windows, one the same as the next. His stomach twisted. Was Herr Hoffel being coy, acting unimpressed as a bargaining technique? Johann wished again that he'd asked for a deposit up front or even a higher price, but he had not known how dear the parts would be, how long it would take. No, he could not afford to negotiate, to go any lower than what he had asked, and still cover the money they needed for their passage.

'The face is porcelain,' he offered, but Herr Hoffel's expression did not change. The man was not haggling over the price, Johann realized suddenly. He simply did not have the eye to appreciate the workmanship, the difference between this treasure and the cheaply made clocks produced by the factories for the department stores. To him, it was just another commodity, like the cloths that covered his tables or the meat he purchased from the butcher for that night's stew.

'When we spoke last year, you said a hundred marks,' Johann offered, reminding the innkeeper of his promise.

Herr Hoffel whistled through his teeth, pushing stale air through his pipe-stained mustache. *'Ja, ja,'* he replied, but his tone was more protest than agreement. 'I had no idea it would take so long, though.' Neither had he, Johann conceded to himself. He had not known that it would take months to save for the materials, or that the work would be so painstaking. 'Business is slow,' Herr Hoffel continued, gesturing around as if to persuade Johann that the empty dining room at mid-morning was indicative of a lack of boarders. 'And Frau Hoffel bought these during our last trip to Munich.' He waved in the direction of the mantel, where the row of figurines stared down.

Anger rose within Johann. Comparing his masterpiece to those trinkets was an insult. He fought the urge to pick up the clock and walk from the inn. 'I suppose I could still take it, but I couldn't afford to pay more than forty for it.'

Forty. Johann's stomach dropped. Forty, though more than he otherwise might see in months, would barely get them to Rotterdam. Herr Hoffel rubbed at a mark on the floor with his foot and suddenly it seemed to Johann that all of his dreams were being ground to dust beneath the innkeeper's boot. His dream for a better life for Rebecca and their child could not possibly come true now.

Looking out through the thick-paned glass of the front window to the street, Johann's vision burned white. The older man was playing him, using his wealth and power to take advantage. But what other choice did he have than to accept the meager offer? Herr Hoffel was the only man in town with the money to buy the clock. But then he turned back to the table and as he looked at the work of art into which he'd poured his sweat and soul, Johann's spine stiffened. He would not part with it for a figure so far short of its worth. He would take the clock to the city, try to sell it to one of the merchants there, before he would let Herr Hoffel steal it from him at such a price.

Unless, of course, Herr Hoffel could be swayed. He took a deep breath, prepared to try again. 'Herr Hoffel, forty is less than half our agreed price,' he began, struggling not to stammer. The innkeeper's eyes widened in fury at the unexpected challenge, but Johann had gone too far to stop now. 'I'm afraid I couldn't possibly...'

'That clock is extraordinary.' A voice behind him interrupted the exchange. Johann and the innkeeper turned toward it. A man whom Johann did not recognize from town stood behind them. 'May I?'

Johann and the innkeeper stepped back, parting to allow the stranger access to the clock. Older than Herr Hoffel, the man had a wide girth

50

that bespoke muscle in his earlier years and a mass of silver-gray beard that seemed to swallow his face. His eyes were a curious pale blue that Johann had seen only once before in the eggshells of a robin's nest, formed in the eaves of the barn.

'Which clockmaker?' the man asked. His German, Johann could tell, was not quite native to the region but from the north, somewhere urban and cosmopolitan.

'Me,' Johann blurted. 'That is, I made it myself.'

The stranger considered Johann for several seconds, not speaking, and Johann realized he had been expecting the name of one of the finer clock-making houses. An odd expression crossed the man's face, as if he doubted the truth of Johann's words. Then he reached out, grazing the top of the clock with considerably more care than Herr Hoffel had done. Though his clothes were dusty from the road, his nails were trimmed and a band of solid gold marked the fourth finger of his right hand. But beneath were calluses that no amount of grooming could mask. Not a laborer's hands, but hands that had known honest work. 'I've never seen anything like it,' the man murmured, more to himself than to the others.

'It's called an anniversary clock,' Johann offered, the confidence and strength in his voice growing. 'A new design from America. It only needs to be wound about every four hundred days.'

'How much?' the stranger asked.

Johann hesitated, resisting the temptation to raise his original price, lest Herr Hoffel think he was gouging his guests. 'One hundred.'

'Now wait a minute,' Herr Hoffel interjected,

his interest piqued by the competition.

The stranger turned to him. 'Are you buying it?'

'I don't—' Herr Hoffel faltered. 'That is, the price—'

'The question is a simple one: yes or no?' Anger flicked across Herr Hoffel's face at the audacity of the stranger using such a tone with him in his own inn, and for a moment Johann thought he would confront the man. But travelers were Hoffel's stock in trade and word got around – an innkeeper reputed as rude would soon find his rooms empty.

'One hundred, then,' Herr Hoffel said, reaching for the till.

But the stranger was not finished. 'One ten.' His eyes glinted, a seasoned trader bargaining for wares.

'One fifteen,' Herr Hoffel replied evenly. To him, the clock was still just a commodity. 'Not a penny more.'

The stranger delivered the final blow. 'One twenty.' A hand squeezed Johann's throat, making it impossible to breathe. Did the man really mean to pay him such a sum?

There was a moment of hesitation. Would Herr Hoffel bid again in spite of himself? But the innkeeper's shoulders slumped in defeat. The stranger reached into his jacket and pulled out a billfold, producing one hundred twenty marks. 'You could have asked several times that,' he said, as he handed the money to Johann. 'Never undersell yourself.'

Johann's eyes darted to Herr Hoffel, wondering if he would protest, but the innkeeper shrugged and turned to the counter, busying himself with the ledger. Without another word, the stranger picked up the clock and carried it carefully from the room. Johann watched, feeling as though a part of himself was leaving too.

'Who was that?' he asked the innkeeper.

Herr Hoffel did not look up. 'Just a boarder. Checked in last night, leaving today. Name is Rosenberg. Don't know where he's from. Hamburg maybe, or Berlin.'

Johann was seized with the urge to run after the stranger, find out where the man would be taking his clock. But it didn't matter – he had his money. Without speaking further, he walked from the inn onto the street, making his way through the wagons and merchants.

Out of sight of the hotel, he opened his hand, half fearing that the bills would have disintegrated into dust, a figment of his imagination. But they were still there, one hundred and twenty marks, more money than he had ever seen at one time. It was enough to buy better passage on the ship, to get Rebecca out of steerage and into a real room where she could rest peacefully and look at the water. She would never let him spend it on that of course; despite her upbringing, she was exceedingly frugal and would insist that they save the money, pointing out the additional expenses they might encounter along the way, the unknown cost of living in America. They could argue about that on the train. He tucked the money back into his pocket and glanced furtively in each direction as if he expected to be accused of some wrongdoing, then hurried onto the road that led out of town before the stranger could change his mind and come after him.

An hour later he emerged on the far side of the forest. The sun was high in the late-morning sky now, warming the grass. He thought of the clock. Where was the man taking it? He imagined a home with a mantelpiece, tried to envision the people who would look at and admire it and take from it the cadence of their day. A piece of himself, going places he would never see.

As Johann reached the final hill, his gait grew light. He and Rebecca could move to America, away from the ghosts that haunted him here, from the hatred that seemed to lurk around every corner. He climbed the gentle slope, his stomach knotting with anticipation as it always did just before he saw his wife. Rebecca would be up, refreshed from sleep, hanging wash or working in the garden. Perhaps he would lure her from her morning chores back to the bed, celebrate by making love to her once more.

He reached the crest, surveying the house and gardens nestled in the dell below, but Rebecca was nowhere to be seen. In the house, surely. Maybe she had even begun to pack.

He opened the door to the cottage, smelling the smoke from the previous night's fire that still lingered in the air. Rebecca had been up for some time, he could tell, from the way the freshly polished table gleamed, and from the basket of folded wash that had not been on the chair when he left. *'Liebchen,'* he called, but only the echo of his own voice rang back at him. He walked through to the bedroom, which was empty and still, the duvet pulled tight and neat. His heart skipped a little in a way he could not quite understand as he retraced his steps through the cottage and stepped outside, closing the door behind him. He made his way around the back of the house to the barn, where she must be watering the mule. 'Rebecca, you'll never guess what—'

It was not until he reached the fence that he saw her, lying on the muddy ground of the chicken coop, body twisted, legs folded awkwardly in the wrong direction beneath her. A scream he did not recognize came from his throat as he tore open the gate and raced to her side, kneeling.

When he lifted her onto his lap, he first saw the blood, great puddles of it seeping through the back of her dress, mixing with the dirt. Had she fallen and hurt herself or had something broken inside her that caused her to collapse? 'Rebecca...' He shook her as if to wake her from deep sleep, and her eyes rolled upward and her mouth opened, a fine thread of spittle running from cheek to chin. He lowered his hand but even before it reached her belly, he knew that it would be still, the gentle kicks he'd felt in recent weeks now gone.

He should not have left her alone, he berated himself. If he'd been here, he could have helped her, or perhaps prevented whatever had befallen her altogether. A great sob of grief tore through him then and he lay down on the sodden earth beside her as though it were their marriage bed, burying his nose in her sun-warmed hair, pressing against the growing coolness of her cheek. He followed her lifeless gaze to the sky as though searching for answers, wondering what to do.

Three

MUNICH, 2009

At eight-thirty Wednesday morning, Charlotte stepped into the terminal at Franz Josef Strauss Airport. As she looked around the gleaming glass and chrome concourse, rubbing the sleep from her eyes, she wondered for the hundredth time what she was doing here. Alone.

Twelve hours earlier, Charlotte had stood by the Lufthansa ticket desk at Newark Airport, holding the boarding pass that had been waiting for her at the counter. Damn Brian, she swore, as she peered through the crowds. She was doing him a favor and his making her wait seemed an affront. She had pulled out her BlackBerry and dialed the number on his business card, but it went directly to voicemail.

A minute later, her phone vibrated. Finally, she thought as she raised it to her ear, preparing to convey her annoyance. But there was only a text message. *Unavoidably delayed,* it read. *Go on without me. Rooms are at the Sofitel. Appointment tomorrow at eleven with Dykmans' attys at 42 Bayerstrasse. I'll catch the later flight and meet you there.*

Charlotte stared at the text message in disbelief. Brian had asked, no, begged her to go with him – and now he was standing her up?

She lowered the phone, fighting against the tide

of emotions that rose up inside her. Brian wasn't going to show. Suddenly, it was as if he was rejecting her all over again. He's just missing the flight, she reminded herself. But the thought gave her little comfort.

I can just go home, Charlotte realized, suddenly set free. This isn't my case and if he's too busy to make the flight, then maybe I am too. But she was still curious – what was the story behind the Dykmans affair? Was Roger guilty? Why would he refuse to aid in his own defense? She glanced down at the boarding pass in her hand, and the lure of Europe called out to her like an old friend. It had been years since she'd strolled Munich's wide thoroughfares, sipped a beer at the Hofbräuhaus. She could practically taste the tortes. At worst it would be a free vacation.

So she'd pushed her doubts aside and boarded the plane. Somewhere over the Atlantic, as she reclined in the comfort of first class, an unexpected wave of gratitude washed over her: she was glad for the empty space beside her, thankful not to have to sleep in such close proximity to Brian. To hear his breathing, see his hair tousled in the way it used to be when he awoke, would have been unbearable.

Now, as she made her way through immigration and customs, her misgivings bubbled up anew. Perhaps she should wait at the airport for Brian to make sure he actually showed. But she had no idea which airline he might be taking or what time his flight would arrive. And he wouldn't really send her all the way to Europe just to stand her up, would he? She withdrew some euros from a cash machine before stepping outside and hailing a cab.

As the taxi merged onto the autobahn toward the city a few minutes later, it picked up speed, traveling with greater ease than might have been expected on the traffic-choked motorway. Charlotte leaned back, staring out the window at the thick pine forest that flanked either side of the road, rising against a hillside, treetops shrouded in morning fog.

She drew her coat closer, trying to decide if it was the chill or the circumstances that made her shiver. Her reaction to Germany as a country had always been conflicted. Over Winnie's objections, she'd taken German in high school because it fit her schedule, and on a class exchange trip to Heidelberg she had found the modern country so far removed from the grainy wartime images as to seem a different planet. It wasn't until later, when she lived in Europe, that she'd noticed the subtle things – how a gruff customs officer on the train demanding a passport could make her cringe, the way she woke in a cold sweat if she heard sirens in the middle of the night, as if she had gone back in time and they were coming for her. Now she was actually here because of a case involving the Nazis. She shuddered. Despite the modern trappings, the historical context was too evident to ignore.

Twenty minutes later, traffic slowed and a sea of red-tiled roofs and Baroque cathedral spires unfurled before them. It had always struck her on her earlier visits to Munich that the reconstructed city was almost too perfect, as if nothing had happened here, and the Dachau concentration camp was not about ten miles away.

The taxi turned onto one of the wide royal thoroughfares, lined seamlessly with imperial government buildings. A minute later, they stopped in front of the Sofitel as she had requested. As she emerged from the cab, she paused, looking down at her khakis and black sweater, wishing she had time to shower and change. But knowing it was too early to check in, she left her suitcase with the bellhop before climbing back in the car with the large leather tote that served as both her handbag and briefcase.

She gave the driver the second address and was surprised when the taxi stopped a moment later just around the corner. 'Here?' she asked. The driver nodded. Close enough to walk, she realized, paying him more than was necessary out of embarrassment. She stepped out onto the pavement, peering in both directions at the generic office buildings, indistinguishable from those found in the business districts of Vienna or Zurich. She patted down her hair and entered the office building.

Once inside the imposing lobby, she hesitated, wondering how far behind Brian was, whether she should wait here for him. But the guard behind the security desk held out his hand. *'Guten Tag...?'* And so she had no choice but to step forward. I don't know who I'm supposed to ask for, she thought, anxiety rising as she handed her passport across the counter. But the guard tapped on the keyboard, then gave it back to her without asking. 'Eighteenth floor,' he said.

Charlotte passed through the metal detector. A minute later, she stepped off the elevator and approached the receptionist's desk. The young woman with short dark hair glanced up from her keyboard. *'Ja?'*

'Guten Morgen.' She faltered, trying to recall some usable German beyond that and failing. 'Charlotte Gold. I'm here for a meeting and not sure who I'm supposed to see,' she said, feeling foolish. 'But my colleague will be joining us too so I can just wait...'

'Herr Warrington called a few minutes ago,' the receptionist replied coolly, cutting her off with clipped English. 'He's been unavoidably detained and urged you to go on and have the meeting without him.'

Have the meeting without him. Charlotte did not reply but stepped back from the desk, her anger rising. Brian had abandoned her – again. And he hadn't even had the decency to call her directly. Of course not; he was too afraid of her reaction to tell her himself. He'd always been like that, a ruthless litigator in the courtroom who would do whatever he could to avoid confrontation in his own life.

As she looked around the elegant reception area, her doubts rose: how could she possibly take the meeting alone? She knew nothing about the case, not even the name of the person she was supposed to see. I need to excuse myself, she thought, figure out what to do next.

But the receptionist was already opening a door and motioning for Charlotte to follow. The woman led her down a hallway, their footsteps muffled by the plush beige carpet. The office, silent except for low voices behind closed doors, was a sharp contrast to Charlotte's own chaotic work atmosphere at the defenders' office. A wave of homesickness washed over her.

They reached the end of the hall and the receptionist ushered her into an office, then retreated wordlessly. Charlotte scanned the corner suite with its floor-to-ceiling glass windows offering a panoramic view of the city. The walls were bare except for a nondescript watercolor of the Alps, none of the usual photographs and diplomas that might have offered a clue about the person with whom she was to meet. Piles of paper and half-drunk cardboard cups of coffee littered the mahogany conference table. Her eyes dropped to the edge of the massive desk and, as they came to rest on the nameplate, widened. She knew then why Brian had been delayed. Why, in fact, he was not going to show at all.

The office belonged to Jack Warrington, Brian's brother.

So that was why Brian had bailed. He and Jack had never gotten along well – Jack, a Yale Law grad two years their senior, was as quiet and intellectual as his brother was brash and athletic. 'He's brilliant,' Brian had conceded, describing Jack before Charlotte had met him. 'If only he'd come out of his own head and live in the real world.' But despite the criticism, Brian's tone betrayed begrudging admiration, even a hint of envy. She wondered later if he hadn't gone to law school in part to keep up with his brother.

But then, sometime toward the end of when

Brian and Charlotte dated, the brothers had stopped talking altogether. Brian had never said exactly what happened, and Charlotte had been too caught up with her mother's illness to ask, but she assumed it was about money or some other family matter that seemed trivial compared to all she was dealing with at the time. Was it possible that they had not spoken in all these years?

What would Jack think of her showing up here now? Did he even know that she was coming? She was seized with the urge to flee, or at a minimum to step out of the office and compose herself. But before she could move, the door opened and there, standing before her, was Jack.

'Hello, Charley,' he said, using the nickname that no one had for years. Not even Brian when he came to see her the other day, and he was the one who had coined it. She could not tell if Jack was surprised to see her alone, or that she was here at all. He bent and kissed her cheek and the faint scent of his cologne, something European and distinctive, sent her hurtling back through the years. When had she been close enough to him back then to recognize his scent?

'Please,' he said as he straightened. He gestured to the conference table, clearing away two of the coffee cups and pulling out a chair.

As she sat, she found herself studying him out of the corner of her eye. The resemblance to Brian was there, not so strong that one would have recognized the connection at opposite ends of a crowded room, but undeniable to those who knew them. Jack shared his brother's broad-shouldered lankiness and his hair was the same shade of chocolate brown as Brian's and parted and flopped at the same angle. But where Brian got a haircut every three weeks religiously, Jack's was shaggy and had more of a curl, combining with the stubble that covered his cheeks and chin to give him an air of intentional disarray. And his eyes were completely different, ice blue and piercing.

Jack started to sit across from her, but before he touched the chair, he sprang up again. 'Coffee?' Without waiting for an answer, he disappeared from the office, closing the door behind him.

She shivered involuntarily. Jack had always intimidated her. On the surface, it seemed illogical; he was the softer-spoken brother, Brian loud and blustery. But there was something behind Jack's impassive exterior, not just his intensity but a quiet bemusement, as though he was in on a joke that the rest of them could not understand or share.

'He's just odd,' Brian had replied offhandedly when Charlotte remarked on Jack's aloofness after meeting him for the first time.

'Why?' Charlotte asked, trying to understand as she always did what was behind a person's behavior, the motive that drove the action.

Brian shrugged. But Charlotte wanted to know more. She was fascinated with peeling back people's exteriors – the more cryptic the better. What lay beneath the layers in which Jack seemed to shroud himself?

It seemed to Charlotte that there was more to it than just his demeanor, though; she suspected that Jack didn't like her. Was it some perceived lack of intellect? Or perhaps it was her background of which he disapproved.

There had been a moment once when she'd joined them for Thanksgiving dinner and the family, who were not the slightest bit religious, said grace. When she was growing up with Winnie, the holiday had consisted of hot turkey sandwiches for two at the local diner, or maybe Ponderosa in the better years. But for the Warringtons it was a formal meal for twenty, with the good china and seating cards. At some point during the blessing, which proved to be not so much a prayer as a long and winding monologue designed to impress upon the guests the family's ancestral connection to the *Mayflower*, Charlotte looked up. Her eyes met Jack's across the table and he lifted his bowed head slightly and raised one eyebrow, a joke shared between them. She blinked and the expression was gone, his head lowered again, and she thought she imagined it. A few weeks later, she learned of her mother's illness and she had not visited with Brian's family or seen Jack again.

Until now. The office door opened and Jack reappeared, balancing two cups. He handed her one and she dipped her head to the unsweetened cappuccino, equally flattered that he remembered her drink and annoyed that he presumed she had not changed. She toggled between the two emotions before finally pushing them both aside and accepting the much-needed caffeine gratefully.

'I'm not sure if we should wait,' she began, as she dropped into the chair he indicated. 'That is, Brian said–'

'Brian,' he pronounced his brother's name with an unmistakable twist, 'won't be joining us. He sent word that he's been detained but that we should get started without him. But I would be surprised if he showed at all.'

'You spoke to him?'

Jack shook his head, fiddling with the top button of his crisp blue shirt. 'Not in years. He left word with my associate.'

'I don't understand.'

'Brian's firm contacted me a few months ago and asked me to work on the Dykmans matter. But on a personal level, my brother and I are, as they say, estranged.' But he still sent you the case, Charlotte thought. Of course. Brian was rational enough to know that Jack was the right person to handle the matter, the same way he knew he needed Charlotte. He would not let his feelings, or in her case, lack thereof, get in the way of providing his client and himself with the best possible chance of winning.

Jack continued, 'Let's not waste time on that, though. How have you been these many years?'

'Fine,' she replied awkwardly. 'I'm a public defender in Philadelphia, handling juvenile cases.' Marquan's face popped into her mind. If Brian had backed out of meeting her here, would he renege on his promise to get Marquan the defense counsel Charlotte had demanded?

'That must be incredibly difficult,' he replied, with more interest than she had expected. There was a spark in his eyes that hadn't been there when she told Brian of her work.

'It is,' she confessed, 'but I love it. I have no

65

idea what I'm doing here, though.' She paused, hoping for an explanation, but Jack just sat there, fingers at his chin, watching her intently, as if prompting a witness at a deposition to say more. 'And I wasn't expecting to find you in private practice,' she continued awkwardly. 'I thought you were at the Tribunal.' Two years ahead of them at law school, Jack had always been focused on war crimes prosecution. He had received the same prestigious fellowship to The Hague that Charlotte later turned down, then became a permanent prosecutor there, gaining international recognition for his successful track record on genocide cases. She had not realized he'd left.

Jack's brow furrowed as though he was surprised himself. 'Yes, well there was a political shakeup at The Hague and the agenda changed. Everything I tried to do got caught up in bureaucracy and politics. And with all of the other things to focus on since 9/11, the Tribunal just doesn't have the support it once did from the rest of the world. I found myself growing frustrated, cynical. Then the firm approached me and offered me the chance to continue doing significant human rights work on a pro bono basis.'

So he had fled too. The realization seemed to level the playing field somehow, made him a hair less intimidating.

'The catch is, of course, I have to deal with the devil,' he added, gesturing around the office. 'How much do you know about Dykmans?'

She shrugged, the irony of the segue not lost on her. She had Googled Roger Dykmans hurriedly before leaving for the airport, scanned a few

66

articles about the indictment. 'Just the public stuff and the bit Brian told me a few days ago. He's a wealthy financier. And his brother was Hans Dykmans, who rescued several thousand Jews out of Prague.'

'Prague and Budapest and just about every other major city in Eastern Europe,' Jack replied curtly. Charlotte bristled at the correction. 'Roger Dykmans emigrated to Canada after the war. He eventually found his way to Manhattan, where he and a friend started Dykmans James in 1949. Using the acumen he had gathered in the German market, he developed a specialty securing financing for the arms industry. It was the right place at the right time, and he was able to leverage the military buildup for the Cold War successfully, finance several major companies, and make a fortune for his clients.'

'And himself,' she noted. 'He never changed his name after the war?'

Jack shook his head. 'He didn't have a reason to. To the contrary, being Hans's brother gave him a kind of legitimacy with the Jewish industrialists.'

She took a sip of cappuccino, processing the information. 'Married? Dykmans, I mean,' she added quickly, worried Jack might think she was asking about him.

But he seemed to take the question in stride. 'Never married, no kids. Some people thought of him as a queer old fellow, others saw him as wrapped up in his work. Anyhow, in 1994, Dykmans suddenly announces that he's moving to Geneva.'

'Just like that?'

'Strange, no? A man in his seventies, leaving his Upper East Side penthouse to relocate. He said it was for the sake of the business, to develop the European presence. But the Geneva office of Dykmans James was never more than a place-holder. His explanation just didn't make sense.'

'Swiss girlfriend, maybe?' she offered jokingly.

But Jack did not respond to her attempt at humor. 'Not that we know of,' he replied, a note of disdain in his voice.

The elder Warrington brother, Charlotte reflected, was seeming less enigmatic by the moment.

Jack continued, 'So he's living in Switzerland, traveling back and forth nonstop to New York because that's where his business is still located.' He drummed his fingers on the table. 'Fast-forward nearly fifteen years. Last spring, a clerk in St. Petersburg claims he found a document showing that Roger was responsible for turning in his brother to the Nazis and for the deaths of the hundreds Hans was trying to save at the time.'

She tilted her head. 'The document surfaced out of nowhere?'

'The archives,' he replied, and Charlotte nodded, understanding. After Communism ended and the Soviet Union and other Eastern Bloc regimes fell apart, a ton of records that had been closed off to Western researchers suddenly became available. He continued, 'Apparently the man tried to extort millions from Dykmans to keep the information quiet, but he wasn't playing. So the man went to the authorities and Dykmans was arrested.'

'In Switzerland?'

'No, Poland.' Before she could respond, Jack turned and reached around to the desk behind him, pulling a file from the countless stacks without looking and handing it to her. She leafed through the first document, a photocopy of Roger Dykmans's passport. The pages were filled with stamps from airports all over the world, the global itinerary of a busy finance executive. But there was one stamp that caught her eye – the entry marker for Poland, which appeared repeatedly on each page.

'That's the odd part,' Jack continued. 'They caught him in Warsaw outside the construction site for the future museum of Jewish history. There was some speculation that he was there to do harm.'

She looked up. 'At his age?'

He nodded. 'Kind of like that crazy old guy who shot up the lobby of the Holocaust museum in Washington a few months ago. Except when they found Dykmans, he was unarmed. They extradited him to Germany.'

'Dykmans went to Poland at least a dozen times in the past two years,' she noted, 'even after the evidence of his alleged complicity surfaced. Why would he do that?'

He leaned back, lacing his hands behind his head in the same way Brian used to. Then he lunged forward again, taking a sip of coffee. 'The guilty are sometimes compelled to return to the scene of the crime.'

'So I've heard.' She found herself irked by the simplistic nature of his statement, and his tone, which bordered on patronizing. Had he forgotten that she worked in criminal defense?

'But I don't think it's that,' he replied, not picking up on or choosing to ignore her sarcasm.

'Then what?'

'That's why you're here.' He set down his cup.

'Have you asked him?'

'Of course. Here's the really baffling part, though: he refuses to help in his own defense, or to say much of anything at all. It's as if he's given up.'

Brian had said as much, Charlotte recalled. 'Strange.'

'That's an understatement. I mean, he's old and alone, but he has his business, his reputation. You'd think he would want to keep those.'

Charlotte thought of her clients back home, kids like Marquan who more often than not refused to talk. But their silence was born out of fear for their safety and that did not seem likely to be the case here.

'Are you ready to meet him?' Jack asked. He did not wait for her response. 'Then what are we waiting for? Let's go.'

Ten minutes later, Charlotte found herself seated in the back of a black sedan beside Jack. One of the benefits of private practice, he'd explained when they climbed into the car at the curb of his office, nodding toward the driver. 'Is it far?' Charlotte asked now, as they wound their way out of the city center.

'Just a few miles.'

As the car skirted the edge of the Marienplatz, Charlotte craned her neck to try to catch a glimpse of the famous glockenspiel. 'Oktoberfest.' Jack gestured toward the square, where workers were stacking tables beneath a massive tent, then rolled his eyes. She wouldn't have minded experiencing the beer festival, Charlotte thought. Events like that, or the Christmas market that filled Kraków's main market square each December, were part of what had made living in Europe so great. But to Jack, the crowds and noise were nothing more than an infuriating distraction.

'Have you heard of the Theresienstadt massacre?' he asked.

Charlotte hesitated, caught off guard by the abrupt change of topic. 'No. I mean, I know about the camp.' Theresienstadt, or Terezin, was the model camp set up by the Nazis in Czechoslovakia. It was intended to demonstrate that the Jewish people weren't being treated that badly, that they were just being temporarily interned. There was a school, with arts and crafts and music, and the students would be trooped out for the Red Cross or other visitors. Of course the moment they were gone, the prisoners were returned to conditions that were nearly as abhorrent as those in the other camps. 'But I've never heard of a massacre there.'

A disapproving look flashed across Jack's face, as though he'd expected her to be better prepared. I would have been, she thought, if I'd had more than twenty-four hours notice.

'Hans Dykmans was stationed as a diplomat in Breslau until the war broke out,' he explained. Charlotte nodded. Breslau was the German name for Wroclaw, a city now part of Poland. 'He became distressed by the plight of the Jews, the

71

failure of almost anyone to do anything to stop it. So working secretly with an international group, he began developing fake papers to help Jews flee. But once they were in the camps, it was almost impossible to do anything to help them. And as the war wore on and the Germans became more desperate, they had less of a reason to maintain the pretense of Terezin.

'Hans knew it was just a matter of time until the Nazis liquidated the camp and sent all of the children to Auschwitz or Treblinka and certain death. So he created a high-level delegation of supposed international emissaries to visit the camp. In fact, they were really people who were working with him and the resistance. The plan was that once in the camp, they were going to ask that the children be permitted to participate in an international exchange with children from a summer camp in Sweden. Put on the spot, the Germans would have no choice but to agree and Hans would be able to sneak the children out of the country. But before the exchange could take place, someone tipped off the Germans. Hans and the delegation were arrested.'

'And the children?' she asked, dreading the answer.

'Well, it's unclear exactly what happened to them, but most people believe they were shot.'

Charlotte was suddenly nauseous. She swallowed, forcing the images from her mind, the way she might when dealing with a client accused of a particularly grisly murder charge. 'And the allegation is that Roger was the one who turned Hans in?' Jack nodded. 'Do you think he did it?' She cringed at her own question. As a defense lawyer, it was axiomatic not to focus on her client's guilt, not to ask. Zealous representation, that was her job.

But if Jack was troubled by the inquiry, he gave no indication. 'Having met him, it's hard to imagine him being so heartless.'

We both know that's no proof, Charlotte thought. She wanted to remind him of people she'd helped to prosecute at The Hague, like the high school math teacher from Pristina who had killed mothers and their children with indifference. But she did not.

Charlotte's mind traveled in another direction. 'You said the massacre happened in Czechoslovakia, yet they picked up Dykmans in Warsaw.'

'He's from Poland and—'

'Polish?' she interrupted. 'I figured he was Scandinavian, or Dutch.'

'You would think so, wouldn't you, judging by the name? I think he had a Swedish grandfather, but the family was mostly Polish. He grew up in the south of the country, about an hour west of Kraków such as it was. But he'd never been back until the mid-nineties.'

A wave of air freshener tickled Charlotte's nose and she stifled a sneeze. 'So why go back now? Maybe out of guilt, or the need to find out what happened to his brother?'

'That we know, I'm afraid.' The car began to slow in front of a walled compound she presumed to be the jail. 'Hans was executed by the Nazis in 1944.'

As the guard processed their entry, Charlotte

took in the high prison walls. 'It's massive,' she remarked as they drove through the gate. The mosaic of large buildings situated around green courtyards, the architecture a mix of old stone and new concrete, could have been a college campus.

'One of the largest in Germany,' Jack agreed. 'And it has a really interesting history too. There were a number of prisoners put to death by guillotine in the late 1800s. And Hitler himself was imprisoned here in the early twenties.'

'After the Beer Hall Putsch,' Charlotte added, feeling, as he nodded, like a student getting the right answer in class.

A minute later, the driver pulled up in front of double glass doors and Charlotte followed Jack from the car. Inside, she watched as he flashed his credentials to the guard at the desk, motioning for her to show her passport as well. The tweed sport coat he'd pulled on as they left his office was more academic than professional, giving him a roguish look.

They were escorted through a metal detector and Charlotte's bag searched, a familiar drill from her visits to clients in prison. Finally, the guard led them down a hallway to a conference room. Cozier than the prison meeting rooms back home, she reflected, with faded brown carpet, matching drapes faded a shade lighter by the sun. It was surprisingly ordinary, save for the bars on the small, high windows.

There was a shuffling sound behind them and another guard led a man in before leaving and closing the door. The first thing that struck Charlotte about Roger Dykmans was how average he looked. A slight, balding man in pressed khaki pants and white collared shirt, he was neither the monster nor the mogul she had imagined. His outfit was one she might have seen on the street, except he did not wear a belt or a tie and his shoes were loafers, no laces required. Nothing with which he could try to hurt himself.

Roger Dykmans had to be close to ninety but he did not look it. The eyes that appraised Charlotte were those of a man decades younger, unclouded and bright. His posture remarkably erect, and beneath the snowy white beard, his skin was eerily smooth, a genetic bounty no surgeon could replicate. It was not a factor that would serve him well at trial. Courts looked with sympathy upon the old and the frail, in part because it seemed unlikely (in Dykmans's case well-nigh impossible) they would repeat their transgressions and in part because jurors felt as though they were imprisoning their own grandparents. But here they would be reminded only of an uncle, and a spry one at that.

'Herr Dykmans,' Jack began, stepping forward. It was then that she saw it, an almost imperceptible flinch, not what one would expect from a polished man of his background. Had someone threatened him in prison or was it a relic of something years earlier? Perhaps he was not so different from her clients back home after all.

'Thank you for agreeing to meet with us on such short notice.' There was a note of deference in Jack's voice Charlotte had not previously heard.

'*Ja*, here I have nothing but time.' His English,

75

though not broken, was still clearly accented, a mark of the old country that the decades in America had not been able to erase, perhaps made stronger again by his recent years on the Continent.

Even here his appearance bespoke a quiet dignity, she noted. His hair was neatly combed and the khaki prison garb looked as though it had been freshly ironed. Money, she realized, lots and lots of money. Brian had said Dykmans was an investment banker and she could see that now in the unmarked hands, the delicate tan. Of course, refinement was hardly an indicator of culpability or innocence. The SS had been doctors, scholars. Closer to home, she had read about a prestigious Main Line physician, rumored to have bludgeoned his wife with a garden hoe, who then sat down to dinner while she bled to death ten feet away, polishing off an expensive bottle of chardonnay before calmly turning himself in. But there was an air of serenity about Dykmans that belied any sort of guilt.

'This is Charlotte Gold. She's been sent by your law firm in America to try to help with your case.' Jack did not, she noticed, reference his brother. Dykmans's eyes flicked over her and then away again, indifferent. Charlotte's annoyance flared; she was here for his benefit, not her own.

'Why don't we sit down?' Jack suggested, setting his briefcase on the table. When Dykmans had taken the seat across from them, he continued. 'As you know, the trial is just a month away. So we were hoping that you might be willing to tell us a bit more. If we could just go over the file again.'

Dykmans did not respond but gazed out the window. He was not dismissive of her, she realized, but of the entire situation. It was as if someone else's life was on the line and it was merely a show that he was watching. She was reminded once more of the inner-city kids she represented – they'd been burned by the system and were understandably wary, and she needed to gain their trust.

She pulled a black-and-white photograph from the file Jack had shared with her at his office, a picture of a group seated before a fireplace. 'Is that your family?' she asked. It was one of the two things she often found she could bond over with clients – family or sports – and the latter seemed unlikely to work here. Of course, family might be a risky topic, given the nature of the allegations against him.

But Dykmans seemed to take the question in stride, reaching for the photo with calm hands. 'That's my *Mutter* and my father.' He mixed his English and German without noticing. 'Of course my brother, Hans, and our sister, Lucy.' He did not speak further but continued to stare at the photo, a faraway look in his eyes.

'Herr Dykmans,' she began again gently. He looked up, as if he'd forgotten she was there. 'We noticed on your passport that you've returned several times to Poland in recent years. Can you tell us why?'

'Business,' he said simply. Charlotte blinked. She didn't know what answer she expected but it wasn't that.

'You mean the emerging capital markets?' Jack

asked, a note of impatience in his voice. Charlotte looked in his direction, annoyed. It took time to get close to a client, earn his or her trust. And she wanted to hear Dykmans's explanation in his own words, without Jack jumping in.

The older man shook his head. 'No, sorry, I misspoke. Not that kind of business. Family matters. Attending to our home in Wadowice.'

'It's still there?' Charlotte interjected, unable to contain her surprise.

'Yes. After the war, it was expropriated by the Communist regime. But ten years ago or so the Polish government passed restitution laws and one could file an application to have property returned. I did, and it was in a terrible state of disrepair, so I'm having it renovated.'

For what purpose, she wanted to ask, but before she could speak further, Dykmans stood. 'I thank you, but I'm growing a bit tired. If you'll excuse me.' He walked to the door and knocked, waiting for the guard.

'So that's it?' Charlotte remarked a few minutes later as they walked through the front door of the prison.

Jack nodded. 'And for Dykmans, that was a long conversation. Probably the most I've heard him say.'

'I see what you meant about him being unhelpful.'

As Charlotte slid into the sedan she caught Jack's eyes darting downward toward her legs, then away again so quickly she thought she might have imagined it. An unexpected spark of electricity ran through her. He's attractive, she realized for the first time, and not just for his resemblance to Brian. What was his deal anyway? She wondered if he was married or seeing someone. He wore no rings, but that didn't mean so much with men these days. She recalled stories from Brian years ago of a rich baroness who'd broken Jack's heart, but other than that he had been alone, always alone. Brian didn't understand his brother, mused more than once if he could be homosexual. 'I'd be fine with that,' he hastened to reassure Charlotte, and she knew he would be in that don't-ask-don't-tell kind of way, but that he would never be best man at his brother's same-sex union ceremony or be comfortable sharing a locker room with him. She'd surmised, though, that Jack wasn't gay, that his brother was mistaking quiet intellect for effeminacy. Now she was sure of it.

Not that it matters, she reminded herself now as the car pulled onto the motorway. Jack's brusque demeanor, bordering on rude, completely negated any possible appeal he might have. And one Warrington man was enough for this lifetime, anyway. She smoothed her pants, forcing herself to concentrate on the conversation. 'It was interesting, though,' she added.

'Was it? I'm not sure he told us anything at all.'

She traced her finger along a trail of condensation that had formed on the opposite side of the glass 'The childhood home in Poland? It doesn't make sense. Why would an international financier with a company to run spend so much time in rural Poland, fixing up an old house?'

'Sentimental value?'

'I don't think so. I think he's been returning to

the house where his family lived before the war because he's looking for something.'

'Like what?'

'I don't know.'

Jack pulled at his chin in a way that suggested more of a beard than was actually present. 'Maybe whatever he's searching for has something to do with his guilt.'

'Or innocence,' she pointed out. 'Don't forget whom we represent.'

'Right. Sorry. My prosecutorial instincts die hard.' But she could tell that it was more than that – Jack believed that Dykmans was guilty. 'So what now?'

A surge of energy ran through Charlotte. This was her case now, and she knew that regardless of whether Brian ever showed, she would see it through. 'Now,' she replied, 'we're going to Poland.'

Four

BERLIN, 1922

Sol ducked farther below the row of men's overcoats, watching the girl behind the counter pass a paper-wrapped package to a customer. As the salesclerk's fingers grazed the elderly man's hand, Sol was instantly filled with envy at the inadvertent touch. She smiled sweetly and said a few words to the customer before turning back to the cash register to finish recording the sale.

He had first seen the girl nearly a week earlier when he had come to the massive Kaufhaus des Westens to pick up some yarn for his mother. He'd balked at the errand – it was nearly four and even with the days lengthening there was not much time to get ready for the Sabbath and make his way to shul. But his mother had insisted – she and the maid were finishing up dinner preparations and without the yarn she would have no way to pass the long day tomorrow. He wanted to remind her that knitting on the Sabbath was an abomination or, from a less principled standpoint, ask why Jake could not go for her instead. But Jake was not yet home from work, Sol could tell from the quiet that still filled the house. Sol's own job at the Gemeinde, checking copy for the obituaries and other non-news items to be printed in the Jewish newspaper, had ended at three that day.

81

Having no excuse, he reluctantly set out for the department store, handing a clerk in notions the fistful of marks necessary to buy anything at all these days, as well as the note from his mother specifying exactly what she wanted so he would not, God forbid, get the wrong shade of blue.

Then, as he carried the yarn toward the exit, he first glimpsed the girl at the counter by the front of the store. Initially he kept walking, his neck burning, feeling as though something was stuck in his throat. Then he stopped and turned back. She was Jewish, he was certain of that, though it was often harder to tell with the women now that most had gotten so liberal in how they dressed. This one was different, though, her sleeves a bit longer, blouse buttoned at the collar, with a modesty he found refreshing. Her skirt, he suspected, would be longer than was fashionable too, if he'd been able to see it. And it wasn't just the tight curl of her raven black hair, which refused to be cowed into the low knot she'd attempted, which signaled her faith. Nor was it the arc of her nose, flanked by dark eyes set just a shade too close, reminding him of a wise owl. No, there was a fearful look, a slight hesitation as she hung back from the other clerks, that told him she was not one of them.

His mind raced as he boarded the streetcar for home and for days after he saw the girl's face in his mind. 'Do you need some more yarn?' he asked his mother the following Friday afternoon, hoping to come up with an excuse to return to the store.

Her brow furrowed with confusion as she patted the still-round skein beside her. *'Nein,* darling.'

Then she smiled, accepting her son's offer at face value for the goodwill it seemed to convey. 'But perhaps some needles.' She reached for her bag, but when she turned back, marks in her out-stretched hand, he was already gone.

Sol loitered now behind the coats, purchased needles in hand, watching as the salesgirl wrapped a parcel for her final customer of the evening. Inhaling the dusty smell of fresh wool, he tried to come up with some excuse to inquire about the fine jewelry the girl sold. In earlier years, he might have turned his nose up at the idea of a shop girl, but he had little room for snobbery now that the family was not so well off. And it took experience and a certain poise to get a job at the city's largest store, especially in such an upscale and centrally placed department.

Not that Sol had ever had the opportunity to consider women in the real sense of the word. Before the war, when he'd been scarcely more than a boy, they were like dangerous animals in the wild, strange creatures to be studied from a great distance. And afterward, well, he'd come back so broken ... it was hard to imagine anyone wanting to share the life of a lone Orthodox clerk who lived at home and had nothing.

The girl was packing up her belongings, he could see, closing out her register for the night. He imagined the conversation that he would never have with her, cursing his own lack of nerve.

'*Mein Herr*,' a voice said behind him as the girl started for the door. It was a salesclerk, nudging him to buy something or move on. Sol did not turn or respond, but started swiftly for the exit.

Outside, he looked toward the bus stop at the corner, hoping the girl might be waiting there, but there was no sign of her.

Defeated, he turned away. He had lingered longer than anticipated and it was almost sundown, so he tucked the needles in his pocket to give to his mother later, then made his way absentmindedly toward shul.

Bypassing the streetcar stop, he navigated the busy thoroughfare and made his way across Wittenbergplatz, past the still fountain. The tinkle of piano music spilled forth from the open door of a *Kaffeehaus*. Sol turned to look through the window at the patrons enjoying their end-of-week gatherings, caught somewhere between envy and disdain. The revelry was unseemly, he thought, in a city where so many people could barely find work, let alone socialize. And it felt forced somehow, like people were acting as they thought they should behave, mimicking what they had read in books or perhaps seen in a movie, if they had been fortunate enough to visit the *kino*, as Sol had managed twice over the years. In the warmer months, when the outdoor beer gardens drew even larger throngs, he avoided the square altogether.

The synagogue, set at the edge of the Jewish quarter, was a large, opulent structure with stained-glass windows and a gold dome on top. As Sol entered, the other men looked up and nodded vaguely in his direction before turning back to their conversations. They were middle class, mostly, or had been in better times, merchants and tradesmen hailing from the surrounding eastern districts of the city, their work clothes pressed a bit more carefully or perhaps covered with a suit coat for the Sabbath.

They thought him odd, he knew. A lone single man who came to shul every Friday night and Saturday was an anomaly among the younger Jews of their once-affluent section of Berlin. The Reform movement had caught on like wildfire, and most young people attended the more modern temple across town, if they went anywhere. Still others, like his brother Jake, went to the Jewish social club on Reisstrasse, where they did not worship at all, but instead had a meal and then debated politics over schnapps and cigarettes late into the night.

Sol pictured his twin brother's face as he made his way down the aisle. Jake, who had shaved his beard to a tiny goatee and trim mustache, was too busy for shul. He traveled in a wide circle of friends, many of whom were non-Jews, and spent long hours at his job at the ministry. Of course, he never explained his lack of observance that way. The Sabbath, Jake said, had traditionally been home-based – it was only in diaspora that Jews had felt the need to come together at the synagogue each week. It was infuriating the way he did that, tried to find nuggets from the Talmud to support his modern views, while ignoring wholesale so much of what the holy text required. But Jake had always done what he wanted, and so each Friday he joined their mother for the Sabbath dinner, making conversation with the handful of guests she assembled, before disappearing to the social club or for drinks with God knows who.

What, Sol wondered, fingering the edge of his

talus, would their father have thought of Jake's lifestyle? But even if he was still alive, Sol likely would not have known. Max Rosenberg had seldom been home and, when he was, had kept his thoughts to himself. Born penniless in a shtetl in Bohemia, Max had spent every waking hour of his life working, building from a single tiny hardware store to a chain, third biggest in Berlin. He had gone to shul dutifully each week when he was in town, not out of a sense of religious obligation but in order to keep the goodwill and patronage of his Jewish customers. No, their father would not have approved of Sol's own observant lifestyle, with its focus on books and study rather than earning money, any more than he would have agreed with Jake's social high jinks.

As the rabbi began to chant, a faint scuffling noise came from the rear of the sanctuary. Sol's eyes darted to the back of the room where a group of men, recent immigrants from the east, shuffled in, clad in work clothes that were crude and worn despite their best efforts to wash the factory dirt from their collars and cuffs. The newcomers had arrived in greater numbers and frequency in recent years, owing to the violence that had worsened under the earlier czarist regime, the harsh economic conditions exacerbated by the war and its aftermath. Their faces still bore the scars of what they had seen, the permanently fixed haggard expressions more telling than anything they could say in their accented Yiddish. Sol doubted that their lives here, living in cramped apartments, often two families to a single room, and working long hours in the factories for little pay, could be any less harsh than in the Pale. But the workers accepted each word or gesture like food offered to a starving man. Berlin's treatment of its Jews, in Sol's estimation, was far from perfect, more of a shove than an embrace. But to the immigrants, the city was worlds away from the barbarism of the shtetls from which they hailed, a haven. Here in modern Berlin, they were safe.

An hour later when the prayers had ended, Sol stepped outside, lowering the brim of his hat and raising the collar of his overcoat against the now-frigid March air. He fought the urge for a cigarette, stopped in equal parts by his desire to avoid his mother's scowl when she smelled the smoke on his breath and the fact that it was *Shabbes*. The streets were emptier now, and the few passersby moved swiftly, heads low to the wind. Sol paused at the corner to fish some coins from his pocket for the homeless man who sat against a building, a one-legged veteran he had seen there before. The man had to eat, after all, even on the Sabbath.

Walking, his thoughts returned to his father once more. Sol recalled Max as a shadowy figure from his childhood, coming home from work late at night, gone on mysterious travels for weeks at a time. Max worked feverishly, and after he died from an unnamed illness at the age of fifty-seven, Sol often wondered if all of the work had killed him. But the gamble paid off in the pecuniary sense of the word – by the time Max was found slumped over his desk, he was president of a prosperous business and had left his beloved Dora with the comfortable house on Rosenthaler

Strasse and what he thought would be more than enough money to see her through her days. It would have been, too, had their mother, naive to begin with and numb with grief, not fallen prey to an investment scam that left her not a year after he had died with a fraction of what he had put away.

Twenty minutes later, Sol entered the house. As he took off his boots in the entranceway, he winced at the sound of laughter that erupted from the dining room. Even as a child, he had felt like his mother's dinner parties were an affront to the quiet dignity of the Sabbath.

'Sol?' his mother called, hearing the door. He cringed. Usually by the time he arrived home from shul, dessert had been served and the wine-tinged conversation was noisy enough that he could sneak up the back stairs unnoticed. Reluctantly, he walked into the dining room.

His brother was still there, he noted instantly. Sol was surprised. Jake should have been long gone to meet his friends by now. But today he lingered, leaning back, running his hand through hair uncovered by a yarmulke, showing no inclination toward leaving. Then, scanning the guests, he saw the reason Jake was still there: a dark-haired young woman, seated beside him, talking animatedly.

Then she turned toward Sol, and as he saw her face he froze. It was the salesgirl from the department store.

No, it wasn't, he realized, taking a closer look, his heart still pounding. The resemblance was striking, though. She had the same dark eyes and curved nose, the same full lips and quick smile.

But her hair was styled in a short, sleek bob, and there was something about her lipstick and rouge that Sol found garish, her sweater tight and immodest, a style that he knew his girl would never wear.

Still, Sol was intrigued. Jake had never brought a girl to dinner before. Who was she: a secretary from the ministry? But she looked nothing like the dour, frumpy women he'd seen leaving the government building the one time he met Jake outside his office. Perhaps she worked at one of the brokerage houses for the bankers who came in every day from the elegant suburb of Grunewald by bus, the Roaring Moses it was called because of the large number of Jews who rode it. Or maybe she was an artist or performer or didn't work at all. With Jake, it was hard to say; he traveled easily through myriad groups, slipping from one mantle to the next seemingly without effort. Even as he disdained his brother's lifestyle, though, there was a part of Sol that secretly wished Jake might for once sweep him up and take him along on the magic carpet ride that was his social life.

'Sit down,' Sol's mother urged. He peered longingly down the table, wishing that he could squeeze past the others and find a seat down by Jake and the girl, but the guests were packed elbow to elbow and so he reluctantly pulled up the only available chair, a low-backed wooden one, and slid into the space his mother indicated beside her.

Sol studied the remnants of dinner that littered the table, crumbs scattered across the lace tablecloth and fine china. On the surface his mother's weekly gatherings had not changed – there had been savory chicken with spaetzle, he could tell from the lingering aroma, delicious chocolate tortes for dessert. Only one who had been there years earlier before the war might notice that the cuts of meat were leaner, the wine not so expensive. The dishes, casseroles and stews, were designed to stretch the expensive ingredients, to hide amidst the gravy and starch the fact that there was less.

The guests themselves were changed too – in earlier years, none would have been caught wearing anything but the latest fashion. Now if he looked closely he could see a bit of hand darning at Frau Leifler's collar, a scuff on the toe of Herr Mittel's dress shoe where the leather had worn thin. No one, it seemed, had been exempt from the economic hardship that followed the war.

Jake caught Sol's gaze and raised a hand in a wave that was friendlier than their relationship might warrant, designed for the benefit of the other guests. Sol did not return the gesture, but nodded and then looked away. He could remember a time when they had once been, if not close, at least not as distant as they had become since their lives took such different paths.

Sol surveyed the room. The house had always been Dora's; even when Max was alive, there was little of their father in the floral upholstery, the too-ornate furnishings. Now, with the passage of the years, there was an unmistakable wornness to it all. The wallpaper had faded and the carpets were frayed at the edges and there was a tarnish to the lamps that no amount of polishing could remove.

Sol's eyes dropped to the mantelpiece. Between the silver candlesticks and the framed photograph of his parents as young newlyweds, now yellow with age, sat a glass-domed clock. It had been a gift from their father to their mother, brought back from a business trip to the south when Sol was a small child. The timepiece was their mother's most prized possession; not only was it a memento of her long-departed husband, but it was one of the few gifts picked with thought and care during their marriage by the otherwise preoccupied Max. Dora forbade the maid from even dusting it, insisting on doing it herself each week with a special chamois cloth.

His thoughts were interrupted by rising voices across the table and he lowered his gaze to Herr Mittel, who was engaged in heated debate with a guest Sol did not recognize. The conversation had descended into politics, a debate on why Germany lost the war, what would have happened if it had won. Almost four years after the armistice, it was a popular topic, the speculation seemingly endless.

Inwardly, Sol bristled. Who else here but he had fought and nearly died in the trenches? 'If the Jews...' Herr Mittel began. Then he stopped, as though he had forgotten for a moment where he was. Clearing his throat, he continued. 'That is, if the foreign populations had fought instead of allying with their interests abroad.'

Sol's anger rose to full boil. The Jews had fought hard alongside the rest of the German men. One survey he'd read at the Gemeinde said more Jews had fought for Germany than any other minority, that twelve thousand had died. But that report had been buried, not published at the 'request' of a government ministry, and so the myth persisted. He looked down the table at Jake, wondering if his brother would correct Herr Mittel. Jake, who worked at the foreign ministry now, knew the older man was wrong. But Jake did not respond. No, of course not – defending the fact that the Jews had served would only point out that he himself had not, make him look cowardly in front of the girl.

Realizing no one else would speak up, Sol opened his mouth to say something, but his mother placed her hand over his, warning him to be silent. It was not politics or even fear on her part – she simply did not want one of her guests to feel unwelcome, or to taint the atmosphere of her party with an awkward moment. Dora Rosenberg loved people and she surrounded herself with company to blunt the force of whatever trauma life threw at her. During the war, she had doggedly persisted, hoarding ration coupons and supplies, holding parties by candlelight when the lighting failed, and starting the dinners in late afternoon when curfews wouldn't let the guests stay after dark. She clung to them even more fiercely after her husband died and the shelter he built around her began slowly to erode.

The gathering devolved into smaller conversations. Jake's voice drifted down the table. 'As I told the minister the other day...' His comments, though directed at the girl, were loud enough for everyone to hear.

Tuning his brother out, Sol grew more annoyed. Everyone already knew about Jake's position. He'd begun working for Walter Rathenau years earlier, long before he became foreign minister. The day he'd gotten the job, he ran home from university, breathless. 'He's amazing,' he told Sol. 'He's going to be the German Disraeli, they say.' Working long days with fervent zeal, Jake had gained Rathenau's favor and ridden his coattails into office as an appointed aide.

'Anti-Semitism in Europe,' Sol heard Jake saying nonchalantly to the girl now, 'is nothing but a passing social phenomenon.'

'Passing for about a thousand years,' Sol muttered under his breath.

'What was that, darling?' his mother asked absently, not looking toward him.

Sol did not answer. He had once believed, as Jake did, that they could be counted among their non-Jewish brethren, more alike than different. As a teenager, he'd been as secular as his brother. When the war broke out, he gamely enlisted with his friend Albert, caught up with everyone else in the Spirit of 1914, convinced that Germany was right and would swiftly prevail. Only then was Sol made aware for the first time in his life that he was not like the others. The lone Jew in his unit, he was hazed with a barbarism that he could not have imagined. They pissed in his water canteen and spat in his rations, which he ate anyway because he was close to starving by then and there was no other food to be had. They stole his extra pair of socks and he had gotten frostbite and trench foot and lost two toes on his right foot as a result.

But perhaps worst of all was the isolation. Shunned by the other soldiers, Sol found himself alone in the most desolate place on earth. Even Albert turned his back out of fear, avoiding his childhood friend until the day Sol cradled his head as he died in the trenches of the Ardennes.

And then he'd returned home. He didn't expect a hero's welcome – the civilians did not know how valiantly they had fought or the hardships they had suffered. But Sol was unprepared for the bile and recriminations: the Jews, the papers said, had not fought for their country. They had allied themselves with foreign interests, surrendered willingly and stabbed the German soldiers, who had treated them like brethren, in the back. Jewish factory owners were supposedly responsible for the shortages of munitions, food, and other supplies that had resulted in the defeat of Germany. Four years later, idiots like Herr Mittel were still repeating those same insidious lies propagated by the media and politicians in order to further their own interests.

Soon the coffee cups were drained and there seemed to be an unspoken cue for the guests to stand and start for their coats, despite his mother's protestations that they should stay a bit longer. 'We're going down to hear some jazz,' Jake announced as he reached Sol's end of the table, already a 'we' with the girl at his side.

'Hello,' Sol said to the girl, a shade too loudly, as she started past. 'I'm Jake's brother, Sol.'

'Miriam,' she offered, extending her hand in the modern custom, and Sol, fighting his natural tendencies, shook it.

'You look familiar,' he began and a look of confusion crossed her face, as if their paths could not possibly have intersected. 'A sister, perhaps?'

'Leah,' she said, and her voice carried the same dismissive note with which Sol had heard his brother speak about him. 'She's older, works at the KaDeWe.'

'Yes,' he replied quickly. 'Will she be joining–'

But before Sol could finish the question, Jake was at Miriam's side, taking her arm. He clapped Sol on the back a shade too hard. 'How's work at the Gemeinde?' he asked in a way that was meant to illustrate to Miriam the difference between Jake's important position at the ministry and his brother's clerical job.

Sol's mind raced as he tried to think of something interesting to say about his work but found nothing. 'We should go,' Miriam said, looking up at Jake.

Sol watched as his brother's expression changed, and there was a submissiveness there he had never seen before. 'Yes, of course.'

He held his breath, waiting for an invitation to join them. He would make an exception, go out on the Sabbath just this once, in hopes that Miriam's sister might be there. It was worth risking the wrath of God if it meant finding her, for the privilege of basking in the light of those brown eyes. But the invitation did not come – Jake and the girl were already brushing past him, making their way to the door, and in that instant Sol was instantly reminded of the vast gulf between his brother's world and his own, the places he could never belong, even if he wanted to.

The next morning, Sol set out for shul once more. On the street, he sniffled, his nose tickled by the acrid odor of the ersatz coal everyone burned to keep warm these days. He had slept poorly, dreaming of the evening in the jazz café that had not taken place, a smiling Leah taking his arm the way Miriam had Jake's, and had awoken strangely warm and empty and exhausted at the same time. His boots scuffed noisily against the cobblestones, carving tracks in the fresh coating of snow that covered the ground.

It was not until he reached the main thoroughfare that he noticed the difference: the street seemed eerily quiet, with a lack of activity more reminiscent of the last few weeks of August, when those Berliners who could fled the city for holiday to the seaside or the mountains, than early March. Inside the synagogue, the change was even more noticeable – the men did not call out to one another as they usually did but clustered in the corners, talking in low voices as if afraid someone might overhear. He stood awkwardly to one side of the room for several minutes, wanting to join in the conversations but not sure how. Nine o'clock, the starting time for worship, came and went, yet the men did not take their seats.

Finally, Herz Stempel broke away from the circle and came to the spot where Sol stood alone. At fifty-four, Herz was one of the younger congregants, less closed off and suspicious of outsiders. 'What is it?' Sol asked.

'You haven't heard?' Sol shook his head. 'Rathe-

96

nau's dead.'

Sol scanned the congregation in his mind, trying to recall which of the men in the sea of gray hair and beards was Rathenau. Then he realized that Herz was not talking about one of their own but rather about the foreign minister, for whom Jake worked. Walter Rathenau was also a Jew. 'How?'

'Shot with machine guns.' A rock pressed against Sol's chest as the image crystallized in his mind. 'Men ambushed his car. That's all we know so far.'

Jake sometimes rode along with the foreign minister, Sol recalled anxiously. 'When?'

'Last night about nine.' Sol inhaled, relaxing slightly. Jake was with Miriam then, on his way to the jazz club.

The rabbi finally signaled the call to worship and Herz retreated. As Sol took his seat, he thought again of his brother. Jake idolized Rathenau, who had mentored him and brought him on board. It was more than just admiration for a single man, though. To Jake, the fact that one of the highest posts in the cabinet was occupied by a Jew was proof that they were fully accepted into German society, that despite the insults and struggles they really were accepted as equals. Did he know yet what had happened?

After the morning service had ended, Sol hurried toward home, his mind still racing. The news of Rathenau's murder, while surprising, was not entirely a shock. Politics had grown more virulent in recent years and assassinations of politicians, either by the ultranationalists on the right or the extreme socialists on the left, were not uncommon. He remembered Jake describing how the esteemed Doktor Einstein and another man had called on Rathenau and begged him not to take the job as foreign minister on peril of his life. But Rathenau insisted, refusing the bodyguards that would encumber his movements and his ability to do his job. And now he was dead.

As Sol rounded the corner onto Rosenthaler Strasse, an arm shot out of a doorway and grabbed him by the shoulder, dragging him into an alley. He froze, certain that he was being attacked. Frantically, he tried to remember the grappling techniques he'd been taught in military training, but his mind was blank.

'It's me, Jake.' His brother's voice broke through the haze.

Sol relaxed slightly. 'Rathenau's dead,' he replied by way of a greeting. The words sounded smug, as if they confirmed everything he had ever believed about assimilation, and his own observant lifestyle choice had been vindicated.

Jake did not answer, but released Sol from his grasp. Sol noticed then the way his brother's hand shook as he lit a cigarette, the paleness of his face. 'I'm sorry,' he added, softening. 'I know you liked Rathenau, respected him.'

'It's not that,' Jake replied, his voice a hoarse whisper. He took a drag from the cigarette and exhaled, letting the smoke unfurl above them. 'I think it's my fault.'

'Your fault?' Sol stared wide-eyed at his brother. 'How could you possibly–'

'I was out at a club a few weeks ago. Miri, the

girl who was at dinner last night, introduced me to some friends of hers. From the university, she said. We were drinking, talking. I think they asked me questions about the minister, his schedule...'

Sol could instantly picture the scene: Jake, his tongue loosened by too much liquor, boasting about his position, saying more than he should. His stomach twisted. 'What about Miri?' he asked, picturing the attractive brunette. 'Have you asked her?'

'Gone. I tried to find her this morning but her flat is deserted.' Jake buried his head in his hands and leaned against the doorway. 'There will be an inquiry. With the information that was given, it's only a matter of time before they figure out it was me. What am I going to do?'

Sol summoned his big brotherness, all four and a half minutes of it. 'You don't know that.' But even as he spoke, he realized Jake was right. The government would be looking for someone to blame and the police force was notoriously anti-Semitic. A Jew betraying Rathenau would be a convenient story; Jake, portrayed as a disgruntled subordinate, would make the perfect scapegoat. 'You need to get out of the country,' Sol said finally, surprised at his own decisiveness, the certainty in his voice.

A light appeared in Jake's eyes and Sol could tell he was thinking of the salons of Paris and London and other grand cities, images gleaned from the boyhood stories their father had told of his travels. 'East,' Sol added authoritatively.

'East?' Jake's shoulders slumped as the visions of cafés and social halls evaporated from his mind.

'Yes. It's easier to cross the border and you'll be less likely to be noticed. And there are Jews there who will help.' Jake's brow wrinkled, imagining the shawl-clad immigrants from the Pale. 'Papa has cousins near Lodz,' Sol persisted, as if making his case. 'Go to them and from there you can arrange a longer journey, by sea to America or somewhere else. I've heard there's a train that goes all the way to China.'

Jake's eyes danced once more as he imagined more exotic adventures. Then his face fell. 'I don't have the money,' he said, confirming, as Sol had long suspected, that the government job did not carry a paycheck that matched its prestige.

'We'll figure that out,' he said, trying to sound reassuring. 'But you have to leave right away and—'

'Miri,' Jake interrupted. His eyes darted back and forth rapidly. 'I have to find her first, make sure she's all right.'

It was the first time Sol had ever heard his brother express concern about anyone but himself. What kind of hold did this girl have on him after such a short time? Then, remembering the effect Miri's sister had on him, he understood.

'And perhaps she can provide an explanation, prove that I had nothing to do with it,' Jake added desperately. 'Maybe we can even leave together.' Sol wanted to tell Jake that his loyalty was misplaced; Miri had clearly abandoned him, perhaps even set him up. But he could tell from his brother's stubbornly set jaw that it was futile; he wouldn't leave without finding her, or at least knowing where she had gone.

Leah, he remembered suddenly. Maybe she

knew where her sister had gone. 'Wait here,' he instructed Jake and started from the alley, nearly slipping in his haste. Steadying himself, he set off hurriedly down the street.

Twenty minutes later, he barreled through the entrance to the department store, then stopped. Did he actually dare speak with her? But there was no time to lose. He steeled himself, then walked toward the counter. The salesclerk, blond and stout, was not Leah. Of course not. She wouldn't be here, surely, on *Shabbes*. And even if she wasn't observant, she might not be working today. His heart fell. But perhaps a coworker might have her contact information, know where Sol could find her.

He started forward. 'Excuse me...' As he neared, he saw a second girl, hunched over a cardboard box. She turned and his breath caught. Behind the counter, as if she had never left, was Leah. She was even more mesmerizing up close, he decided as she straightened. A mix of surprise and delight filled him.

A flicker of what Sol thought resembled recognition crossed her face and for a moment he hoped that perhaps she had noticed him too on his previous visits to the store. 'May I help you?' she said, and her voice, which he had imagined so often in his mind these past few days, was even more lyrical than he had dreamt. But her tone was formal, as though she were speaking to anyone.

He stifled his disappointment. 'Leah,' he blurted, and the girl seemed so taken aback that he wondered if he had made a mistake. 'You are Leah, aren't you?'

101

'Yes.' She blinked, as if unaccustomed to being known. 'Have we met?'

'No. I'm acquainted with Miri.' She looked annoyed then, having been asked too many times about her sister by young men, he suspected. 'She's a friend of my brother, Jake.' Leah's expression relaxed slightly. 'Do you know where I can find her?'

'She's left,' Leah replied evenly, her eyes narrowing. It seemed to Sol then that he might spend his entire life watching her face. 'On holiday, she said.' Her emphasis on the last word made clear that she did not believe her sister's story.

'Do you know where she's gone? So that I might tell Jake,' he added quickly.

'I would think that he should already know,' she retorted, and whether Leah was just being protective of her younger sister or was aware of what had happened, Sol could not tell, but he knew she would say nothing further.

'I've seen you working here before,' he ventured. 'But I would not have thought today...'

'I don't normally work Saturdays,' she replied, a touch of defensiveness creeping into her voice. 'But the other girl called in sick. I didn't have a choice.'

No, he agreed silently, forgiving her transgression more readily than might be expected, given his steadfast beliefs. Principle had to give way to practicality on occasion, if one hoped to keep working in this economy.

She was watching him, he noticed then. Her gaze held his without wavering and there was a spark of interest there that he had never seen before – from anyone. Adrenaline surged through his veins and, pushed forward by it, he took a deep breath. 'What time do you finish working?' he asked, the words tumbling out atop one another. 'Perhaps–'

'Leah,' the other salesclerk called, interrupting before he could finish his invitation for coffee.

'I have to go,' Leah said, glancing over her shoulder nervously. 'But I'll tell Miri that Jake asked for her. If I see her,' she added, then turned away.

Sol fought the urge to call after her, then stopped, knowing further conversation might put her job at risk. The momentary surge of confidence receded and he walked quickly from the store. Outside, he shivered, cold and lonely once more.

As he headed back to Jake, his mind raced. He had done it, spoken to Leah, perhaps even laid the groundwork for future encounters. Then, remembering the purpose of his visit to the store, his heart sank a little. He was no closer to finding Miri for his brother. She was gone; he was sure of it. And he had to persuade Jake to leave, now. His brother needed money for the journey, too, and the meager amount he saved from his job at the Gemeinde would come nowhere close to being enough.

Perhaps *Mutter* ... he thought, then stopped. Telling their mother was impossible – she'd have too many questions, and would insist that he stay. Surely her boy, her beautiful Jake, could never have done such a thing and the world would see if only he explained. No, she wouldn't understand, and even if she did, she did not have that kind of cash. Dora had a houseful of things she treasured but individually none was worth much.

Except the clock, he remembered suddenly. He pictured the domed timepiece that sat on the mantel. A treasure, his father called it more than once, when no one but Sol seemed to be listening, proud of the bargain he'd wagered. He had bought it from a provincial clockmaker who was unaware of its full value, which had surely increased with time.

Inside, the parlor was quiet, the smell of eggs from breakfast lingering in the air. He paused to listen for their mother who, God willing, should still be at market with the maid if the lines were long. Then he rushed into the dining room, where the silver from the previous evening's meal lay neatly stacked and polished, waiting to be put away. Reaching the mantelpiece, he stopped. Beneath the glass dome the four pendulums of the clock rotated in one direction, then stopped and continued in the other direction on their endless journey.

Sol hesitated, picturing the clock on the mantelpiece for generations to come, his mother showing it to her grandchildren. (He was surprised that in the vision, the children were his, girls with dark curly hair and close-set eyes.) She would be devastated to find it gone. But Jake needed to go, and this was his only hope. He grabbed the clock and carried it out under his jacket.

He walked back down the street as quickly as he could without attracting attention, and slipped into the alleyway where his brother crouched low to the ground, smoking another cigarette. 'Miri?' Jake asked hopefully, standing up.

Sol shook his head. 'I spoke to her sister. She's left the country for good. Leah didn't know where.'

Jake's face sagged and Sol felt a stab of guilt at the lie. But Jake would never leave if he held out hope of finding Miri. 'Here.' Sol produced the clock.

Jake paused, and for a moment Sol expected him to object. But his brother, never one to question what was given to him, took the clock. 'If Mama asks...' Jake began, then faltered. Then without another word, he turned and ran.

'*Auf Wiedersehen,*' Sol said under his breath as his brother disappeared around the corner. Jake had not, he realized, even bothered to thank him.

He started slowly back toward the house. From the foyer, he could hear two voices, his mother's high-pitched and the maid's higher, back from market, recounting the previous night's festivities as they put away the silver. There was a pause in the conversation, a moment of silence followed by a scream. Steeling himself, Sol walked toward them.

'Gone,' his mother said simply as he entered the dining room, and for a minute Sol thought she was talking about Jake. But Dora had gotten so used to her sons coming and going it would be days until she remarked upon the lack of Jake's shadowy presence, the fact that his bedclothes seemed undisturbed. 'The clock is gone.'

'*Ja, Mutter.*' He faltered as the moment he had waited for his entire life unfurled before his eyes.

Now he could tell her Jake had taken it, vilify the golden child who was no longer here to defend himself and finally claim his rightful place as the favored son. But then he saw Jake in the alley, vulnerable and helpless, and he could not bring himself to do it. It was best if their mother knew nothing when the police came asking questions about his whereabouts anyway. 'I saw that the latch to the back door was open this morning so I expect someone may have broken in and snatched it.'

Her complexion paled. 'We were robbed?' she asked, disbelieving.

'I don't think it was that serious. More likely someone who saw the door left ajar and seized the moment. Nothing else was taken. But I'll report it to the police first thing.' He watched remorsefully as a torrent of emotions washed across her face, shock then sorrow and anger. But her expression soon slackened to one of resignation. The clock was her most beloved possession, but in the end it was only an object and no one could afford to get very attached in these troubled times. The blow of Jake's unannounced departure would come much harder and he was grateful that in the moment she did not ask.

There seemed to be nothing more to say, so Sol started up the stairs. As he reached the landing, optimism surged through him suddenly. He had done it – helped Jake and taken the clock and gotten away with it. And after *Shabbes* he would stop by the department store to see if Leah was working again, follow through on his invitation to coffee. He didn't require an introduction now.

For years the notion of someone who might share his life had been a concept so foreign and remote he'd scarcely entertained it. But now as he saw Leah's face in his mind, new possibilities stirred inside him.

Sol pictured Jake running with the clock and recited silently the prayer for safe travel, while half suspecting that it was better than his selfish, mercurial brother deserved. But there was no need to be petty – he was here in Berlin and Jake was not, and the house and the family and all of this would be his for the rest of his life.

Five

WADOWICE, 2009

Charlotte brushed the wrinkles from the front of her pants as she stepped out of the cab that had picked her and Jack up from the Katowice Airport just over an hour earlier. She groaned inwardly, noticing a smudge of gray dirt across the front of the khaki fabric. Amazing that despite all of the economic development, the wider roads and gleaming shopping centers they had seen along the way, the same fine coat of coal soot seemed to cover everything here as it had years ago.

As Jack paid the driver, Charlotte inhaled deeply, welcoming back the familiar crisp morning air, tainted by the odor of burning brush. Wadowice, she reflected as she studied the main square, was something of an anomaly. Bigger than a village yet too small to be a city, it seemed to hover in between, attracting enterprising new businesses to its narrow, traffic-clogged streets while stubbornly clinging to its provincial, Old World character. She had passed through on research trips before the motorway was built, when the road between Krakow and the other cities still ran through dozens of little places exactly like this one.

They walked from the square in the direction of the address that she had Googled before leaving.

'Wadowice is where Pope John Paul II was born,' Jack noted, pointing to a plaque in front of one of the houses.

Charlotte nodded, more than a little pleased to be the one with more background knowledge this time. 'And the interesting part is, when he was a boy here, his best friends were a Jewish family, the Turnowiczes. One of the sons, Ryszard, later became head of Kraków's Jewish community. The pope used to stop and visit him on his return trips from the Vatican. And when Turnowicz died in the early nineties, the pope sent three cardinals as emissaries to the funeral.'

'That's a side of Polish–Jewish relations you don't hear much about,' he replied, a hint of interest in his voice.

'Most people don't take the time to learn it,' she agreed. 'They come to Poland, visit the con-centration camps, and leave again. There's so much more to it than that.'

'I wonder if Roger knew the pope as a boy,' Jack mused. 'They would have been about the same age.'

'Good question.' She stopped. 'This is it.'

She looked up at the house before them. Three stories high, with a sloping wood roof and freshly planted flower boxes in the windows, it was set close to the road, as was the fashion in these parts. Jack came to her side and knocked on the door. 'Roger said that the caretaker would be here to let us in.'

At the Munich airport that morning, Jack indi-cated that he had spoken to Roger and told him of their plan to go to Wadowice. Roger had seemed indifferent to the idea, Jack reported, but had made arrangements so the caretaker would be expecting them. 'Maybe he's having a late lunch,' Charlotte suggested when no one answered, looking at her watch.

Jack raised his hand but before he could knock again, the front door flew open and a woman with short dark hair and a square, stocky build, reminiscent of an Olympic volleyball player from the Eastern Bloc days, appeared. *'Tak?'*

Charlotte hesitated. *'Dzień dobry,'* she said, then paused, fumbling for the right words in Polish. 'We are friends of Pan Dykmans.'

The woman cocked her head as she listened. 'Nice to meet you. I'm Beata,' she said in surprisingly good English. 'Come in.'

She led them up a set of polished wood steps into a sitting room. At the far end was the very mantelpiece in front of which the photograph of the Dykmans family that Charlotte had shown Roger had been taken. The house had been immaculately restored, the furniture, curtains, and other decor an exact replica of what they must have looked like just before the war. But everything was in such good condition; Charlotte could not imagine that these things had been here and survived the decades so unscathed. Roger, she suspected, must have scoured the antique stores, paid a fortune to find the identical pieces.

As she looked around the pristine living room, Charlotte's anxiety rose. The house was a museum – how could they possibly find anything useful here? She turned to Beata. 'Was your family in Wadowice during the war?'

110

'*Nie*,' Beata replied. 'I mean, no. My parents came from Warsaw in the fifties and stayed.'

So the woman could not personally offer anything helpful, Charlotte thought with more than a twinge of disappointment. 'Is there a basement or attic?' she asked.

'No basement.'

'Can you show us the attic, then?' Beata gestured that they should follow her up another flight of stairs. On the next floor there were four bedrooms, also perfectly restored. Through one of the doorways, Charlotte glimpsed two narrow beds, toys stacked on a shelf. She could almost imagine young Roger and Hans playing there. What had their relationship been like as boys?

Beata pulled a rope from the ceiling and brought down a set of wooden attic steps that unfolded to the ground. She gestured that they could go up in a way that suggested she had no intention of joining them. 'I'll check later back,' she said, her reversed word order betraying the fact that she was not a native English speaker.

Charlotte went first, climbing the ladder and stepping into the darkness at the top of the stairs. 'There must be a light,' she said, feeling for the wall. But the fixture that she found was empty, the slot where the bulb should have been bare. She walked forward, slamming into a crate. 'Oww!' she cried, clutching her shin, her voice echoing, then fading into the shadows.

'Careful,' Jack said, now at her side, his hand warm on her shoulder. But he did not ask if she was all right, and his tone was more critical than concerned. As they spent more time together, she

111

reflected, he seemed not so much enigmatic as just plain rude.

Jack navigated past her with ease. There was a rustling sound as he reached the lone window and pulled back the thick, yellowed curtains, allowing light to filter in.

Charlotte surveyed the attic. In contrast to the rest of the house, it was a mess. Wooden boxes, stacked haphazardly from floor to sloped ceiling, ran the length of the cavernous space. A fine layer of dust covered everything like a sheet.

Jack walked across the floor, sending a sea of particles dancing through the air. 'How on earth are we ever going to find anything? This could take weeks.' There was a note of rebuke in his voice, as if reminding her that the trip had been her idea. 'And more to the point,' he paused to stifle a sneeze, 'what are we looking for?'

You could have disagreed with my suggestion to come here, she wanted to say. But an argument with Jack was not going to help their case. 'I'm not sure, but we need to put ourselves in Roger's shoes,' she offered instead. 'Why did he keep coming back here?'

'He said it was to restore the house.'

'Yes, but why leave the attic in such a state? And what could be so important–' She paused in front of a waist-high stack of boxes. 'Look.' The top box had been swept clean with a cloth, or perhaps a hand. 'Someone's been here, and recently. Maybe Roger?'

Jack shook his head. 'He's been in jail for months.'

'How about her?' Charlotte tilted her head

downward, indicating the caretaker.

'I don't think so.' He sneezed. 'She's had access to this place for years. Why would she suddenly be interested?'

A chill ran down Charlotte's spine. Who else was looking into Roger's past?

'We might as well get started.' Jack lifted the box that had been wiped off and put it down on a narrow swath of unoccupied floor.

Charlotte started for the next box in the stack, then stopped again. 'I need to make a quick phone call. Be right back.' Jack bit his lip, as though he wanted to ask who she was calling but had thought better of it.

She climbed back down the ladder and, not seeing the caretaker, stepped into what appeared to be the master bedroom. Pulling her Black-Berry from her bag, she found Brian's number in the call history, then hesitated. She needed to know that he had kept up his end of the bargain by getting Kate Dolgenos to represent Marquan, but she really didn't want to call. It wasn't that she was nervous about speaking with him. In truth she wouldn't have minded getting him on the phone to give him a piece of her mind for standing her up. No, she just didn't want to discuss the fact that she was in Poland with Jack. It was her investigation now and she didn't need to justify her decisions to him.

She dialed a different number instead. 'Defenders' office,' Doreen blared. Her voice crackled, though whether from her perpetual gum chewing or the quality of the connection, Charlotte could not tell.

'Doreen, it's Charlotte. Is Mitch around by any chance?'

'Not in yet,' the receptionist replied and Charlotte, calculating the time difference, realized that she was right.

'Has anyone called about my client, Marquan Jones?'

'Nah.' She could hear Doreen's nails clacking against the keyboard, updating her Facebook status, undoubtedly. Charlotte's anger flared. Brian had reneged on his promise after all, leaving Marquan without counsel and her thousands of miles away, unable to help. 'But there's a whole team set up in the conference room.'

'Team?'

'Yeah. Showed up yesterday. Kit or Kath or someone, big shot from New York.'

'Kate Dolgenos?'

'That's her. Comes in all dressed up in a fancy suit with three baby lawyers following her like mice and says your office is too small. So Ramirez gave them the conference room.' Charlotte cringed, wondering if Mitch was annoyed by the intrusion or grateful for the help. She should have given him a heads-up but hadn't wanted to say anything until she was sure Brian would come through. 'They've been in there ever since,' Doreen added.

Charlotte exhaled. 'Thanks, Doreen.' So Brian had kept his promise and Marquan had the very best counsel available. She only hoped it would be enough.

She climbed back up the stairs to the attic. 'Everything okay?' Jack asked. He had moved on

114

to a different box and did not look up.

He thought that I called Brian, she realized, hearing the tightness in his voice. She was suddenly aware of the magnitude of the rift between the two brothers, which seemed to have been worsened by the years. 'Just checking in on a client,' she explained as she knelt before the box once more. 'There's this kid, Marquan, and I repped him a few years ago on something minor. I'd gotten him into an after-school program and he really seemed to be turning it around. Only now he's gotten caught up in a carjacking that went bad, and two little kids got killed.'

'That's hard,' Jack replied, his voice neutral.

'He's a really good kid,' she insisted, kneeling by one of the boxes and opening it. 'Smart, so much potential.'

'Sure.' But she could tell that he was not convinced.

'You don't believe me.'

He shrugged. 'I just never saw you doing crimnal defense work, that's all. Crossing over to the dark side.' He did not bother to keep from sounding judgmental now.

Of course. Jack had known her in law school, when she thought she would spend her career as a prosecutor. That was so long ago it felt like another lifetime. And Jack viewed defenders as mercenary sharks, willing to represent anyone for money. She had felt that way herself once upon a time. 'It's not that way at all.' But even as she spoke, she knew there were plenty of lawyers just like that. So what made her think she was different? 'I'm a public defender, for one thing,' she said aloud, though as much for herself as for Jack. 'So clearly this isn't about the money.'

He rubbed his nose with the back of his sleeve. 'But you have to represent everyone who comes along, even the really rotten cases.'

That was true, she conceded inwardly. The public defender's office was the last stop for those who couldn't afford an attorney. Everyone was entitled to a fair defense and so for many people they were it.

'It must be better, though, working with juveniles,' he offered, seeming to sense her inner conflict. 'I mean, most of them aren't hardened criminals, at least not yet.'

She looked up at him, surprised by the note of empathy in his voice, the first sign of warmth she'd detected since her arrival. There are some pretty tough kids where I come from, she wanted to say, but didn't. Of course in some ways it was easier representing the Marquans of the world, with their youthful soft voices and gentle eyes suggesting that they were not yet beyond reach. But there was always a specter of fear looming over her, that she would open the newspaper and read about a murder committed by someone she'd successfully gotten off of a charge, or for whom she'd negotiated a reduced sentence. The knowledge that the person was on the street because of her.

That had not happened yet, thankfully, but there had been something just as bad, maybe worse. Last February when it was bitterly cold and sleeting, she had walked the underground concourse between Locust Street and City Hall, trying to breathe shallowly to make its urine-soaked stench bearable. As she passed the row of homeless people, mostly black men, that lined the passageway, her guilt rose and she fought the urge to stop and give them each something. Would they spend the money on food or drugs? She could not help them all, she thought, reminding herself of the regular donations she made to charities like Project H.O.M.E. and Philabundance.

'Please,' one of the men said and there was something familiar about the voice.

She looked down and her heart broke as she recognized a boy she had represented on a drug charge three years earlier. She stopped and knelt, heedless of the filthy floor. 'James?'

'Hullo, Miz Charlotte.' His voice was the same. She managed a smile, but inwardly she screamed. She had not asked James what had happened to him, how he had come to be there, not wanting to embarrass him. Instead she had bought him breakfast at the nearest hot dog stand, then had given him the rest of the money she had in her wallet, not in fact caring what he spent it on. She wrote down the phone numbers to the shelters and soup kitchens from memory and made him promise to come see her in the office later that day so she could help him further. As she walked away, leaving her heart behind on the concourse floor, she knew he would not show and after he had not, she returned to the same spot but he was gone. The image had haunted her for months. How had he come to be there? Could she have done something different to change his fate?

'What is it?' Jack asked, interrupting her

thoughts, and for a minute she considered telling him about James. But she didn't, knowing it would only reinforce his perceptions of her work.

She lifted a stack of documents from the box. 'Nothing.'

'I'm sorry if I offended you,' he offered. 'I just always saw you as a prosecutor.'

She shook her head. 'I never had the stomach for it. I mean, the big war criminals, sure. But I interned one semester at the U.S. attorney's office and I found I just didn't like putting people away, especially when I looked at their families in the back of the courtroom.'

'Those kids killed in the carjacking had families too.' His brusque tone had returned, any sign of the understanding he'd exhibited a few minutes earlier now gone.

'I know that.' Her frustration grew. 'I'm not saying it's black and white. Anyway, you're a defender now too,' she pointed out.

'Only for this case.' He waved his hand, refusing to acknowledge the conflict. 'This is just a stopping place for me until I figure out what I am going to do next.' She waited for him to elaborate, but he turned wordlessly back to the box.

She looked down at the stack of yellowed papers before her, setting them on the floor so as not to jostle them. It was the first rule of research, whether poring over documents in a dusty archive in Kiev or going through a police locker in North Philly: preserve the materials intact in order not to destroy their evidentiary value.

'Well, this is interesting,' Jack said, straightening. Charlotte looked up to see him holding a brown leather portfolio. 'Roger's papers from when he was a student at the university in Breslau.'

Where Hans had also been stationed as a diplomat, she recalled. 'And...'

He unfolded a piece of paper, which had yellowed with age. 'My dearest Magda,' he began, translating from German.

'Dearest,' Charlotte repeated. 'Who's Magda, I wonder?'

'No idea. But I guess our Roger wasn't such a loner after all.'

'What does it say?'

Jack shrugged indifferently. 'Nothing much. Some routine talk about summer in Wadowice.' He paused, an eyebrow raised. 'And that he's counting the days until September.'

'When he could return to school,' she surmised. 'Magda must have been in Breslau. But why would the letter Roger wrote still be in his folder?'

Jack turned over the envelope. 'Because for whatever reason, he never sent it.' He set the paper aside. 'Not sure it has much relevance to the case, though.'

Charlotte wanted to disagree. A relationship, or even an unrequited crush, could go to the very essence of who Roger Dykmans was, why he might or might not be guilty. But Jack had lowered his head and was engrossed in the papers before him once more, so she returned to the box before her. The documents appeared to be routine, she observed. Bills that had been paid, a ledger recording household expenses, recipes held together by a rusty clip. The Dykmanses, it seemed, had not thrown anything out.

Pausing again, Charlotte peered at Jack out of the corner of her eye. He was more attractive than Brian now, she decided. His lean figure had not given way to paunchiness, as his brother's had, and the lines that had formed at the corners of his eyes gave him a more interesting look than he had years ago.

She looked down at the papers once more, but her eyes, dry from the dust and reading, blurred. 'Tell me more about the case,' she said, leaning back on her heels, eager for a break.

He lifted his head. 'Well, generally speaking, Nazi war crimes prosecutions are a crapshoot. Some countries, like Syria and unbelievably Austria, refuse to cooperate with the international community at all. Sweden has a statute of limitations and takes the position that it cannot prosecute for that reason. Others, like the Baltic states, participate in a token manner but never really bring a case against anyone who is fit to stand trial. They're really more interested in prosecuting former Communist leaders.'

Of course, she thought. Those crimes are so much fresher and more personal for the living population. Naturally there's more of a mandate to pursue those cases than to vindicate Jews gone for decades, whom they never wanted in the first place.

'And even where there is a will,' Jack continued, 'prosecuting crimes against Nazi war criminals is a ticking time bomb. Fewer and fewer are still alive and of those many are medically unfit to stand trial.

'The United States created a group at Justice in

120

the seventies, the Office of Special Investigations, to track down Nazis who had somehow slipped into the U.S. and were living there undetected.' His face grew more animated as he delved into the topic, picking up steam. 'They're unable to prosecute the Nazis for actual war crimes that took place outside their jurisdiction. So instead they use the tactic of having them denaturalized and deported.'

'I've read about it,' she said, recalling something from the files she'd reviewed at the hotel the previous evening. The approach had worked and the United States had successfully prosecuted several dozen cases, more than all of the other countries combined. But it was a drop of sand compared to the millions who had died, the thousands who had perpetrated the crimes against them. She had wondered several times if it was worthwhile, spending all of the money bringing to justice a handful of senior citizens while war crimes continued unabated in the Sudan and elsewhere. But it sent a message, symbolic and important: *We have not forgotten.*

'The cases seemed to flag for several years,' Jack explained. 'Then the Soviet Union collapsed and a vast number of documents suddenly became available to help identify and find the former Nazis.'

She opened her mouth to ask how it all related to Roger's case. But Jack had turned back to his documents and seemed to be concentrating deeply. They worked intensely for some time, the silence broken only by the sound of a bird chirping in the eaves. 'Nothing in this box,' Jack announced sometime later. She could sense his frustration – so much time wasted and nothing to show for it. At this pace, they could be here for weeks, which was time they didn't have.

'Mine either.' She stood up, stretching her right foot to relieve a cramp in her leg. 'Are we missing something? Are there people, maybe, who we should be talking to, who could point us in the right direction?'

'I don't think so,' Jack replied. 'I asked Roger that when I told him we were coming here, but he said that it's been so many years, everyone who knew his family has either emigrated or died.'

Charlotte nodded. It was one of the great challenges of researching the Holocaust. The generation that had witnessed it all was dying off by the thousands each day, their experiences slipping away like sand through one's fingers. 'Maybe we should approach this differently,' she suggested, scanning the attic once more. He tilted his head. 'I mean, the box that someone has been through is probably least likely to have what we're looking for, because if there was something relevant, the person likely would have taken it, right?'

'Assuming they were looking for the same thing as us.'

'Assuming. So maybe if we try the places they didn't get to...' She wove her way through the maze of boxes toward the far end of the attic. The light was dimmer there, making it difficult to see. She noticed something smaller then, wedged between the last stack of boxes and the wall. A trunk, she realized, reaching for it. But her reach was too short. 'Help me, will you?'

Jack came to her side, his arm pressed against hers in the narrow space. 'Let me,' he said.

She stepped back and he pulled the trunk out and dragged it back toward the window, where the light was better. 'Is it locked?' she asked.

He pulled hard on the clasp at the front until there was a loud popping sound. 'Not anymore.'

As Jack returned to the box he'd been searching, Charlotte knelt down, then opened the trunk and peered inside. It was filled with photographs, mostly loose, some in frames or albums. She began to rifle through them. The albums contained the older pictures, Dykmans family ancestors, she presumed. There were photographs of Hans and Roger and Lucy, too, as infants, then growing through the years. A normal, happy family, or at least they had been, until the war destroyed everything. And they hadn't even been Jewish.

She picked up a pile of loose photographs. There was one of Hans and a striking, dark-haired woman in a white dress standing before a fireplace, holding hands. A clock with a dome of glass sat on the mantelpiece behind the couple.

'Was Hans married?' she asked Jack, holding up the photograph. 'I don't remember reading anything about a wife.'

He nodded. 'Briefly, in the years before his death. But I'm not sure what happened to her after he was arrested.' He looked down at the box he'd been searching once more, then stood up, brushing the dust from his pants. 'This is pointless,' he declared. 'I mean, what is it that we're looking for exactly? A photo, a document, or

123

something else? We don't even know that there's anything here worth finding at all.'

'There has to be,' Charlotte replied defensively. She searched for some evidentiary support for her assertion, but found none.

'Anyway, it's getting late,' he added.

She looked past him out the window. Beyond the gritty rooftops and the trees, the sun was sinking into the mountains, faint in the distance. She blinked in surprise. 'What time is it?'

Jack looked at his watch. 'Almost seven.'

She blinked. 'I had no idea we'd been at it so long.'

He stood, stretching. 'We'll have to come back and continue in the morning.'

'But you just said this is futile.'

'And maybe it is. But we're here, so we might as well finish what we've started.' His expression was dogged. 'I booked us hotel rooms in Kato-wice for the night, so we should try to find a cab and make our way back there.'

Why not Kraków, she wanted to ask. For the same drive, they could have enjoyed decent food and a stroll through the Old City rather than a bad hotel restaurant by the industrial airport. But she did not want to sound like a tourist. 'All right,' she said, replacing the photographs. 'Let's go.'

They found Beata cutting some fresh flowers outside in the garden, which stretched expans-ively behind the house. 'We needed to stop for the day,' Jack explained. 'But we'd like to come back and look some more tomorrow morning, if you don't mind.'

Beata nodded. 'Certainly. Come with me.' She led them through the backyard to a small cottage. This must be where she lives, Charlotte realized. As Beata opened the door, then stepped aside to let them in, Charlotte hesitated. Katowice was a good hour away, and that was after they somehow found a taxi. She just wanted to get to the hotel, take a hot shower, and sleep. Exchanging glances with Jack, she could tell he felt the same way. But it would not do to offend the caretaker when they wanted to come back and search again tomorrow. Perhaps she was even going to give them a key to let themselves in the next morning. Reluctantly, Charlotte stepped inside.

The cottage was more spacious than its compact exterior suggested. A single room with a high vaulted ceiling, it had a small kitchenette at one end and a neatly made futon at the other. In the middle, a long table had been set for twelve, a collection of mismatched chairs crowded tightly around it. 'Sit, sit,' Beata urged before disappearing through a door into what could only be the washroom.

'What are we doing here?' Charlotte whispered to Jack in a low voice.

'I don't know.' He gestured toward the table with his head. 'Must be a dinner or party of some sort.' He pulled out a chair for her. 'We'll stay for just a few minutes and then excuse ourselves.'

'Oh, Jack...' She wanted to tell him that there was no such thing as a brief social call at Polish gatherings, that one drink meant six and a casual stop by someone's house invariably resulted in staying long into the night. She recalled going out for lunch with friends at Kraków's main market square one day and the next thing she knew the whole night had passed. She'd woken up in the morning with very little recollection of how she'd gotten home and some fuzzy memories of a nightclub that were so strange she thought she had dreamt them. Even the performers at Polish concerts were obliged to return for about six encores as the audience remained on their feet, clapping methodically, refusing to leave.

Before she could speak, Beata reappeared in a floral dress. 'This is very kind of you,' Charlotte began to demur, 'but we really must–' She was interrupted by the ringing of a doorbell. The caretaker hastened to greet her guests.

A steady stream of people of various ages, arriving alone or in pairs, poured through the front door, and as they crowded around the table Charlotte doubted that they could all possibly fit, but there miraculously seemed to be a chair for everyone. When they were seated, Beata produced a bottle of vodka from the freezer and it was passed around, shots poured. Charlotte's *'nie, dziękuję'* was ignored, the tiny glass before her filled to the brim.

'Na zdrowie!' someone proposed, raising his glass in Beata's direction, and as the group erupted into an off-key but enthusiastic rendition of *'Sto Lat'* ('May You Live to Be a Hundred') Charlotte realized that it must be the caretaker's birthday.

She turned to Jack, and was surprised to find him watching her. He smiled then, and there was a softness to his eyes that she had not expected.

Her cheeks flushed.

She raised her glass in his direction. 'Cheers,' she said, then looked away, downing the liquor with resignation. It was the first real drink she'd had since leaving Philadelphia and she welcomed the searing burn, putting at a distance for a moment all that had happened.

Soon trays of deli meats and cheese were produced, along with cucumber and cabbage and beets in sour cream, always sour cream. Charlotte took some of everything that came in her direction, hungry and uncertain of when they would have the chance to eat again.

Underneath the table, Jack's leg brushed against hers. She looked up. Was he trying to tell her something? But he was gazing off in the distance, seemingly distracted.

As they ate, introductions were made in Polish, too rapidly for Charlotte to follow. A white-haired man across the table gestured to the younger woman beside him, attractive despite the fiery shade of unnaturally red hair that seemed to still be popular here. *'Moja żona.''*

My wife. Charlotte checked to make sure she had heard him correctly. The man had to be fifty years her senior. 'Are you from Wadowice?' she asked in Polish, wondering if he had perhaps known the Dykmans family.

He shook his head. 'No, I'm from Przemyśl.' Charlotte nodded, recalling the small city on the Ukrainian border. 'My wife and children were taken to Auschwitz, so after the war I came here looking for them. I never found them but I stayed.'

'Are you Jewish?' She hoped he wouldn't mind the question.

'No, Catholic, but that didn't seem to matter when the Nazis cleared our town. Anyway, sometime later I met Jola.' He patted the hand of the woman next to him.

Much later, Charlotte hoped. Jola would not even have been born when the war ended. 'And we have a son, Pawel,' Jola added in accented English. 'He's ten.'

Charlotte stared at the elderly man. It was hard to believe he had a child so young. Well good for him, she thought, taking in his proud smile. Everyone deserved a second chance.

Jack's leg met hers again, and this time it stayed. It's the crowded table, she told herself, making it hard to keep a distance. Heat rose within her and she struggled to focus on the conversation. We should leave. She was more eager than ever now to escape the too-warm room. But she knew it was impossible. It would be easier to climb out of a quicksand pit wearing heavy Wellingtons than to flee the hospitality of their well-intentioned host.

'So you are visiting the Dykmanses' house?' a man to her right asked in Polish.

'Yes.' She waited for him to press her for the reason but he did not. People in this part of the world, still scarred from the decades of Communism when one kept one's head down to avoid trouble, tended to ask less of strangers and mind their own business.

She wondered then if it bothered these people that Roger, now a foreigner, was reclaiming such a big house in the midst of their town. 'It's lovely really,' a woman seated across the table said, seeming to read her thoughts. 'For Pan Dykmans to come back and spend so much time and money restoring the place. It was an eyesore for so many years.'

The man to Charlotte's right made a strange guttural sound, somewhere between a cough and a snort, signaling something other than approval. 'Like the Jews,' he mumbled.

Charlotte's cheeks flushed. Poles were supposedly past the war. Some even professed a new-found interest in Jewish life and culture, at least in the big cities. But here in the provinces when the alcohol flowed and they thought they were among their own, the anti-Semitism that had lain dormant in the intervening years flared up. She wanted to tell the man that the Jews had only been permitted to reclaim the properties that were not occupied, and those were mostly the synagogues and cemeteries and community centers no one wanted. But Jack put his foot on hers beneath the table, willing her to be silent. He was right, she realized, biting her tongue. Why waste her breath when nothing was going to change the entrenched views here?

Jack's hand brushed against her leg, rested. She inhaled sharply. Was he hitting on her? Highly improbable, she concluded. It must be the vodka. She considered pulling away, then decided against it.

'The Dykmanses were good people,' Jola said. 'At least that's what my mother said.'

'Really?'

'Yes. My grandmother and Pani Dykmans, Hans

129

and Roger's mother, were close.' Jola paused, glancing self-consciously from side to side, as if aware for the first time of all the eyes upon her. 'Well, everyone knows about Hans, the work he did during the war. But Roger, he was another story.' Charlotte cringed, wondering if maybe the information was something she didn't need to hear about her client. 'Roger was a good friend of my mother's older cousin. He was a kind man, according to her. Just very quiet.'

'A loner?' Jack suggested.

But the woman shook her head. 'Not necessarily. I mean, he kept to himself – especially after he met Magda.'

Charlotte and Jack exchanged glances. 'Magda?' she repeated, feigning surprise.

Jola looked around the table again, as if afraid to say too much. 'Magda was a beautiful young woman. They met when Roger was a student at the university in Warsaw, I think.' Wroclaw, Charlotte corrected silently. 'Roger only had eyes for her. That was a very well-kept secret, though he confided in my cousin once when he was home from university. You see, Magda was married.'

Charlotte looked down the table at the caretaker, Beata. Had she set up the meeting with Jola purposely? Perhaps knowing they were trying to find evidence of Roger's innocence, she had arranged for them to meet the one person who might be able to help. Or maybe I'm reading too much into it, she decided, watching Beata's simple face, now gone slack from the vodka.

'What happened to Magda?' Jack asked.

'I don't know. Taken to the camps, I would

130

guess, along with the other Jews.'

Charlotte's breath caught. Surely Roger could not have been in love with a Jewish woman and yet conspired with the Nazis to have all of those children killed. This bit of information, more than anything else that she and Jack had learned so far, seemed to speak to their client's innocence.

Suddenly Charlotte grew very warm and nausea rose up within her. 'Need ... air...' she managed, pushing back from the table and rushing to the door. Outside, the cool night air rushed against her face and she gulped it in greedily, fighting the urge to vomit.

A moment later, Jack was at her side. 'Are you okay?'

She nodded, too embarrassed to speak. What had come over her? Was it the alcohol or Jola's story, or something else entirely? 'Fine,' she said at last. 'I thought I might be sick. I think it was the shots of vodka on an empty stomach.'

'Heady stuff, especially on top of jet lag,' he agreed. 'It was a good exit strategy, anyway. You must be exhausted. Which brings us to an important point: Where are we going to stay tonight?'

'I thought you said you reserved us a couple of rooms in Katowice.'

'I did, but it's after eleven, and I don't think we're going to get a cab at this hour.'

She resisted the urge to rebuke him for his lack of planning. 'We could see if someone could give us a ride...' But she did not finish the thought. If they went back inside they would be cajoled into staying for more vodka, the party likely lasting

131

well into the night. And there was no one in that gathering who was in any shape to drive them anyway.

'What about there?' Jack suggested, pointing toward the Dykmanses' house.

She paused, looking up at him. 'Are you seriously suggesting that we stay here?'

'The house is empty,' he retorted, annoyed by the challenge. 'Do you have a better idea?'

In point of fact, she did not. 'I'm assuming it's locked.'

'Let's go see.' They walked back and pushed against the solid oak door, which did not move. Polish houses were not like the quickly assembled particleboard dwellings back home. They were made with granite and stone, built with painstaking care over many years and passed down. It was not uncommon for three or four generations to live under one roof.

Jack disappeared around the side of the house. Charlotte followed and found him working at the edge of a large window. 'What are you doing?' He pulled harder and for a moment she was afraid that the glass might break, but he tugged again with a grunt and the window slid open. With great effort, he climbed over the ledge, hoisting one leg, then the other.

'But–' she started, surprised. She had not imagined breaking and entering to be part of his skill set.

Charlotte expected him to reach back and offer a hand to help her over, but he disappeared into the darkness. She waited outside alone for several seconds, hearing the laughter spill forth from the caretaker's cottage, certain that they would be caught at any moment. But then Jack appeared around the side of the house, gesturing toward the now-open back door.

Inside, the darkened house was eerie and still. A chill ran up Charlotte's spine, and she fought the urge to feel for a light switch, not wanting to attract attention from the outside.

'I don't feel right staying in their beds,' she whispered.

'Too risky,' he agreed. 'Let's go to the attic. I saw a mattress there.'

As they climbed the ladder, Charlotte wondered how they would find their way around the cluttered attic in the dark. But moonlight shone brightly through the lone window, illuminating the boxes in pale gray. Jack moved around the now-familiar space with ease, pulling out a mattress from against one of the walls and clearing some of the boxes to one side to make a space for it.

'Not exactly the Ritz,' he commented, unbuttoning his shirt as he sank to the mattress.

And awkward, she thought, to say the least. She took off her shoes and sat down. As she lay on her back, she tried to maintain a few inches of distance between them. The room began to wobble slightly from the vodka and she placed one foot on the floor beside the mattress so that it wouldn't spin.

He turned toward her. 'Is it hard for you, being here and working on the case?'

'Because I'm Jewish, you mean?' She stared up toward the ceiling. 'It used to be. The first time I came to Poland in the early nineties, everything was so gray and old. It looked like something right out of the war. And the signs of the past were everywhere – the police sirens, the concentration camp site I had to pass on my way to the archives. It was hard not to see life as a graveyard.' The words seemed to spill out as she recalled the images she hadn't thought of in years. 'But eventually I had to put it in context or I would have gone crazy. It still crept up on me though. You expect to feel something the first time you walk through Auschwitz. But maybe not the fiftieth and that's when it gets you.'

'That's nearby, isn't it?'

She nodded. 'Half an hour, forty-five minutes from here, tops.'

'Jesus.'

'I'm always conflicted,' Charlotte continued. She was rambling, she knew, but the answer to Jack's question was not a short or simple one. 'I mean, I'm the descendant of Holocaust victims. My mom's whole family died here. But when I came back, I found that the truth was so much more nuanced than I ever expected. The people you wanted to call evil had humanity and the heroes were flawed. There was gray everywhere. That's what I found so appealing about the work. The broad brushstrokes of history were misleading. I really felt that by studying and recasting things in a finer light, I was doing more of a service to the truth and to those who died. But as for Roger...' She paused, turning to face him. 'It's too soon to tell, I think.'

'Yet you still want to defend him?'

'I do. Everyone deserves a fair trial. It sounds clichéd, I know. And often it isn't pretty. The kids I see, lots of them have done some really awful things – they've hurt family members, strangers, animals, other kids. Maybe there's a reason, maybe not. But they all deserve to be heard.'

'Is that why you're doing it?' Jack asked. 'I mean, helping Brian, after all that happened.' The painful history suddenly loomed large between them. 'It's not like you owe him anything.'

So that was his real question. 'I don't know.' She shifted uneasily. 'I don't think of it that way. It's not for him,' she added quickly. But the question lingered. Even with the passage of time, perhaps there was still some small part of her that wanted Brian's approval, reveled in having something to offer that he needed.

Jack seemed to exhale, so slightly she thought she imagined it. She remembered then his expression earlier that day when he thought she was calling Brian. Was he worried that she might still have feelings for his married brother? And why should he care? Was it just sibling rivalry, or was the acrimony between them still so strong after all of these years?

'I could ask you the same thing,' she countered, changing the subject.

'True,' he acknowledged. She could hear him stroking his chin. 'I'm not sure why I'm helping. It's most decidedly not because I care whether Brian makes partner in that firm of his. I guess it's out of some sort of sense of obligation – family, not personal.'

'But you haven't spoken in years.'

'He's still my brother,' he replied simply. 'And he asked for my help.'

'It was curiosity,' she said abruptly. 'For me, I mean. The story was so intriguing and it was a chance to do something overseas again.'

'Do you miss it?'

She hesitated, knowing that he was talking about her former life, the international work she'd left behind. 'Not so much. It's like the stuff in these boxes.' She gestured around the attic. 'You pack a dream away so that it doesn't see light and pretty soon it's just part of your past, like an old art project. Most days you don't even think of it.'

'And then someone comes along and opens the trunk and takes it out and gives life to it again,' Jack replied. 'You wonder if you will be able to put it away.' There was an undercurrent to his voice that made her think that he was talking about something else.

As they lay in the darkness, the question nagged at her. She had left her ghosts buried all of these years for a reason. Would coming back here and stirring things up change that somehow? 'I have a life in Philadelphia,' she said aloud, as if responding to an argument that had not been made. 'I've got work that matters, people who need me.'

'Of course.' She searched his voice for a hint of condescension but found none. He rolled slightly away then and a moment later began to breathe more deeply, air whistling softly through his teeth.

Charlotte looked around the darkened attic, hearing in her mind the whispers of those who had been here before them. She wondered what they had thought when they tucked their belongings away, the things they had thought important enough to save. Had they known they might not be coming back? Her skin prickled.

There was a scuffling sound by her feet then. She sat up, alarmed. A mouse, perhaps, or something bigger? The noise came again, closer now. Impulsively, she grabbed Jack's hand. 'Wha–?' he started, then turned toward her. As he did, his face drew close and his lips brushed hers. She froze, waiting for the awkward leap back, the apology. But his mouth stayed, grew stronger on hers, and she found herself responding. His hand came to her hair, then her face.

A moment later, they broke apart. 'I thought I heard a rat,' she managed, as if that explained everything. He did not respond but lay back again, as if still asleep. But she could hear his breathing, quicker and heavier than it had been.

Charlotte turned away, heart pounding. What had happened? The kiss was so out of left field. Even with the slight thaw that seemed to take place as they'd spoken in the darkness of the attic, it was almost impossible to reconcile the prickly, aloof man she'd come to know over the past two days with the one who had kissed her so passionately just now. Had the moment been born of sleep or alcohol or both? Surely it could not have been something more. He didn't even like her.

She lay awake in the darkness, uncertain of what to do. The thought of staying here next to him the rest of the night was unbearable. But she didn't know the rest of the house well enough to go traipsing around in the dark and didn't want to risk the wrath of whatever had been scurrying around, now that it seemed to have disappeared. She turned toward the window, studying the webbed branches, covered with crisp fall leaves, that seemed to form a canopy beneath the pale gray sky. It had to be after three, she guessed. In a few hours it would be light and they could resume their search. She closed her eyes and forced herself to sleep.

Sometime later, Charlotte blinked her eyes against the bright sunlight that beamed in through the open curtains. 'Ahh,' she moaned as a dagger seemed to shoot through her head. It was, she realized, the kind of hangover brought on by cheap Polish potato vodka, compounded by the fact that she could no longer drink like she was twenty-two.

She became aware then of something warm pressed against her back. Jack, she remembered. Without rolling over, she could see his tousled hair and rumpled T-shirt out of the corner of her eye. What had happened? A series of images flooded her mind: she grabbing his hand, his lips on hers.

She lay still for several seconds, feeling his breath warm and slightly sour against her neck. It was the vodka that had caused it all, she decided. Best to say nothing about it. She pulled away and sat up, studying him again. Watching him sleep now, arms flung over his head, it was impossible to remember how he had ever seemed intimidating at all.

Charlotte carried her bag down the stairs and found the washroom, then changed into the fresh

138

blouse and jeans she'd brought with her. She ran her tongue over the fuzz that had formed on her teeth. Then she cringed at her own reflection, which shared none of Jack's sleepy, roguish charm. Instead, her hair was pressed flat against her head, sticking out awkwardly at her neck, and there was a crease across her cheek left by the pillow. She opened the medicine cabinet looking for an aspirin, or at least some toothpaste, but it was completely bare. Of course it was. She rinsed her mouth with some water, then splashed some on her face and smoothed her hair before returning upstairs.

Taking in the still-sleeping Jack once more, she debated waking him, then decided against it. Instead, she sat down beside the box of photographs she'd been examining the previous evening and continued to sort through the pile.

A few minutes later, Jack stirred. 'Mmph,' he mumbled, shielding his eyes with his forearm.

'What time is it?'

'Morning.'

'You have a keen insight into the obvious,' he remarked dryly. Their eyes met, and if he felt at all awkward about what had transpired between then the previous night, he didn't show it. Perhaps the drinks had blurred his recollection. Or maybe to him it was just no big deal.

'Do you think we should leave before Beata returns?' she asked.

'You mean, knock and ask to be let in again? I don't think that's necessary. We'll just tell her we got here early and the door was unlocked.'

He stood up and pulled on his shirt. As he knelt

beside her to open another box, her heart seemed to skip once. 'This is futile,' he said, picking up their debate from the previous day. 'Why don't we decide which ones we want to look through, and I'll arrange to have them shipped back to Munich?'

'I don't know.' She looked around. It seemed such a shame to disturb the order of the attic that had lain largely untouched all these years. But before she could reply, she was interrupted by a clattering below. Beata, she thought, expecting the caretaker to appear at the top of the steps. Instead, a head of bright red hair came into view. *'Dzień dobry.'*

'Dzień dobry.' Charlotte returned the greeting, confused. It was the woman from the party last night, the one who knew about Roger and Magda. But what was she doing here?

Jola, Charlotte recalled suddenly. The woman looked fresh, as though she had gotten a sound night's sleep instead of drinking vodka into the wee hours. 'I remembered something else,' she said, her voice more confident now than it had been in front of the group at Beata's. 'Last evening I said that Roger was a student in Warsaw, but that was wrong. Roger studied in Wroclaw, or Breslau it was called then. His brother Hans was living there at the time and Roger stayed with him.'

'And that's where he met Magda?' Charlotte asked.

Jola did not answer, but looked over Charlotte's shoulder with interest at the pile of photographs. Charlotte cringed, not sure if they should be sharing the Dykmanses' intimate family belongings

140

with this woman. But Jola reached past her, picking up one of the photos. 'That's her.'

'Magda?' Charlotte followed the woman's finger, wondering if she had misheard. 'Are you sure?'

'Yes,' the woman replied firmly, handing it back to Charlotte. 'I saw her once in a photo my grandmother had from Pani Dykmans.'

Exchanging uneasy glances with Jack, Charlotte held up Hans's wedding picture, which they had seen last night. Roger, it seemed, had been in love with his brother's wife.

Six

BRESLAU, 1940

Roger wiped his boots on the mat and looked up expectantly. Forty-three, the number above the doorway of the row house read. He compared it to the slip of paper in his hand once more. The address was correct. He raised his arm, then hesitated, wondering if it was too soon to knock again.

As he reached forward, the door swung open, leaving his hand flailing in midair. A slight woman with dark hair and pale skin appeared in the doorway. They stared at each other for a moment, not speaking. Roger had never met his brother's wife. There had been a photograph of an impromptu wedding in Geneva, a hastily scrawled letter, as Hans's invariably were, apologizing that circumstances had not enabled them to have proper nuptials, or at least come to Wadowice and make introductions to the family before they wed. Their mother, always eager to find an excuse for Hans's inattentiveness, had speculated in a more outspoken way than was proper that perhaps his bride might be with child. But six months later, the woman who stood before him was willowy, showing no evidence of an impending birth.

'You must be Roger,' she said, stepping aside. 'I'm Magda. Come in.'

'*Vielen Dank.*' She was taller than he had imagined. In the photograph she had appeared more slight, clinging to Hans's side in the shadow of an alpine slope, gazing up at him with an expression that seemed midway between trepidation and awe. Here in her own home without her husband, she seemed to fill the space, moving through the light-filled house with ease.

'I can show you to your room, if you're tired from the journey,' she offered, as she led him into the sitting room. 'Or perhaps some tea.'

'Tea would be nice,' he replied, setting down his bag and taking the chair she indicated. 'If it isn't too much trouble.'

'Not at all. Hans would have been here, but he's been called away on business.' Business, Roger reflected, as Magda disappeared into the kitchen. No one was quite sure what his brother did, and Roger often had the sense that it was better not to ask. Hans, five years Roger's senior, had studied politics, choosing not to enroll in the university here and taking off instead for Berlin. After graduation, he had gone into the diplomatic service and been detailed to the consulate in Breslau, an office that had ceased to exist now that Germany had invaded Poland and no longer recognized its national sovereignty. Hans kept his official residence here but seemed to travel endlessly throughout the country and abroad, meeting with contacts.

Roger looked around the house, simply furnished with a scarcity of personal effects, which reflected the fact that Hans and Magda hadn't been here long. It was more spacious than he had imagined, given Hans's modest government salary and his refusal to accept help from their mother. Of course the location, in the Jewish quarter and close to the synagogue, could hardly be considered ideal in light of the present German administration, and that likely kept the value low.

The invitation to stay with his brother had come as a surprise to Roger, prompted, he was sure, by their mother's urging. It wasn't that Hans was inhospitable – he simply moved in his own orbit and it would have never occurred to him to ask. Roger felt awkward about being an interloper between the newlyweds. But the coincidence of his brother having a house in the city was too fortuitous to ignore, and the price of rent too dear for their mother to pay when it wasn't necessary.

Not that it seemed, Roger observed now, as if his presence would be much of an intrusion. The few touches that did decorate the house were all Magda's, from the embroidered slipcovers to the handful of framed photographs scattered about the room. There did not seem to be a trace of his brother anywhere, not his pipe or shoes or any of the usual clutter that Hans had left in his wake for most of their youth. Roger imagined Magda alone in the large house night after night, and considered, with more empathy than he expected to feel for the woman he had just met, if she was lonely here.

Magda returned with a tea tray, which she set on the low table in front of him. There was not any sugar and he wondered if it was due to rationing. Surely the shortages here could not be as bad as back home. He picked up one of the

144

cups. 'That's a beautiful timepiece,' he remarked, pointing to the clock on the mantel.

She sat down in the chair opposite him. 'It was my father's dearest possession. We found him holding it when he died.'

He waited to see if there was something more she wanted to say, but her expression turned vague as she picked up her teacup, lost in private thoughts. 'Where are you from?' he asked, realizing how little he knew about his brother's wife.

'Frankfurt, originally.'

'How did you and Hans meet?' The question sounded more intrusive than he had intended.

But Magda did not seem offended. 'I worked in a café in Berlin. Your brother used to come in when he was a student.' Her eyes seemed to dance at the memory. Sipping his tea, Roger imagined the meeting. He pictured Hans holding court at a table, a circle of onlookers watching as he pontificated on current events, debated politics long into the night. Magda could not have helped but been smitten. And what had drawn Hans to Magda? Her beauty, for starters. Magda, with her perfect posture and luminous blue-gray eyes, had a quiet grace that would have made her the focus of attention over other women who were more flirtatious or better dressed. Even his brother, so often preoccupied, could not have failed to notice her.

'After Hans graduated, we lived some distance apart for a while after he took this assignment. And then we married and I moved here.' She spoke hurriedly, fidgeting with the cuffs of her dress, offering more information in response than the question necessitated. Was she nervous at his

145

presence? He wondered if she minded the intrusion.

'It's very gracious of you to have me in your home. I hope it isn't too much of a bother.' He felt certain from her contemplative expression that it was the first time anyone had asked.

'Not at all.' Her voice sounded sincere. 'It will be good to have someone else here.' She closed her mouth quickly, raising a hand to her flushed cheeks as if she had said too much.

She stood abruptly, setting down her still-full teacup and gesturing for him to follow her. There was something striking about her gait as she climbed the stairs, a way of walking that was so smooth and effortless, she traveled without seeming to really move at all.

As they passed the second-floor landing, he counted through the open doors three rooms, a bedroom and a study and another room that seemed in disuse. 'The water closet is just here,' she said, pointing to a fourth, closed door. She continued up the stairs to the third floor, opening the door at the top. 'This is yours.'

They started forward at the same time. 'Oh!' Magda said, as they jostled against one another in the doorway, which was too small for both to pass. They stood motionless for a second, her arm warm against his side.

'Excuse me,' he said finally, feeling his face go red as he leapt back to let her pass. He berated himself inwardly, certain that she must be appalled by his lack of manners.

But Magda let out a tinkling laugh, as though his misstep was an intentional joke, and her good nature instantly put him at ease. She walked into the room and gestured to the expanse of space beneath a sloping roof. A simple bed, chair, and desk were the only furnishings, giving the space an uncluttered feel that he rather liked. The smell of fresh lemon cleanser filled the air.

'It's lovely,' he remarked.

Neither spoke for several seconds. 'I'll leave you to get settled,' she said at last. She paused, mouth still open, as though there were something more she wanted to say. Then she turned and vanished down the stairs, leaving a sense of emptiness in her wake.

The next afternoon, Roger stood on the doorstep of the house once more, unsure of whether to knock or walk right in this time. He settled somewhere in between, rapping once lightly, then opening the door a crack without waiting. 'Hello,' he called.

Something was different, he sensed immediately as he stepped into the foyer. He had left early that morning without seeing Magda and spent the better part of the day at the university, picking up the required texts, making contact with his tutor about their first meeting. Now, as he started up the steps, juggling an armful of books, he detected an unmistakable energy in the air that had not been present previously.

'Good afternoon.' Magda greeted him hurriedly, not stopping as she passed him on her way down the steps. He stared after her, puzzled at her coolness. Had he done something to offend her? But she had already disappeared into the kitchen. He proceeded upward. As he reached the second-floor landing, he heard a male voice, muffled and deep, through the now-closed door to the study and he knew then the reason for the change: Hans had returned.

As Roger continued on to the third floor, the door to the study below flew open. 'My brother!' Hans bounded up the stairs, clapping Roger on the back. 'Welcome to my home.' There was a proprietary note in his brother's voice that was impossible to ignore.

'Thank you,' Roger managed, struggling not to drop the books. Hans had always seemed so confident and self-assured, giving the impression that he was well older than twenty-four. And he had aged in the almost two years since their last meeting. With his broad-shouldered build, he still had a youthful air, but his sandy hair had thinned and there were new lines beneath his hazel eyes.

Hans swept the stack of books from Roger's arms. 'Come, let's catch up.'

Reluctantly, Roger followed Hans into the study. The desk and floor were covered with papers, and the familiar smell of pipe smoke hung sickly sweet in the air.

'You've settled in all right, I take it?' He slipped seamlessly from German into their native Polish. 'Found everything you need?'

'Indeed. Magda has been most hospitable.' She entered the room as he spoke, hesitating as though caught off guard by her own name. With shaking hands, she set down two cups of tea between the stacks of paper on the desk. Did her husband make her nervous? She had not seemed this way the day before.

As Magda straightened, Hans caught her hand and their eyes met. *'Danke, Liebchen.'* There was a genuine look of affection that passed between them, making Roger squirm and filling him with a strange sense of disappointment.

'So,' Hans said, turning back to Roger when Magda had gone. His white shirt was rumpled, the sleeves rolled up, a faint gray line of dirt at the collar. And his jaw, usually clean shaven, had a fine coat of stubble. Where had he been? Roger did not ask, of course, knowing Hans would not say.

Hans's smile was more disarming, his perfect teeth whiter, than Roger recalled. The Dykmans boys had been blond as children, owing to their Scandinavian roots. But where Roger's coloring had darkened with adolescence, Hans remained fair. That, along with his crisp, unaccented German, was an asset that enabled him to blend in, causing people to forget the fact that he was a foreigner here.

A foreigner, sort of. Breslau, or Wroclaw as the Poles called it, had been batted back and forth between the Poles and Germans and their neighbors like a ball in a game of table tennis for centuries. Though the city, part of Upper Silesia, was predominantly German now, it maintained a distinctly Polish undercurrent, and signs of the Slavic culture were everywhere – in the shops, the cuisine – even if people did speak the language a bit less and in a softer tone these days.

'So Mother is well?' Hans asked, interrupting Roger's thoughts. His expression and tone seemed to convey genuine concern, in sharp contrast to the infrequency of his letters and almost non-existent visits. That was the thing about Hans – despite the fact that he was self-absorbed, he was almost impossible to dislike. He was never arrogant or dismissive, and had a way of winning people to his side while making them think that his ideas were their own. The worst that one could say about him was that his work, whatever that was exactly, consumed him with a kind of passion that made him distracted, unable to ever be entirely present.

Hans's charisma had translated well into his professional world. He was a diplomat in the truest sense of the word, and he managed to keep the goodwill of the present German administration even as he worked, Roger suspected, covertly against them. In fact, it was likely Hans's influence that enabled Roger to come to Breslau and study at the university during a time when Poles were less than welcome here.

'I'm sorry to have been gone and not able to greet you,' Hans apologized, not waiting for an answer to his previous question. 'The situation right now...' He waved his hand around his head in the direction of the front window. 'It's terribly bad and getting worse, I'm afraid.'

Hans spoke as though Roger knew what he meant, and in some sense he did. Germany had been under control of the Reich for more than seven years. The changes were perhaps less abrupt here than in the countries the Nazis had come to occupy more recently, such as Poland. Roger had been there when they marched into Wadowice, the tanks preposterously large in the narrow town streets, Great Danes in a china shop. Here, he imagined, the shift had been gradual: shops closed one by one, people who had intermingled quietly for decades suddenly forced to wear armbands and associate only with their own.

Roger recalled the previous morning as he arrived at the train station a family with four small children clustered around a pile of luggage. The mother's face was drawn with exhaustion, her lips pressed tightly together, and she seemed to barely have the strength to thank him as he held the door for them. She carried a sizable toddler who bore his own tiny version of the armband with the Star of David, and Roger noticed then that they had no pram. He did not know how they had gotten to their final destination from the train station since the Jews were banned from streetcars. At the time, the woman had struck him as just a harried mother traveling with children. But now he wondered if it was something more. Where were they going and was it by choice?

'Well, it's getting late,' Hans said, standing, and that was Roger's cue to do the same. As they walked into the hallway, they encountered Magda, returning to clear the cups.

'Dinner at six?' she asked, looking up at Hans, her face bright. 'I've managed to find some cutlets for schnitzel.'

But Hans shook his head. 'I'll just take a tray.' He turned to Roger. 'You'll forgive me for not joining you,' he said. 'I need to leave again first thing in the morning and there's much to be done before then.' Roger could not help but notice how Magda's face fell as her husband brushed past her.

151

He held his breath, waiting for her to turn to him and ask him to join her for dinner. But she retreated silently from the study.

Having been dismissed, Roger picked up his books and carried them to the third floor, settling down at the desk to read. He gazed out the window, across the soot-blackened chimneys at the gray late-afternoon sky. His eyes dropped to the courtyard below, which was adjacent to the White Stork Synagogue. The three-story neoclassical structure with its high arched windows stood in sharp contrast to the modest Jewish house of worship in their home town of Wadowice. It was magnificent, or at least it had been, Roger could tell, before the mobs that took to the street on Kristallnacht almost two years earlier ravaged the building, shattering the windows and burning the prayer books within. But it had not been entirely destroyed and was, perhaps, the city's only still-functioning synagogue.

Today was Friday, the beginning of their Sabbath, and a small group of men had clustered outside the desecrated synagogue, talking. Roger marveled that they could be so nonchalant, as if nothing had changed and their very presence there might not be putting their lives in danger. But maybe, he reflected, this was the one place where they could feel as if life as they once knew it still existed.

A beam of sunlight broke through the clouds then, illuminating the jagged remnants of the synagogue's stained-glass windows. He could see into the women's section, a raised balcony on the second story, separated from the main sanctuary with a thin lace curtain that had somehow survived unscathed. Tonight the balcony was empty, but he could imagine it coming to life on the holidays, the pews filled with women hugging and talking, children scampering restlessly beneath their feet before being cowed into sitting still.

His thoughts returned to Magda and her disappointed expression. As if on cue, he heard her on the floor below, her presence given away by the quiet scratching of her shoes. He would have eaten with her, if only she had asked. But of course it wouldn't be proper for him to suggest it. He looked down at his books. He should work through the evening anyway, prepare for the first of his lectures the following day.

That evening a tray appeared outside his door, though he did not hear Magda leave it. The house was eerily still and the Victrola did not play below, as it had the previous night. How odd, he reflected, that a house could be quieter with three people in it than it had been with two.

When his eyes had grown bleary from reading, he carried his tray down to the kitchen. As he started back upstairs, he passed Magda, who had come from the washroom on the second-floor landing. Her face was freshly scrubbed, cheeks flushed. He saw her then as scarcely more than a girl, with an innocence and vulnerability to her that tugged at his heart. He cleared his throat as though there was something he wanted to say, and she looked at him expectantly. But no words came out and a moment later she opened the door to the bedroom. A thin sliver of the room

153

appeared, the intimacy of the space she and his brother shared somehow an affront. She did not look up again but closed the door with a click, leaving him in the hallway alone.

The next morning he started down the stairs on his way to the university. Roger could tell before he even reached the second-floor landing that Hans was gone by the calm that seemed to have been restored. Indeed, the visit had been so swift it might never have happened at all.

The door to Hans and Magda's bedroom was ajar and through the opening he could see Magda. He moved nearer, drawn in by her sure, fluid movements. He wondered if her mood had brightened, or if she was even more bereft by her husband's departure. Impulsively, he walked to the door. 'Magda?' He knocked, then pushed the door open slightly. 'I'll take dinner with you this evening, if–'

He stopped short. Magda had pulled a large mahogany armoire from the wall – how she had managed to move such a heavy object he could not fathom – and she was kneeling behind it. Had she lost something? Startled, she jumped to her feet and started to push the armoire back into place.

'Can I help?' he asked, moving closer.

'*N-nein, danke,*' she managed, clearly flustered. 'I was just trying to dust.' But she held no cloth or other cleaning supplies. He leaned forward, peering over her shoulder. She moved to the side, trying to block his view, but he could see that there was a large, gaping hole in the wall.

'What's that?' he asked. The question was per-

154

haps too intrusive to be asked of this woman he had only just met. But there was something about her that caused him to feel like they had known each other much longer, a sense that he had met her long before. She did not respond. He walked to the spot beside her and together they slid the armoire back against the wall. As they did, their fingers brushed and she pulled back quickly. He hoped that he had not offended her. 'Magda, what's behind the wall?' She did not answer and for a second he wondered if she was angry.

'A place,' she said simply. 'For hiding things.'

'Things?'

Her face seemed to crumple. 'Or people,' she replied reluctantly.

People. His mind whirled. Was she scared that the Nazis might arrest them in retribution for Hans's work? It had to be something more than that. There were people who hid Jews from the Nazis. Perhaps Magda was somehow involved.

He studied the space behind her once more. It was narrow, just big enough for one person, maybe two if the second was a child. No, the hiding place was too small to be of use to others. It was intended for Magda herself.

The realization hit him in the stomach like a rock. Surely Magda wasn't ... he pictured the Jews as the yarmulke-clad men he had seen lingering outside the White Stork Synagogue, or their shawl-covered wives. 'Magda, are you ...?' He did not finish the question.

'My father was killed during Kristallnacht,' she said, her voice a monotone. 'When the rioting started, he insisted upon going to the shop where he worked to rescue his beloved clock. We begged him not to go out, but he insisted and the next morning we found him in the back room of the shop, murdered.' Her eyes did not meet his. 'After that, I managed to leave.'

'And the rest of your family?'

'My mother, Hannah, passed a few years ago from a heart condition. And my older brother, Stefan, left Germany before the war. He was trying to make it to England, or at least that's what we thought; I've not heard from him since he went.'

Roger studied Magda, considering her anew. The raven hair now seemed a liability, a sign that somehow she did not fit in. He was seized with the longing to shave her locks, for even shorn she would still be beautiful.

'Does Hans know?'

She nodded. 'We spoke about it once, long ago. We don't talk about it anymore, though. He has enough to worry about.'

Roger contemplated what she had said. Suddenly he imagined standing in her shoes, living with the fear day by day, alone. Then a vision swept him of Magda disappearing, and he was seized with an emptiness and terror such as he had never known in his entire life.

'Magda.' He took a step toward her and wordlessly she folded into his arms, trembling like a bird that might break if he held her too hard. She pulled back and looked up at him and in that moment it was impossible to breathe.

Then without speaking further, she turned on her heel and was gone.

Seven

MUNICH, 2009

'So Roger was in love with Hans's wife,' Charlotte remarked as the taxi sped down the autobahn. It was not, of course, the first time they had discussed it. After Jola left, Charlotte and Jack had agreed that the best approach would be to return to Munich and confront Roger with what they had found. So they had inventoried the rest of the attic hurriedly, bringing back with them a few of the boxes that seemed more significant than the rest.

'Yeah,' Jack replied, drumming his fingers against his knee. 'Talk about motive.'

'The fact that Roger had an affair with Hans's wife doesn't mean he turned his own brother in to the Nazis,' Charlotte said, her defender instincts rising.

'We don't even know if there was an affair,' Jack pointed out. 'The feelings could have been one-sided, or perhaps things never went that far.' There was a pull to his voice that Charlotte could not quite comprehend.

'Regardless, he was in love with a Jewish woman, which suggests he wouldn't have been in collaboration with the Nazis,' she insisted, hearing her own exasperation. Despite the kiss, arguing still seemed to be their default state.

'But why didn't he mention it to us?'

'It's not exactly something that one brings up in casual conversation,' she retorted. 'He was probably embarrassed. Anyway it was so long ago. Maybe he just forgot, or didn't think it was relevant.' But the words did not ring true, even to her. Magda, from what they knew, had been Roger's only love. One didn't simply neglect to mention something like that.

'Well, I certainly wouldn't want it coming out in court,' Jack replied grimly. With this Charlotte could not disagree. 'We need to find something to clear his name, and fast.'

She did not respond but faced forward, trying not to fidget in what now seemed like an uncomfortably close confinement with Jack. They had not spoken of what happened the night before, and a few times she wondered if the fleeting kiss had been a dream. Earlier as they busily combed the attic and made preparations to leave, the tension between them had been easier to push aside. But sitting beside each other on the plane and in the cab, it had grown until it was impossible to ignore.

Her thoughts were interrupted by the low ringing of Jack's phone. *'Ja?'* he said, turning away and lowering his head. *'Jetzt? Aber–'* Charlotte could tell that he wanted to argue with whoever was on the other end of the line but couldn't. *'Danke schön.'* He closed the phone. 'This just keeps getting better,' he muttered in a low voice.

'What is it?'

'That was the lead judge's clerk,' he answered. 'The prosecutor has filed an emergency motion to elevate Roger's case to the higher court. The judge wants to have a telephone conference at once.'

'Now?' That seemed quick, even by the standards of the rough-and-tumble criminal justice system in which she was used to practicing.

He nodded. 'The clerk said she would call me back momentarily and get both parties on the line.' He looked out the window for several seconds, stroking his chin.

'Are you all right?' she asked, sounding more concerned than she'd intended.

'This isn't good,' he replied. 'So far Roger's case has been before the Landgericht, or regional court. But the fact that the prosecutor's office wants to raise the case to the appellate level – and that the court seems inclined to entertain the notion – suggests that they're contemplating a guilty verdict.'

And a far more serious sentence, Charlotte thought. 'Appellate court?' she asked. 'But we haven't even had a trial yet. What is there to appeal?'

'The word *appellate* is just a rough translation,' Jack explained. 'Really it's the next-higher-level court, the Oberlandgericht. They do have original jurisdiction over certain more significant matters, as well as hearing appeals.'

'And they're just beneath the national or supreme court, right?' Charlotte asked, mustering her scant knowledge of the German legal system. Jack nodded. 'What's driving this?'

'Politics, I suspect. The German foreign minister was just in Washington for meetings with the secretary of state and there's a lot of pressure from the States for the chancellor to show she's serious about war crimes prosecutions. A case like Roger's is a chance to do just that. Plus there are elections here next spring.' He trailed off, looking down at some notes that he'd pulled from his bag.

A minute later Jack's phone rang again and he set down the papers and answered it. 'Can you put it on speaker?' she asked, wanting to hear what was going on.

'Too much noise,' he replied, tilting his head toward the window. He turned up the volume on the phone and gestured for her to come closer to hear. She hesitated, then slid across the seat, trying to get as close to the phone as possible without touching him. His now-familiar scent, cotton and tweed with a hint of sweat from the night spent in the attic, tickled her nose.

On the other end of the line, a woman spoke shrilly in German, too quickly for Charlotte to understand what she was saying. 'Prosecutor,' Jack mouthed, his breath warm against her neck.

When the woman finished, Jack cleared his throat and began to speak at a speed and in a dialect that made it somewhat easier for Charlotte to comprehend. The prosecution's motion was without basis, he argued, and would unfairly prejudice his client, who had spent months preparing for trial before this court. And, he added, the transfer of the case would result in inevitable delay, needless further incarceration of an old man.

He's amazing, Charlotte realized as she listened. It was more than just Jack's ease with the foreign language. He had the perfect balance of advocacy

160

and reserve, his easygoing style a sharp contrast to the prosecutor's hawkish tone. And he seemed to come alive, as if he were actually before the court, any doubts he might have about Roger's case thoroughly undetectable. She had seen dozens if not hundreds of litigators in action and Jack was clearly among the best.

'What if,' the judge asked, interrupting, 'the appellate court could expedite the case?'

Charlotte's breath caught. Jack's argument about the potential delay had backfired. In fact, they needed as much time as possible to find any evidence that might help exonerate Roger. 'Even if the court could guarantee such a speedy trial,' Jack began, 'there is simply no basis to elevate the case.' He was speaking slowly, as if trying to find the right words in German, but Charlotte could tell that he was actually stalling for time, trying to collect his thoughts. 'We're still gathering evidence and we believe that we will have something shortly that will exonerate our client without having to burden this court – or the higher court – further.'

Charlotte stifled a gasp. What was he doing? They had just come from Roger's boyhood home and had nothing – other than the arguably damaging discovery that Roger was in love with Hans's wife.

'What evidence?' the judge asked.

'Respectfully,' Jack replied, 'I'd rather not say until I can present the court with something more concrete.'

The prosecutor jumped in, speaking rapidly, and though Charlotte could not understand her exact words, she could tell the woman was arguing that

Jack had months to produce evidence to support Roger's defense and had failed to do so.

'*Wie lange?*' the judge asked Jack. How long will this take?

This time Jack did not hesitate. 'One week.'

'One week,' the judge said, relenting. 'If there's no new evidence to support the defense of the accused, we will proceed to grant the prosecution's request to elevate the case.'

'A week?' Charlotte asked incredulously after Jack hung up a minute later. 'How can we possibly work that quickly?'

'I don't think we have a choice. We talk to Roger again, go through the last few boxes. Either we're going to find something that proves his innocence or not.'

He was playing all in, Charlotte realized, the ultimate hand in a poker game. Only so far, all they had was a bluff. It was guts ball, the dangerous kind of stakes for which she herself almost never had the stomach. But he hadn't asked her. She was suddenly angry. It was her case too. For a minute, she considered calling him on it, but there was no point – he had already made the representation to the court and she would have to live with it.

One week, she thought. When she'd accepted Brian's invitation to come here, a week was all she wanted to put in before fleeing home. But now it seemed a drop in the bucket, hardly enough time to do what they needed to do.

'Are you going to tell Roger?' Charlotte asked.

'Not right now,' Jack said. 'I don't see the point. If we find what we're looking for, then the case will stay here and it's all a moot point.'

'And if not?'

Jack pressed his lips together. 'I'd rather not think about it.'

Twenty minutes later they entered the prison. As they reached the door to the conference room, Charlotte's arm brushed against Jack's. 'After you,' he said, stepping back, his eyes not meeting hers.

Roger sat at the far end of the room. Seeing them, he rose. 'You visited the house in Poland? A lovely restoration, isn't it, if I do say so myself?'

Charlotte fought the urge to jump in and barrage him with questions as she might a witness on the stand. 'You've done a beautiful job,' she agreed instead, trying to build his trust.

'Herr Dykmans,' Jack began, and she could hear the edge of impatience in his voice. 'Can you tell us about Magda?'

An indescribable mix of pleasure and pain crossed Roger's face. Charlotte's stomach twisted. She recognized the emotion as one she had felt for Brian over the years, the paradox of reconciling a memory so filled with joy with the tragic ending it had suffered. 'Magda,' he said slowly and with great effort, 'was my brother's wife.'

Charlotte empathized silently with how hard it was for Roger to acknowledge that marriage, which carried more legitimacy than his own relationship with Magda, whatever that had been. Like admitting to herself that Brian and Danielle were married. Enough, she thought. This isn't about me. She forced her attention to the elderly man seated across from her. 'Herr Dykmans,' she

163

tried gently, 'we understand that Magda may have been something more to you.'

'No, no,' he said, his first reaction after all these years still to deny it.

Jack pulled out the letter and slid it across the table. As Roger scanned the paper, the years seemed to unfold across his face, his misgivings about committing such things to writing in the first place, the strong emotions that had prompted him to take the risk. 'This was nothing,' he protested, lifting his eyes from the paper. 'The foolish musings of a young man. I never even sent it.'

'Herr Dykmans,' Charlotte said, 'we understand from someone we met in Wadowice that what existed between you and Magda was more than just feelings, that there was a relationship.' She willed her expression to be neutral, hoping he would not see through the bluff.

'But that's impossible...' His voice rose, then trailed off.

She met his gaze, held it. 'It's true though, isn't it?' A jolt of energy surged through her. This was where she was at her best, getting inside of a witness.

He sat back, resigned, still clutching the letter. 'Yes,' he confessed weakly. Charlotte glanced upward at Jack, signaling the significance of the admission. 'We were close.'

An affair with his brother's wife that caused him to risk everything. 'Close' was a gross understatement. But he would not be more explicit, Charlotte knew, and dishonor the memory of the woman he loved. 'What happened?'

'When I was a student at the university in

Breslau, I stayed with my brother and his wife. But Hans was traveling most of the time for his work and Magda and I became close. She disappeared one day, taken by the Nazis. I was never able to find out what became of her.'

'She was Jewish?' Jack asked, confirming what they already knew.

'Yes. When the Nazis started rounding up the Jews in Breslau, I went to Hans and begged him to help her. Even though Magda's heritage was not well known, and being Hans's wife offered her some degree of protection, I was concerned that the Germans would stop at nothing, that it was only a matter of time. But Hans said he couldn't do anything without jeopardizing the fate of thousands.' Roger bit his lip, angry at the memory. 'My brother was very principled that way. I wanted to help her myself, but I was just a student; there was nothing that I could do. Then one day she was gone.'

'What happened to her?'

His shoulders slumped. 'I honestly don't know. I've tried for years to find out, searching through records from Berlin to Moscow. I had fresh hope, after the Cold War ended and the archives that had been buried in the former Soviet Union became available for the first time, that I might discover additional information.'

A light dawned in Charlotte's mind. 'Herr Dykmans, is that why you kept returning to Poland?'

He nodded slightly. 'Yes. But I never found anything.'

'What did you do? Afterward, I mean?' Jack asked.

'Soon after Magda disappeared, I received word that my brother had been arrested too.' Charlotte held her breath. Embedded in that very statement were the answers they needed to know. How had the Nazis come to seize Hans? Had Roger had something to do with it, and if so, why? She leaned forward, willing him to say more.

'I thought I might be in danger too, so I headed east,' Roger continued, treading just shy of the heart of the matter. 'I tried to make contact with some of Hans's partisan allies.' To do what, exactly – try to make amends for betraying his brother, or to warn the others before it was too late? 'But I was unsuccessful.' A guilty look washed across his face and Charlotte could not help but wonder what he had really done. Roger was not Hans, did not share his bravery or his strength. 'I couldn't bear to return to the house in Breslau after Magda was gone, and I didn't want to risk going back to my mother's house for fear of putting her at risk. So I lived in different places until the war was over, not staying in any one location for very long.'

'You didn't flee to the West,' Jack observed.

'No, not until a few years later.' Until, Charlotte realized, he had finished turning over every lead. He could have fled to a non-extradition country in South America or elsewhere. But he hadn't. He had stayed behind in Europe, at great peril to himself, in hopes of still finding information about Magda – or perhaps even Magda herself.

What had he done in the years between then and now? she wanted to ask. Not for a living – they already knew, and knew that he hadn't married.

But had he loved again? It seemed unlikely. Perhaps he tried and found it impossible, or maybe after Magda he had simply given up. She studied Roger's face as she often did with her juvenile clients as if reading a map, looking for signs of the places he'd been and things he had seen. But his expression was impassive and unyielding. Maybe that explained the absence of lines – he hadn't allowed himself to laugh and live and do the things that wore impressions on the faces of others, like water coursing endlessly through a canyon over time.

'Did you look for information on Hans also?' Jack asked.

'Yes, yes, of course,' Roger replied hastily. 'But with Hans, we soon knew what had happened. The Polish government had notified my mother of his death in a Nazi prison and they returned some personal effects that seemed to leave little doubt as to the truth of their explanation.'

Whereas with Magda, Charlotte reflected, Roger had nothing. No information about her whereabouts, the fate that had ultimately befallen her. 'We're sorry about Magda,' she said gently. Roger's mouth tilted faintly upward, the first time she had seen him attempt anything remotely approximating a smile.

'Our priority, though, must still be defending you against these very serious allegations,' Jack interjected. Charlotte cringed at his brusque tone. 'Can you tell us anything that might help?'

Roger hesitated, staring down at his fingers. Then he seemed to relent slightly. 'When I returned east, in addition to restoring the house and trying to learn about Magda, I was also looking for something.'

'Something?' Jack repeated, struggling to keep the frustration from his voice.

Charlotte reviewed the contents of the attic in her mind. 'Was it a letter?' Roger shook his head. 'A photograph?'

He pressed his lips together. 'A clock.'

She considered his response. Then, remembering the photograph of Hans and Magda, she reached in her bag. She leapt up, thrusting the picture at the old man so abruptly that he reared back. 'Sorry.' She pointed to the clock on the mantelpiece in the background. 'Is this the one?'

A pained look crossed his face as he studied the image of the couple. Was it grief, Charlotte wondered, or jealousy, even after all of these years? 'Yes.'

Charlotte and Jack exchanged looks above his head and she knew he was picturing all of the boxes that remained in the attic. 'Would it have been at your family home?' she asked.

'No, it was in Wroclaw.' He spoke more freely now – it was as if once they knew about the affair, he had little reason to be silent. Had his refusal to cooperate in his defense come from his loyalty to Magda, his unwillingness to tarnish her name? 'I went to my brother's former house, but the new owners knew nothing of it,' he added.

'How does the clock relate to the allegations against you?' Jack pressed.

'I've tracked down a possible lead to a clock shop in Salzburg,' Roger added, ignoring the question. 'I was about to travel there when–' He held up his shackled ankles.

'What does the clock have to do with the case?' She could hear the exasperation rising in Jack's voice, close below the surface now.

'It contains proof that I–' He faltered. 'It helps to explain what happened with Hans.'

She leaned forward. 'Does the clock have something to do with Magda?'

'Charley, can I speak with you for a second?' Jack asked before the older man could answer. 'Privately?' He pulled her into the hall. 'Do you think that's wise? Pushing Roger on Magda, I mean. I guess I'm just not sure where you're going, and with so little time left we need to focus on the charges against him.'

'I'm not the one that told the court we could prove this case in a week,' she retorted.

'I had no choice on that, and you know it.'

She brushed her hair from her forehead impatiently. 'Anyway, Magda's a soft spot for Roger, a way to possibly win his trust.'

'But we need to keep him focused.'

Her frustration exploded. 'Dammit, Jack, I'm the one who's good with witnesses, remember?'

'And I'm not?' She could hear the irritation in his voice.

'I'm just saying that's why Brian brought me in.' Jack's jaw clenched. 'You think that was a mistake?' she pressed.

'Not at all,' he replied quickly.

But she was not mollified.

'You never liked me, or thought I was very good.'

'That's not it at all,' he protested. 'But it isn't

Brian's call. Or yours. This is my case.'

Charlotte felt as though she'd been slapped. All the while she'd been thinking of the two of them as a team, Jack had perceived her involvement as an intrusion on his turf. 'Well, I'm here now, so why don't you let me do my job?'

'Because you seem to be going off on all sorts of tangents. First the trip to Poland for the house...'

'Which proved to be a good lead.'

He shrugged his shoulders. 'It provided some anecdotal information about Roger's personal life, nothing more.'

The information about Roger's affair, she thought, was considerably more than an anecdote. But before she could disagree, he continued. 'And now this clock. You want to go to Salzburg, too?'

'Actually, I do.'

He threw up his hands. 'This isn't a goddamn Eurorail trip!'

He was treating her like some kind of novice. Charlotte's rage seared white hot. 'Or maybe it's not about that at all,' Jack added, throwing fuel on the fire.

'What's that supposed to mean?' But even as she asked the question, she knew.

'I'm just saying that coming halfway around the world on a moment's notice ...' He looked at her levelly. 'Well, that's not something one would do for just anyone, is it?'

He was implying, of course, that she was here because of her feelings for Brian. 'How dare you? If you think you can do better on your own, then be my guest.' Not waiting for a response, she turned and walked from the prison.

Outside she paused, inhaling the fresh cool air, trying to compose herself. Fighting with Jack felt wrong somehow. She wasn't even sure what their disagreement was really about. And it certainly wasn't helping their case. But he could be so infuriating. She paused, wondering whether to go back inside and make amends.

Then she spotted the car waiting at the edge of the parking lot. She approached the driver, who leaned on the bumper, smoking a cigarette. 'Can you take me back to the hotel?' she asked.

He looked puzzled. *'Und* Herr Warrington?'

'He's staying for a while.'

A few minutes later, she sat back in the car, still seething. Jack's words replayed in her mind: *not something one would do for just anyone.* Had he been goading her? She recalled his expression as he said it, which bore no sign of sarcasm or malice. No, he genuinely thought she had gotten on a plane and traveled thousands of miles because she still had feelings for his brother. Had she? No, she decided quickly. It wasn't like that, not anymore.

At the hotel, Charlotte dropped onto the crisply made bed. The jet lag and nonstop travel of the past few days seemed to finally be catching up to her. She pulled out her cell phone and for a moment considered calling Jack. To say what, exactly? It wasn't as if she had something to apologize for, and if he was still in the prison with Roger, his phone would be turned off anyway. No, best to let things cool off for a while.

Her thoughts turned to the information they had learned in Wadowice, the picture made more complete by Roger's reluctant admissions. His

171

one true love had been his brother's wife. What had become of Magda? Perhaps if she could learn some of the truth, the information might help to give Roger some comfort and win his trust. But how?

Charlotte mentally ran through her list of contacts who worked in the Holocaust area, most of whom she'd lost touch with over the years. There was a Polish woman, Alicja Recka, who had worked at the Auschwitz-Birkenau site and had been very helpful to Charlotte in her research. Charlotte recalled reading several years later that Recka had become the research director for the Jewish Historical Institute in Warsaw. Of course, the information was years old now; there was no telling if Recka had moved on. But it was worth a try.

Charlotte accessed the Internet on her phone and found the Jewish Historical Institute. She dialed the main number. 'Alicja Recka, *prosze,*'she requested when the operator answered. There was a moment of silence, then a click as she was connected to another line. Charlotte's hopes rose, then fell again, as the phone rang four times before dropping her into voicemail.

'Hello, Alicja,' she said when the prerecorded greeting had ended. Recka's English was good enough that she did not bother to leave the message in Polish. 'This is Charlotte Gold. I don't know if you remember me but you helped me on some Holocaust research at Oświęcim many years ago.' She spoke faster now, not wanting to run out of recording space. 'I'm trying to find out the fate of a woman who was interned in the camps, name of Magda Dykmans. Any information you could provide would be greatly appreciated.' She finished by leaving both her cell phone number and e-mail address.

Setting down the phone, she lay back on top of the duvet, closed her eyes. It was a long shot, the odds of finding information on Magda slim to none. Roger said he had looked everywhere and he undoubtedly had the benefit of additional information, such as Magda's date of birth and maiden name. But she had to try.

Suddenly, there was a loud knock at the door. She stood up groggily. How much time had passed? The heavy closed curtains shrouded the room in semidarkness, making the hour impossible to gauge. She opened the door. Standing there, juggling an armful of files, was Jack.

She braced herself, expecting a continuation of their earlier argument or at least a comment about the fact that she had stalked out. 'Roger was feeling tired and asked to excuse himself,' he said, as if that explained everything. 'We can get more time with him tomorrow.'

So they were done for the day. Then what was he doing here? He shifted his weight awkwardly from one foot to the other. 'Can I come in?'

'Sure.' She stepped aside, watching him as he set the files on the edge of the now-rumpled bed.

He turned back to her, bit his lip. 'I don't want to fight anymore.' Neither, Charlotte realized, did she. But he had not apologized. In that way at least, the Warrington brothers were alike. 'It's been a long day,' he added.

Charlotte's mind reeled back and suddenly it

seemed impossible that just this morning they were in the attic, searching the boxes – and waking up beside each other.

'I brought some of the files from Wadowice with me. Why don't we grab some dinner?' he suggested. 'Then we can look these over, regroup, and figure out what to do next. Or do you want to rest some more?'

Exhaustion swept over her then, vying with hunger for primacy. It was an old joke she'd shared with a roommate at college, the battle of sloth versus gluttony. But she was unwilling to admit to Jack that she was tired, lest he perceive it as a sign of weakness. 'I'm going to hop in the shower and try to freshen up,' she said. 'Why don't you order some room service and we can go over the files.' She felt the blush creep up into her cheeks, worried about how her suggestion might sound. 'I just meant it might be easier to spread out the documents here.'

Twenty minutes later, she emerged from the bathroom, drying her hair, clad in a Philadelphia Eagles T-shirt. Jack sat on the edge of the bed, a series of papers from the files spread before him. 'I ordered some dinner and–' He looked up then and faltered.

What was it, she wondered? Her rumpled sweatpants and wet, tangled hair could hardly be considered alluring.

He cleared his throat. 'Food should be here in a few minutes.'

'Great.' She dropped to the far side of the bed. 'So when we last left off, you were saying you didn't think we should necessarily go to Salzburg.'

He nodded. 'It just seems so improbable. The notion that the clock Roger is searching for still exists, or that this clockmaker might actually have it, or that even if it is still there, it would somehow help his case. I mean, how can a clock prove anything?'

'He didn't say the clock was the proof. He said it contained the proof.'

'Proof of what?'

'I don't know,' she conceded. Roger had not said, in fact, that the clock contained evidence of his innocence.

'It just seems like a needle in a haystack to me.'

'You have a better idea?'

He gestured to the papers before him. 'Stay here, keep pressing Roger. Go over the evidence again to see what we missed.'

'You've done that a half dozen times already. The clock is something new.'

'I just don't see it, Charley.' His voice was a note softer now. They stared at each other for several seconds, neither yielding. 'Well then, maybe we split up. You can go to Salzburg and I'll stay here and keep plugging away at the files.'

Her stomach sank unexpectedly hard. She was not, she realized with discomfort, ready to separate from Jack. 'What about Wroclaw?' she asked, searching for another option. 'If Roger lived there with Hans and Magda during the war, do we need to search that house too?'

'I already looked into that. After Hans's arrest, the Nazis confiscated the property. Anything of value that was left there is gone.'

Before she could reply, there was a knock at the

door. She leapt up, grateful for the interruption. 'That was fast.'

'I didn't know what you wanted,' Jack apologized, as she signed for the food. 'So I ordered a bunch of stuff.'

'I'll say.' She surveyed the half-dozen dishes that crowded the tray. She lifted a cover off the first plate to reveal a veal cutlet bathed in savory sauce. 'Why not? Brian's firm is footing the bill.' She reached for one of the small bottles of wine that accompanied the meal.

'I hope they're paying you well, by the way,' he remarked as they sat down with their plates, she in the chair by the night table, he on the edge of the bed. 'I mean, not that it's any of my business, but you did sort of drop your life to do this for him.'

Charlotte considered this last comment, searching for signs of judgment or reproach and finding none. 'They aren't. Paying me, that is.'

He cocked his head. 'Seriously?'

She shrugged. 'I guess they would have. I didn't ask. I just negotiated Kate Dolgenos to handle Marquan's case while I'm gone.' Which was worth, she reflected, more than she made in a year. But thinking now of the new roof her townhouse needed, the student loans that lingered accruing interest, she cursed herself for not driving a harder bargain. 'He just caught me off guard, I guess.'

'Brian can be very persuasive,' Jack agreed, chewing. 'It wasn't easy, you know, growing up with a brother like that. He was so much larger than life.'

Charlotte paused. She had always thought of it

176

the other way, Jack being the older and more intimidating of the two. But now she saw it through his eyes for the first time, living in the shadow of boisterous, confident Brian. 'Is that why–' she hesitated, considering whether the question was too personal. 'Is that why you stopped speaking?'

He gave a laugh that came out equal parts chuckle and snort. 'Sibling rivalry? Hardly.' Charlotte bristled, deciding whether to take offense at his derisive tone. In that moment, he seemed like the Jack of old, all of the warmth that had developed between them in the past day or so gone. But he didn't mean it that way, she realized quickly. Rather, the topic was a raw one, and her question had touched a nerve.

'And your family?' she pressed. 'What do they think of you and Brian not speaking?'

Jack shrugged. 'No idea. Brian sort of won them in the custody dispute. That is, I still keep in touch, holiday cards and the like. But Brian's so much nearer geographically, it just made sense that he would be the one to keep close.'

'So you're on your own.' He nodded. And as alone as I am, she thought. 'I didn't know, that is, I always wondered why you never–' She stopped, fumbling over the question.

'Why I'm single?'

'I suppose.' She finished the last of the roast potatoes that had accompanied the dish, then returned her plate to the cart. 'Not that it's any of my business.'

He rubbed his chin. 'I never did date much. You know, in the early years when we were teenagers, it was so awkward and Brian was such a natural at it. For me it was easier to bury my nose in a book. And then I guess the pattern just kind of stuck.' He laughed once, a short huff that seemed to bounce off the walls. 'Brian asked me once if I was gay.'

'Really?' She tried her best to feign surprise.

'Yes, and he did it in that trying-to-be-concerned-but-rather-afraid-of-the-answer kind of way.'

Charlotte smiled, picturing the conversation. 'I know just what you mean.'

'I'm not,' he added quickly. 'In case you were wondering.' She did not know quite how to respond. She had never seriously considered the possibility and any doubts she might have had were erased by the kiss in the attic. He continued, 'Anyway, love finds all of us, even if we aren't looking for it. There was someone once...' His voice trailed off in the silent ellipses of pain she recognized from her own narrative. 'Meeting people over here is just so difficult.'

She nodded in understanding. Dating at home was awkward enough with the cheesy bar scene and posturing. Once upon a time she had thought that Europe, with its sophistication, might be better. But it was hard being the foreigner, dealing with the nuances of a different language and trying to fit in with the cultural norms, which in Poland had been right out of the 1950s. And there was always a sense of uncertainty whether a person was legitimately interested or just wanted something. One man had asked her on a date only to request midway through dinner that she go to the embassy the next day and pretend to be his cousin to improve his chances of getting a visa to the States. After that she had stopped trying.

'What about you?' he asked. 'Has there been anyone since my brother?'

'Oh, yes,' she replied hurriedly. She could not bear to have him think that she had spent all of these years pining for Brian. And really she hadn't – she seldom thought of him anymore, at least not until he appeared in her office a few days ago. She had gone on the blind dates that had been offered over the years, joined a running club that met once a week to jog the banks of the Schuylkill, even tried one of those crazy online dating services that everyone recommended, the one with all of the compatibility questions. There had been the obligatory first meetings over drinks, and once or twice even a second dinner leading to awkward sex. But there was never a connection and she soon retreated home with her cat. It was easier to be alone than in bad company. 'I just never found anyone...' – she searched for the word – '...right.'

He held her gaze for several seconds, not blinking. *Until now,* she thought, stunned. Despite her view of Jack from years ago and their frequent bickering now, she felt more comfortable with him than she had with just about anyone. But why was he staring at her? He could not possibly be thinking the same thing.

'Are you sorry you came?' Jack asked, changing the subject abruptly.

She looked at him, caught off guard by the question. Did he mean because of the nature of Roger's case, or leaving Philadelphia? Or was he referring to something else entirely? She waited for a clarification and when none was forthcoming decided to take the easiest interpretation.

'No. It's a fascinating case. Fun to be back in Europe. And,' she swallowed, then spoke before she could decide whether or not to let the words come out, 'it's good to see you again after so many years.'

She held her breath, wondering how he would take this last comment. A moment of silence passed between them.

'Yeah, it's great,' he replied wryly, 'to meet up not in the shadow of my brother.' She looked at him, puzzled. He's joking, she realized, as his face broke into a smile. He chuckled then, a lone scratchy sound that seemed wholly foreign to his being. The full irony of the situation descended upon her then, and she too began laughing, welcoming the indescribable sense of release from all of the tension and stress that had been building, within herself and between them, over the past few days.

A moment later, their laughter subsided. He cleared his throat. 'Earlier, when you said I didn't like you...' He looked away.

'You don't – I mean, you didn't,' she insisted, emboldened by the wine.

A look of confusion crossed his face, so immediate and genuine she thought she had been wrong. 'That's not it.' He faltered, then shook his head. 'Never mind. It's getting late,' he said, rising. 'I should go.'

'Okay.' She stood up, stung by the abruptness of his announcement. It was after eleven, she noted, looking at the clock on the nightstand.

He gathered his files, not looking back. 'Good night.'

She closed the door behind him. As she listened to his footsteps recede down the hall, she was surprised by a wave of disappointment at his departure. Well, what had she expected? This was not rural Poland; his apartment, located somewhere in the compact city center, was likely not more than a few minutes from here. There was simply no reason for him to stay.

What's wrong with me, she wondered? Jack's effect on her felt unexpected and strange. It was just the history, she decided, his resemblance to Brian and the memories his presence generated. But he was what to her, exactly? She considered the question. A colleague, she decided, for the limited purposes of this case. And at some point in the days or weeks to come they would go their separate ways. But an uneasiness continued to tug at her stomach as she brushed her teeth.

As she climbed into bed, there was a knock at the door. 'Jack,' she said, surprised to see him standing there when she opened it. She scanned the room over her shoulder: Had he forgotten something?

'Sorry to bother you again,' he said, then looked away, fumbling. 'But I wanted to tell you, earlier, when you said I didn't like you, well, nothing could be further from the truth.'

There was a pause that seemed to last both a second and a lifetime, and suddenly his lips were on hers, with none of the hesitation or strangeness that there had been in the attic in Poland.

Later, she could not remember who had kissed whom, or how the door had gotten closed behind him, but they were in bed, and this time there was no question of stopping.

As his mouth trailed her neck, she reached out and caressed his cheek. He shuddered then, sort of a heavy sigh and a tremble that was visible in his lower lip. In that second, she knew how hard this was for him, how terrifying it was to let someone in. Knew because she realized that it was just as hard for her too. It was as if she had looked over the abyss, seeing for the first time how high up she was standing, how far down she had to fall.

Afterward neither spoke. Charlotte lay in the crook of Jack's arm, staring at the ceiling, letting the emotions – pleasure and confusion and awkwardness and doubt – wash against her like waves, waiting to see which one would stick. Terror swept over her then. What was she doing? This was exactly what she didn't want to have happen. She rolled away, stiffening, fighting the urge to leap from the bed.

'What is it?' he asked, turning to face her.

'Nothing,' she said, but then the words seemed to spill from within her, from a place too deep to control. 'It's just that being here again... I ran away, Jack,' she confessed. 'From all of this. I ran home years ago and I hid and this is the first time I've been out since.'

'And it terrifies you,' he concluded for her. She looked up. 'Surprised? Don't be. I ran too, though I think retreated would be the fairer characterization.'

'You?' she asked, perplexed. 'How can you say

182

that? You're still out here, in the Great Wide World, living and working.'

He smiled ruefully. 'Retreat is more than a question of geography, Charley. Years ago, I met a woman,' he said. 'The baroness.' Charlotte's breath caught and she held it expectantly, waiting to hear the story at long last. 'She was beautiful and cultured, but it was more than that. Caroline was brilliant, made me see the world in a way I never had before. But she was married, and she strung me along for years with promises of a future together. Not that I was innocent. I knew what I was doing, the lives that I was compromising with my selfishness.'

He reached up, running his hand through his hair. 'Anyhow, her son died suddenly of an illness at the age of seven. It was a freak virus, and one of those things that all the money in the world, the very best doctors, couldn't prevent. She decided that it was God's way of punishing her for her transgressions with me. So she returned to her husband and I never saw her again.'

Hearing the hollowness in his voice, Charlotte tried to imagine his pain, the guilt of the affair, and the heartbreak he could share with no one. 'Afterward, I returned to work and tried to function as well as I could. But I was drinking too much, and things just spiraled downward. I was handling a major trial at The Hague and... I blew it, Charley,' he said, his face falling. 'I mishandled a key witness and compromised her testimony, and as a result a war criminal who had slaughtered dozens of innocents was allowed to go free.'

So that was the story, she thought, as the last

183

piece of the puzzle fell into place. Not just about the baroness, but how he had come to be here. 'Of course there was no question of my staying on after that,' he continued. 'They let me resign and I was able to get the job at the firm. It's safer, you know. The stakes aren't as high.'

At least until now, she reflected. Now someone's life was in his hands once more. 'I stopped drinking too, in case you're wondering,' he added. She realized then that he had not touched the wine that had come on the tray with dinner.

And what of their initial night together in the attic in Wadowice? She had presumed that the kiss had come as a result of them both being intoxicated. But now, looking back through the haze of the vodka at the events that had transpired, she could not remember him downing a single shot at the dinner party. Suddenly the portrait of the evening shifted, her drunk, him watching bemusedly. 'So you see,' he said, 'I retreated too.'

'I just feel like such a coward,' she said, speaking before thinking. She had not meant to include him in that characterization.

But he did not seem offended by the association. 'Hardly,' he said. 'You're still out there on the front lines, defending people's lives. The fact that you've chosen to do it in Philadelphia and not at The Hague doesn't make it any less admirable. Perhaps more so, because there just aren't that many great attorneys willing to do what you do.'

She flushed, flattered by the compliment. 'There are, actually,' she protested, thinking of her colleagues back home. There was the usual

184

smattering of tired civil servants of course. But the public defenders with whom she worked were among the most talented legal minds she'd ever known.

'I have to wonder, though, do you ever get bored?'

'No, not at all,' she replied quickly.

'I didn't mean any offense. It's just that after traveling the world, doing such exciting work–'

'I like it there,' she insisted. And she really did, she realized, as an unexpected pang of longing shot through her. 'There's my job and home and friends and such.' She found herself speaking in a way that made her solitary life in Philadelphia sound much more exciting than it really was. 'I guess I've always been a little conflicted. Like I'm torn between my two selves, the globe-trotter – or gypsy, as my mother used to say, though I guess that's not an acceptable term anymore – and the homebody. I love being here, hopping on a plane, the freedom of going to places unknown where nobody knows me. But the other life is nice too,' she added.

'I know what you mean,' Jack said, surprising her again. She had never thought of him as anything but a world traveler. 'Caroline and I talked about settling down together someday, getting a place in Amsterdam on one of the canals.' He looked vulnerable then, the cool exterior stripped bare by his memories.

She wanted to tell him that she understood, but couldn't find the words. Instead, she reached out and touched his hair, then dropped her hand, interlacing her fingers with his, a communion of the once wounded. It all made sense then – his terseness, the way he seemed to hold himself apart. He was still out in the world, but he'd built such a protective barrier internally that no one could get close enough to hurt him.

But if that was true, then what did everything that had just transpired between them mean? Was it just a fling between two lonely people that had come about as a result of spending too much time together? There was something in the way he looked at her, though, that suggested something more, if that was possible.

Overwhelmed, she fell into a deep, dreamless sleep, still holding his hand. Rustling sounds awakened her and she rolled over to find the space beside her empty. 'I'm going to go back to my place for a shower and a change of clothes,' he said from the darkness above.

'Okay.' She searched his voice for signs of awkwardness but found none. His hand grazed her shoulder and then he slipped out the door.

She dozed off and sometime later was awakened by a knocking. 'Mmph,' she managed, standing up and reaching for her clothes. Faint daylight pushed through the curtains. Jack must have returned. Had she overslept? Being a compulsive early riser, she seldom bothered to place a wake-up call or set an alarm unless rushing for a flight. But they had not, she realized, said whether they were meeting here or at the prison, or at what time.

'Jack, I–' she began, pulling open the door. She stopped in mid-sentence, caught by surprise.

There, standing in the hallway, was Brian.

Eight

BRESLAU, 1942

Roger set down his notes and looked out the window, chewing on the end of his pencil, a schoolboy's habit he had never been able to break. The courtyard below was empty now, but he knew that the men would soon appear. He had gotten used to the quiet routine of the synagogue over the past eighteen months; it had become a timepiece of sorts, marking the hours like the clock on the mantel in the living room two floors below, or the neighbor's rooster that crowed mornings back home in Wadowice. The men came to worship in small groups in the weekday evenings, with larger crowds on their Sabbath and holidays.

Or they used to, anyway. The change had come quietly at first, and it was so subtle that he might have missed it had he been studying for exams and not looking out the window most days, daydreaming and putting himself in danger of failing out of the university altogether. Attendance had decreased to a trickle and then a handful of men, and the few that did still come moved swiftly through the courtyard to the synagogue entrance, not stopping to look up at the magnificent structure but glancing furtively behind them and ducking inside, afraid to be seen.

From below came a familiar scratching sound.

187

Roger held his breath, gauging with an appraising ear the nearness of Magda's footsteps, whether they were growing louder as she climbed the stairs. But they faded again and he heard a door shut as she walked into the kitchen. He exhaled, trying to contain his disappointment.

The dwindling presence of the Jews was not the only thing that had changed in the time since Roger had lived here. The realization that he was in love with his brother's wife had come swiftly, falling upon him like a sudden weight from above. It had started innocently enough: often in the evenings when Hans was out of town and the study had grown too cold to work, or when he did not dare to leave his light on because the sirens had signaled an air raid, Roger would join Magda in the parlor, reading for class by candlelight while she knitted.

Occasionally one or the other would make a comment and they would break from their respective activities. Their conversation ventured from one subject to the next, minutes bleeding into hours as his reading lay unfinished and she had to redo the stitches she'd dropped while distracted. He didn't mind the time that seemed to evaporate between them, leaving him working harder and faster at his studies the next day to accomplish all that needed to be done. Those evenings, as they sat across from each other, the Victrola playing softly in the background, were the most peaceful that he had ever known.

It was more than just her beauty that had drawn Hans to Magda, Roger decided as he got to know her better. She had an intelligence and wit about her that in other circumstances might have opened worlds of possibility. Instead she was here, alone in this house, waiting for a husband who scarcely noticed her. He oftentimes found himself angry on her behalf, wanting to fill the voids left by his brother's absences and inattention.

'Here,' he said one January evening, as they sat at their usual stations in the parlor. He pulled from behind his back the wrapped brown paper package he'd been hiding and held it out to her.

Magda looked at the parcel uncertainly. He extended his hand further in her direction. 'For you.'

Tentatively, she took it and opened the paper with shaking hands. Inside was a small skein of gray wool yarn. 'I thought you could use it for knitting,' he said awkwardly, explaining the obvious when she did not speak.

'Oh.' She stared blankly at the yarn, which lay in her lap, and for a moment he wondered, crestfallen, if she did not like it, or perhaps it was the wrong type or color. He had bought it on impulse that afternoon, stopping in a notions store on his way back from the university to see if there was any to be had. He knew from watching Magda knit that she had been unraveling old sweaters to get the yarn she needed.

But perhaps the gesture had been a mistake. Was the gift too forward or perhaps not what she wanted? It had cost him the better part of his spending money for the remainder of the month and he hoped he could return it if it wasn't right.

But she had picked up the yarn and fingered it

189

gently now, as if making sure it was real. 'It's lovely,' she said, her voice low and hoarse.

It was not that she didn't like the yarn, Roger realized then. Rather, she was just so unaccustomed to being given gifts, or to anyone noticing what she wanted or needed. His resentment of his brother loomed larger than ever.

A few weeks later, Roger woke one morning to find the same brown paper parcel lying outside the door to his room. He picked it up, puzzled. Had she returned the gift? Unwrapping the package, he found a single mitten, made from the gray yarn.

After he'd dressed, he carried the package down to the kitchen, where Magda was polishing silver. 'You left this for me?'

She nodded, not looking up. 'You lost one of yours, I think, some time ago.'

'Yes.' He'd made do through the winter, burying his bare left hand in his pocket to keep warm. He held up the mitten, which was just a few shades lighter than his other one. A torrent of emotions washed over him: surprise that she had noticed what he needed, remorse that she had not used the new wool on something for herself. Most of all he was touched by the time and work she had put into making the mitten for him. He had noticed her working on the piece, but he had assumed that it was for Hans.

She looked up then, searching his face for a reaction to the gift. 'Beautiful,' he said as their eyes met and held. He cleared his throat. 'That is, thank you.'

A troubled expression flickered across her face,

then disappeared again. She turned and picked up the silver and carried it into the dining room.

The following evening as they sat together, he glanced up from his work and saw her hands moving gently above the knitting needles, making something new with brown yarn unraveled from a sweater. He was stunned by the familiarity of her fingers, the soft oval shape of the cuticle beds. In that moment he realized that he knew everything about her, each exquisite detail from the curve of her hips to the corners of her mouth, as if they were his own.

'Excuse me,' he said, standing up so abruptly that she stopped mid-stitch. She looked up at him puzzled, needles suspended in the air. Usually neither of them retired to bed until the candle had burned too low to see, at least an hour or two from now. 'I'm quite tired.' He felt his way upstairs in the darkness, then sank to the bed, shaking. What was happening? It was loneliness, he decided, the stress of the war and his studies and the lack of a woman's warmth. But there were plenty of girls at the university who made clear that they would be only too receptive to his attention if it was forthcoming. No, this was something more. He knew then, even though he had never felt it for anyone before, that he was absolutely in love with Magda.

The next morning, after a long and fitful night's sleep, Roger awoke before dawn, the renewed realization a cold cloak of guilt against his skin. Magda was his brother's wife – he could not, would not have feelings for her. After that, he tried to take an interest in other women, actually asking a few out for coffee, one even to a second

191

dinner date. But the conversation always fell flat and he found himself looking at the clock, counting the minutes until he could return to the house. He avoided the evenings downstairs for a time, but eventually he was pulled back to the warmth of Magda's company.

At least, he consoled himself, the feelings were all one-sided.

One night a few weeks later, after he had retreated to bed, he was awakened by a low rumbling sound. Bombs, he thought. They had started a few months earlier, distant and occasional. But they came with greater frequency now, almost every night. These were closer than anything he remembered, shaking the walls, knocking his books from the desk to the floor.

He should go to the cellar. He groaned inwardly, thinking of the hours that might be spent sitting in the darkness on the cold, damp concrete floor. But Magda went faithfully downstairs with each raid and she shouldn't have to be alone. Reluctantly, he made his way to the second floor and stopped in front of her bedroom door to see if she was still there. 'Magda?' he called through the opening. 'It's getting rather close. Perhaps we should go down to the cellar?'

His question was met with silence and he wondered if she had already gone. He pushed the door open a crack further. As his eyes adjusted to the darkness, he could see that the armoire was pushed away from the wall. He went to the opening behind it. She was huddled in the tiny crawl space, arms wrapped tightly around her knees. 'Magda?'

She did not answer, but rocked back and forth, keeping her head low. What was she doing? The space might offer some protection if one needed to hide, but was useless if a bomb should hit. Yet to her it seemed to represent safety against all perils. He dropped to her side. 'Come with me.' When she did not move, he put his arms around her and lifted her up. She was shaking, Roger noticed as he straightened with effort. He hesitated, debating whether he should carry her to the cellar. Better to try and calm her here in the familiar surroundings of her own room. She seemed to relax slightly as he carried her to the bed, but when he tried to set her down, she clung to him.

'It's all right,' he said softly, sitting down himself, still holding her, their faces just inches apart. Something inside him stirred and seemed to break loose from its moorings.

Her eyes darted back and forth, searching his face, trying to decide whether to believe him. Then she blinked, as if awakening from a dream. 'What happened?'

He opened his mouth to answer but found that he could not. Instead, he drew closer, as if pulled by an unseen hand. As his lips neared hers, she pulled away. 'Roger...' There was a note of warning in her voice.

'*Es tut mir leid*,' he apologized, leaping up. He fled the room and raced back to the third floor, heedless of any danger, the roaring in his ears drowning out the exploding bombs in the distance. He climbed into bed, shaken. What had happened? Magda clung to him only out of fear,

193

surely. And he had taken advantage of the situation, or so it would seem to her. How could he ever face her again after behaving so improperly?

He could not stay here any longer, Roger decided. He would get a room at the university, find a job to pay for it. He didn't know how he would explain it to Hans, but he would think of something.

The explosions outside grew louder, drawing him from his thoughts and making his stomach jump. Then there came another noise beneath, a scratching from the stairway, lower and more persistent. He walked to the door and, opening it, was surprised to find Magda on the other side of it in her housecoat. She did not speak, but came into his room and slipped into the bed.

He stood in the center of the room uncertainly. He slid into bed beside her, trying to maintain a respectful distance, an almost impossible feat given the narrow space. She trembled beside him in the darkness. He lay frozen, too stunned to move, afraid that the slightest word or gesture would give away his reaction. She's just here for comfort, he thought, willing himself to be calm. But then she turned to him and her lips were on his, her body pressed close, and everything he had scarcely allowed himself to dream became reality.

In the morning she was gone, her slight frame leaving a sheet so unwrinkled he wondered if he had imagined the encounter. The house was still as he left for the university. That day, as he attempted to work in the library, he could think of little else but the previous night. Desire surged

194

in him as he remembered the lilac scent of her hair, the way she cried out with more force than he'd thought possible. Surely it had been an accident, borne of the terror of the bombing raid. He returned home late, preferring to linger in his memories rather than face the inevitable return to the status quo he was sure awaited him.

But she came again that night too, even though the bombs no longer rang out. He was still at his desk when she appeared at the door that he'd deliberately left open. Her hair was neatly combed and she wore a blue dressing gown that made her eyes look even more luminous. She lingered in the doorway until he came to her. 'We can't–' she began, but the words caught in her throat as he drew her in by the hand.

Their encounter this time seemed even more surreal. Once, however forbidden, could be written off to the terror of the bombing raid, to an impulsive need for comfort. There had been an air of intention about this second night, though, that was impossible to deny. Afterward, he could tell from her uneven breathing beside him that she was not asleep either, and he considered asking her why she had come back. But the question seemed too personal, not his to ask.

Her visits became nightly after that and often, once she had slipped from his bed, he would lie awake, adrenaline still racing, marveling at what had transpired between them. But the question nagged: Why did she do it? Boredom, or loneliness, would have been the easy answers. Magda was too principled a woman, though, to betray her marriage on a whim – and the way she clung to him in the brief moments they shared afterward suggested something more. He desperately wanted to know, yet he fought the urge to press for an explanation, fearful that if he shone a light on what was happening it would disintegrate like dust.

It was not for several months, when the weather had given way to early summer, that Roger noticed for the first time the growing roundness of Magda's belly. He wished he knew how to calculate such things, to know if the child was conceived during one of Hans's lengthy absences. Surely, given the infrequency of his brother's visits, the many nights that he and Magda had shared... Roger was instantly ashamed at his selfishness. A child that was his would be a stigma, yet another secret for Magda to carry when her burden in that regard was already heavy enough.

He did not ask her, of course. He wondered if, given her condition, she would come to him less, but she still climbed the stairs to his room each night, the growing belly pressed unmentioned between them.

The child was born on a cold morning in November. Roger loitered outside the room for what seemed like endless hours, waiting for something to do, and he was almost relieved when the midwife appeared and asked him to send a telegram to Hans that he had a daughter and all was well.

'Would you like to hold her?' Magda asked one afternoon. The child, Anna, as she had been named after one of Magda's grandmothers, was now three weeks old.

He hesitated. Anna seemed as delicate as a china doll, so tiny and perfect that the faintest wind might shatter her. But then he saw the fatigue in Magda's eyes and knew she needed the respite. 'Certainly,' he said, taking the child with trembling arms. He studied her face. Thankfully there was enough of a resemblance between the brothers that no one would question whether Hans could be the father. Roger could tell, though, that beneath the lips that were so like Magda's, the chin with the minute dimple was his. He shifted the child to his other arm, struggling to find the right way to hold her strange, delicate shape. But Anna sought out the crevice between his chest and chin and nestled in with a sigh, making sucking noises until she fell asleep there. Magda smiled knowingly, confirming his speculation about the child's parentage, and it seemed all was complete.

In the months that had followed, they had fallen into a sort of life, he and Magda and Anna, and it sometimes seemed possible, on those nights when they sat together in the living room, that it was real. Magda would put on some music, singing softly as she rocked the child. He could almost pretend that they were a normal happy family and that all of this was his. But in the cold light of morning when she was gone from his side he was always reminded that it was just a fiction.

How would it end? he wondered now. He dropped his pencil, disarmed by the thought. It had to happen sometime. The conclusion of the school year was looming fast and without a job in the city he would have no excuse to stay here, but rather would be expected to return home to help their mother or to travel elsewhere in search of work. Of course he would be back in the autumn, but the notion of being separated from Magda for days, much less weeks or months, not being able to see her and protect her, was unfathomable.

And even if they could get through the summer, what then? He'd imagined a thousand times asking Magda to leave Hans and run away with him. But even if he could get past the guilt at trying to steal his brother's family while Hans was off fighting the Nazis, Roger knew it was futile. Magda was, in her own ironic way, fiercely loyal to her husband and too practical to put sentiment above reality. She would not leave him. So at some point, Roger would graduate or the war would end and Hans would be home, and Roger would have to leave. No, things couldn't go on like this forever, but how and when they would end was something he could not and did not want to see.

Pushing these disturbing thoughts from his mind, Roger looked out the window once more and saw a number of people massing in the synagogue courtyard below. The group had grown to close to a hundred, milling about. His spirits rose. Perhaps the persecution that had been afflicting the Jewish community had somehow waned and the people were returning to their routine. Something was different, though. The crowd was unusually large for the middle of the week and it wasn't any holiday of which he was aware. And the men and women stood mixed, not separate, as they sat inside, holding their children fast to them.

It was then that he noticed the suitcases, bags

at their feet. His stomach tightened. A group holiday of some sort, maybe, to the mountains or the lake. But even as he thought this, he knew with a sinking sensation that they were not here by choice.

He saw then one tall, uniformed Gestapo officer and then another, moving through the crowd, directing the people into lines. Roger was flooded with alarm. He had heard stories, of course, of the deportations of Jews. But those relocations were from the villages to the cities and only whispered about, nothing confirmed. Despite all that had happened, it didn't seem possible that the Jews of Breslau, cultured merchants and scholars and artisans, were being rounded up before his very eyes, in the heart of the city center in broad daylight.

His thoughts were interrupted by rising voices below. Toward the back of the crowd, he saw a scuffle, a man who had not gotten into line quickly enough being kicked and beaten. One Nazi drew a pistol and Roger braced himself. But the Nazi would not fire a shot that might attract attention on the street. Instead, he used the gun as a blunt weapon, striking the man on the head until he lay motionless.

Roger turned away sickened. There was a scuffling noise behind him and he turned to see Magda standing at the door, which he had not realized was ajar, fidgeting with her cuffs. He leapt up in front of the window, hoping to shield her from the scene below. But he could tell from her expression that she had already seen it.

'Darling,' he began, stepping forward, forgetting

the need for discretion in his desire to comfort her. She turned and fled without responding.

She did not come to sit in the parlor that evening, but made excuses about being tired and put the baby hurriedly to bed. He did not linger downstairs either, finding the space they usually shared unbearable in her absence and instead working late at his desk.

The next morning he looked for Magda but the house was still. As he left for lectures, the sun shone brightly through branches, casting shadows on the cobblestones below. Roger kept his head low, trying to avoid looking up at the wall that separated the synagogue courtyard from the street. It might have been any morning, but for the disturbing scene he had seen from his window. He should have done something more than stand by like a coward – but what? He thought then of Hans. Suddenly he understood his brother's tireless work, the magnitude of what he was trying to do.

And what about Magda? The Nazis had been taking Jews for several years now, but the scope and swiftness of the deportation he'd witnessed suggested a new level of aggression. Hans's protection could go only so far. Roger returned to the idea of asking her to leave with him. She wouldn't do it just because she had feelings for him, but if he could convince her that fleeing was in the best interests of herself and the baby...

Lost in his thoughts, he was almost at the trolley stop when he realized he'd forgotten the paper he was supposed to turn in at his tutorial that day. He paused, considering. Going back for it would surely make him tardy, but Professor

Helm did not suffer late work. He turned and began walking rapidly back toward the house.

Ten minutes later, as he rounded the corner by the synagogue, he stopped. Halfway down the block, in front of Hans and Magda's house, sat a large black Mercedes, adorned with a swastika flag on either side of the hood. His breathing ceased. Easy, he thought, willing himself to remain upright. The Nazis could be at the synagogue again, following up from the previous day's raid. But they had parked on the adjacent street then, not this one. No, this was different.

He stood, paralyzed and uncertain. His first instinct was to get help, but even as he thought this, he knew that the notion was laughable. There had been no aid here for years. And Hans was too far away to do anything now.

Steeling himself, he started forward. As he drew nearer, the front door to the house opened. He leapt back, hiding behind a delivery truck. Roger's panic solidified as three German officers made their way to the sedan. What were they doing here? He could not hear what they were saying, but he could sense their frustration. Whatever they had come for, they had not gotten it.

He forced himself to remain motionless as the car engine started, barely managing to wait until it had pulled away before running into the house. 'Magda?' he called. There was no response. He ran up the steps to the second floor. 'Magda?'

He found her in the nursery, standing over the crib, clutching Anna and rocking her silently. He walked to her and she fell wordlessly against him with her full weight. A few minutes later, when he sensed she could stand, he led her into her bedroom and onto the floral settee. Though the child slept peacefully, he did not suggest putting her in the crib, knowing that it was out of the question, that Magda would not let Anna out of sight now.

'Wait here.' He went down to the kitchen and made tea, then pulled a bottle of brandy from the shelf above the stove and added some. Upstairs, he took the baby from Magda gently and laid her on the bed. Then he pressed the teacup into Magda's hands before sitting down beside her. 'What happened?' he asked, when she had taken a sip.

'They came...' She faltered, setting down the cup on the floor and reaching for his hand. 'I'm not sure why, really. They first wanted to speak with Hans, but when they realized he wasn't here they kept asking questions about activities in the neighborhood, whether I had seen anyone helping Jews.' Her fingers tightened around his. 'I didn't have anything to tell them, of course.'

Of course. But the Nazis would kill those who they thought were holding back information, regardless of faith. Thank God the officers seemed to have believed her or the two of them might not be sitting here having this conversation. A chill ran down his spine as he processed the gravity of the situation. 'Do you think they knew–?'

'About me?' He nodded. 'Not that they let on. And Anna was asleep upstairs the whole time, thankfully, so I don't think they even knew she was here.' Roger processed the information, wanting to find relief in it. But he could not.

Suddenly Magda's face crumpled. 'Oh, Roger,' she cried. She leaned forward against the bed, her dark hair grazing the baby's stomach. She began to shake, clutching the rose-colored duvet in her fist.

He froze, caught off guard by her uncharacteristic outburst. Then, as he sensed the depths of her anguish, the need to comfort her rose up inside him. 'There, there,' he said, wrapping himself around her back and drawing her close. 'You're safe now.'

'It's not that,' she said, her voice muffled in the bedding.

'Then what?'

'I'm worried about Hans.'

The unexpected response slammed into his chest. He straightened. 'Yes, of course you are.' It made sense, really, a wife worried about her husband. Who could argue with that? But he turned away, facing the wall.

'Please don't.' She touched his shoulder. 'I'm just concerned about his safety. That's all. I do care for him,' she added quickly, her tone defensive.

'Then why?' he asked abruptly. For a moment he didn't think she would understand the question, but he could tell from the quiver of her lip that she knew just what he meant.

'You? Us?' She paused, as though considering him for the first time and Roger braced for the answer. She leaned back in his arms, her body slack with surrender. 'You're the great love of my life.' A lump formed in his throat, making it impossible to breathe. 'I only wish I hadn't found out when it was too late.'

Roger's heart swelled until he felt as if it was about to burst. It was him that she loved, not Hans, and she wished as he did that they might have met first so that things could be different. Then his joy was extinguished by a tidal wave of regret as her words echoed in his mind: *too late.* He imagined a life married to Magda, not having to hide, but openly proud of his family. If only he had met Magda before Hans did – but it was that way with the two of them, his older brother always better, more important. Of course the irony was that without Hans, Roger reflected, he never would have met Magda in the first place.

But his concerns right now went well beyond jealousy. 'What about you?' he asked. 'With all that has happened, it isn't safe for you to remain here.' Roger thought then of his brother. Some time ago, on the day he'd discovered her hiding place, Magda had said that Hans knew she was Jewish. With his connections, surely he could help. 'Have you talked to Hans?'

She nodded, seeming to burrow deeper in his embrace. 'I tried once. I didn't mention myself directly of course, but friends in need of assistance. But he said that it was impossible, that the organization had to focus on large groups and couldn't compromise operations to help individuals.'

'Maybe it would be different, though, if he knew you were asking for yourself and Anna.'

'No.' She was right. Hans, principled and remote, would not make an exception, even for his own family. 'Promise you won't say anything.'

Roger bit his lip. 'I promise.'

'Such help is better than I deserve in any event.' A look of self-loathing and recrimination twisted her face then, and Roger knew she was thinking of the affair. Magda did not consider herself worthy of Hans's sanctuary while betraying his trust.

'Magda, don't–'

She waved her hand. 'I'll answer someday for what I've done here – no matter how real my feelings are for you.' Her voice was heavy with resignation. He thought then about his own lack of remorse. A better man might have felt guiltier about taking his brother's wife while living in his house. But Hans had everything and appreciated none of it.

'It is only for Anna that I am worried,' Magda added, changing the subject. Roger nodded. With a Jewish mother, the child would be considered Jewish too. 'I've made inquiries with the neighbors.' There had long been speculation that the Baders, the elderly couple next door, were somehow involved with protecting Jews. Not that he'd ever spoken with them. There was a kind of unease among people these days, as though each was watching the other, unsure who could be trusted.

'I can care for Anna,' he protested.

'Darling,' she said gently, reaching up to graze his cheek, 'I know that you want to. But she would have to be hidden, in ways that you couldn't possibly manage.' A knife ripped through his chest then as he contemplated for the first time what a life without Magda and their daughter might be like. 'It won't come to that,' she added firmly, sensing his unease.

'Let me talk to Hans,' Roger said suddenly. 'If he can arrange for papers, we can get you out of the country. Geneva, maybe, or Paris.' Though he did not say so, it was clear that he would be going with them, that he would not let them travel alone.

'No,' she said firmly. 'We need to be here for Hans.'

Who isn't here for you, he wanted to point out, but he did not. Equality was not a condition for which Magda had bartered in this marriage. 'But surely he would feel better if he knew you were safe.'

'No,' she snapped, more forcefully than he had ever heard her speak. 'Don't you see,' she hissed, dropping her voice to a low whisper though they were the only ones in the house, other than the baby. 'You're barely able to contain yourself when he is around. Your expression, the way you watch me.' Roger turned away, sheepish. He wanted to deny what she said but he could not.

'It's not just you,' she hastened to add, softening her words with a smile. 'I'm no better. Don't you know that if you go to him, he's going to figure it out?' She was right about that too. Roger wanted to claim that he would go to Hans as a concerned brother-in-law. But surely the intensity of his panic would give it all away.

'I won't say anything,' he relented, attempting to placate her.

'Everything will be fine,' she said. But her words rang hollow.

Roger could tell from Magda's voice that there was more to it, something she was not saying. Though she confided in him more than in her husband, it was also clear that even after all they had been through, everything they had shared, she still did not completely trust him. There would always be some part of Magda that he could not know.

'But–' He prepared to try to reason with her once more. Before he could finish the thought, there was a sound in the foyer below, the door opening, heavy footsteps. He froze. Had the Gestapo come back? Magda lunged for the child on the bed but Roger tightened his grip, restraining her. They needed Anna to remain asleep so she would not cry out.

'Shhh...' he whispered. His eyes darted around the room uncertainly, coming to rest on the armoire. He had to get Magda and Anna into the hiding space behind it, but there was no way to move the heavy piece of furniture without making noise that would attract attention.

The footsteps were on the stairs now, moving rapidly, growing closer. Was there something he could use as a weapon? He would die fighting before letting Magda and the child be taken.

'Hello?' Hans's blond head appeared in the doorway.

Roger's entire body went limp with relief. 'My brother,' he said, feeling more warmth toward Hans than he could remember. 'Thank goodness!'

But Hans did not appear to share the sentiment. He stared at Roger and Magda, the lines in his brow deepening. Each time Hans had returned home previously, Roger had been certain that his brother would discern what had happened, that events of such magnitude could not go undetected. Hans had always seemed oblivious, though, retreating to his study with excuses about urgent matters. Roger was suddenly aware of how strange the scenario must appear – he and Magda in the intimacy of the bedroom, with her draped around his neck in a way that suggested it was not the first time. Surely Hans would know now.

Magda leapt to her feet, smoothing her hair. 'I thought you were returning this evening.' But for the redness around her eyes, there was no sign of the despair that had wracked her body just a few minutes earlier. She walked quickly to Hans, her face lighting up as she took his coat. Roger searched for a sign that Magda's enthusiasm wasn't genuine, or that her smile was forced. But he found none.

Hans stroked his wife's hair. 'I was able to get an earlier ride.' Hans turned to Roger. 'Shouldn't you be at your lectures?'

Hearing the paternalistic tone in his brother's voice, Roger grew annoyed. 'I stopped back to get a paper I'd forgotten. And a good thing too – the Gestapo was here.' He realized as the words came out that he had exaggerated his role, as though he had personally encountered the Germans.

Concern flashed across Hans's face. 'Oh?'

'Mostly they were asking about activities in the neighborhood,' Magda explained, in a voice calmer than Roger thought possible under the circumstances. He could see the relief on his brother's face as Hans comprehended that they had not come to jeopardize his operations. Roger grew angry. Surely the safety of his family should mean more to Hans than his work.

As Magda continued telling him about the encounter in a low voice, Hans wrapped his arms around her, leading her to the bed. She picked up the child and the three of them sat together, a family reunited. He had been forgotten, Roger realized, with a sense of disappointment. Part of him wanted Hans to find out what was going on between him and Magda, to destroy the status quo of the arrangement in which Roger could never win.

But that had not happened, and Roger would not force the situation. Magda needed the protection that her marriage to Hans afforded her now more than ever. Defeated, he slipped from the room.

That evening, Roger stood at the door of Hans's study, waiting for his brother to notice him. He looked back over his shoulder. Magda would be furious if she knew that Roger was disregarding her wishes, as well as his promise to her. But after today he had no choice. And he was counting on the fact that Hans was preoccupied and told his wife little. Hans would not say anything to Magda unless he was actually able to do something and then it would no longer matter. Roger had to take the chance.

When several minutes had passed and Hans had not looked up, Roger cleared his throat. 'Come in,' Hans said, but his affability was forced, as though he was trying to hide annoyance at the interruption. 'How are your studies?'

'Fine,' he replied dutifully, more aware than ever of his brother's benevolence, the imbalance of power that had always existed between them.

'Do you need some extra money?'

'No, thank you.' Roger fought to keep the indignation from his voice. He had asked for some money once just to make it until the end of the month when he received his stipend, and then he had repaid it promptly. 'It's about Magda.'

Hans glanced up from the papers momentarily. 'What is it?'

He took a deep breath. 'I'm concerned about her safety and Anna's too.' But Hans continued to stare at him blankly. Did he really not see the connection between his own work and the danger that threatened his family? 'After all that happened today–' he pressed.

Hans straightened. 'Magda was not the target of the Gestapo inquiry. And with my position as a diplomat, they would not dare to touch my wife.'

He was not trying to be arrogant, Roger realized. He was just giving his honest assessment. But how could he be sure? 'If you could arrange some papers–'

Hans shook his head. 'Even if I could manage that, Magda would refuse to go.' In that one regard, at least, Hans seemed to know his wife. 'And her departure would attract too much attention.'

Roger's anger flared. Was his brother seriously more worried about appearances for the sake of his work than about his family's safety?

Roger hesitated, yearning to say more. But he

had already said more than Magda wanted and he would gain no further ground with Hans. He turned. 'Good evening.'

'Wait,' Hans called after him as he reached the door.

He turned back, the dutiful brother summoned. 'About Magda – I understand your concerns.' Hans's face softened. 'And I'm going to be traveling a good deal these next few months.'

Meaning that Hans was going to be absent even more than he was already? Roger wondered with a mixture of hope and disbelief. It hardly seemed possible.

'I want you to look after her.'

I already do, Roger wanted to say. Hans continued. 'That is, if something should happen to me...' Hans's voice trailed off and his face clouded, betraying more concern than he had previously been willing to admit.

'Is there something–?'

'Nothing that I know of. No imminent danger.' But Hans sounded like he was trying to convince himself as much as Roger. 'Just in case, there's a drawer at the bottom of my desk with a false bottom. Beneath it you will find some money, as well as papers detailing my various contacts in different places. Don't go there unless it's absolutely critical. There are other things there too, and you would endanger yourself and Magda by knowing about them.'

'Of course.' Another man might have pushed for more information or perhaps even been tempted to look. But Hans would say no more – and Roger had learned the value of keeping his head low.

Roger retreated from the study, and eyed the stairs to the third floor reluctantly. Nights with Hans home were the hardest, and on the occasions when Roger knew his brother was coming, he would remain at the university for as long as he could, working until the librarian patiently reminded him that the building would be closing. Later, he would invariably lie awake, trying to shut out the sound of voices talking softly below, unable to accept that the moment of Magda's arrival would not come.

He started for the stairs now. Behind him there came a noise from the water closet and he looked back to see Magda emerging in her housecoat. She made her way to the bedroom, head down.

As Roger forced himself to continue on, his boot scuffled loudly against the floor. He turned back. Magda glanced over her shoulder from the doorway and when their eyes met, he could see a longing that tugged at his heart.

He stepped closer, emboldened. 'Magda.' His lips formed her name without sound. He held his breath, wishing that she might dare to whisper his name as well. Seconds passed. Then the silence was broken by the shuffling of papers behind the closed study door, Hans clearing his throat.

'*Gute Nacht,*' Magda said hurriedly. Roger opened his mouth, but before he could respond, she disappeared into the darkness behind her.

Nine

MUNICH, 2009

Charlotte stared up wordlessly at Brian, a thousand conflicting emotions roaring through her. There was the usual jump in her stomach. But at the same time she wanted to slap him, hard, for standing her up at the airport. Everything he had done to her years earlier came rushing back, amplified even more due to his most recent transgression. Underneath it all, a small flicker of desire burned, the attraction she felt to him undimmed by time or pain. And then, just as suddenly as they had come, the feelings receded like a tide, leaving her hollow and drained. Inwardly she started to crumble.

'Good morning,' Brian said, as though there was nothing unusual about his unannounced appearance, or the circumstances that had caused them to meet here. He walked past her into the room. She was suddenly mindful of her sweatpants and sleep-tousled hair, as well as the musky smell that seemed to linger in the air. He walked to the windows, pushing the curtains aside, and bright sunlight illuminated the unmade bed. He had just missed his brother, she realized with relief. What would have happened if he had arrived a little earlier?

'When did you get in?'

213

'About an hour ago.' But with his pressed suit and fresh shave, he showed no signs of having taken an overnight flight. 'You were expecting Jack?'

'I – that is, we – never said where we were meeting this morning.' The half-eaten food on the room-service trays that still sat in the corner seemed somehow like incriminating evidence. But Brian did not seem to notice. Anger replaced her uneasiness. It was he who had stood her up, sent her on to deal with the case on her own. He was the one who owed explanations.

'Why don't you take a shower?' he suggested before she could speak. 'I'm going to grab some coffee in the lobby and wait for you there.'

Ninety minutes later they entered the prison conference room. Jack looked up and at the sight of her began to smile. Then as he saw his brother, his face clouded over and his brow furrowed. His gaze dropped to Charlotte once more and his expression changed – to what exactly she could not say. Awkwardness? Desire? Regret?

Jack stood. 'Hello Brian,' he said evenly, his voice neutral, devoid of any reference to the decade of unexplained acrimony between them. The two men did not shake hands.

'I just got in,' Brian said. 'I was delayed by an emergency hearing.' As usual with Brian, there was no apology. 'I heard that you were in Poland?'

'Yes. It's a long story and–'

But Brian brushed by without giving him the chance to finish. 'Roger,' he said warmly, extending his hand as though they were meeting on the golf course. It was the first time Charlotte had heard anyone address the older man by his first name.

Then Brian stopped, noticing the ankle chains. 'What's this?' he demanded, turning around, as if Charlotte and Jack were personally responsible for Roger's incarceration. 'My client is a respected businessman, an industry leader. He shouldn't be treated like a common criminal.'

His client, Charlotte repeated silently, annoyed. 'I'm going to get the judge on the phone,' Brian blustered. 'This is an outrage.'

'You,' Jack replied quietly, his voice steely, 'will do no such thing. You aren't in New York anymore. This is a foreign country and they have their own rules and customs and throwing your weight around is only going to make things worse.'

Brian's mouth opened and Charlotte braced herself for an obscenity-laced retort, but then he sat back, seemingly subdued by his brother's admonition. 'So what are we doing now?'

'Charley and I–' Jack faltered, flustered by his own use of the intimate nickname. Brian looked from Jack to Charlotte, then back again, a scowl crossing his face.

'Yesterday Herr Dykmans was telling us about a clock that may contain some helpful information,' Charlotte interjected. 'He thinks it might be in Salzburg and I thought we should go there to check out the lead.'

'And I think it's a wild goose chase,' Jack chimed in.

'It's not as if we have a better lead here,' she countered suddenly, feeling like she was arguing

215

her case before a judge.

'I agree with Charlotte,' Brian pronounced, as though the call was his. He was, she conceded inwardly, the tie-breaking vote. But did he really agree with her, or was he simply trying to out-maneuver his brother?

Out of the corner of her eye, she caught the look of anger that imprinted itself upon Jack's face. This was the frustration he'd described before – it was his case and in waltzed Brian at the last minute, taking over. It was more than that, though. She could feel Jack shooting waves of recrimination in her direction across the room. To him, it was as if she had betrayed him, which seemed unfair, seeing as going to Salzburg had been her idea all along, and given that he'd brought up their disagreement. Still, she didn't want him to think she was siding with Brian. I'm sorry, she tried to mouth to him silently.

But Jack looked away. 'Fine,' he said at last. 'I'll book the train.'

'You don't have to go,' Brian replied. 'You can stay here and work the case and Charlotte and I can go to Salzburg.'

As she stood back and watched them argue, dread rose in her. She wanted to be alone with Brian even less than she wanted to be separated from Jack, and the combination of both seemed unthinkable. The deluge of emotions she'd been holding back surged forth then, nearly knocking her off her feet.

'No,' Jack replied firmly. 'We should all go.' Charlotte exhaled silently. 'Anyway, my German is the best.'

'Then what are we waiting for?' Brian asked.

Charlotte cringed. She had still hoped that he might back out of this part of the trip. 'But your case in New York – don't you have to get back?'

Brian waved his hand dismissively. 'Nonsense. I just arrived. And there's no matter more important to me than Roger's,' he said, loudly enough for the older man to hear. But Charlotte could tell that it went beyond concern for his client. Brian simply wanted what Jack had, insisted on taking control. This was the tension she had sensed between the brothers years ago, only instead of easing with the passage of time, the gamesmanship was even more pronounced now, laid bare. And it wasn't just about the case – seeing the closeness that had developed between her and Jack in the past few days had fueled Brian's competitive instinct. The thought gave her little comfort. It wasn't that Brian wanted her. He just didn't want his brother to win.

But there's nothing between me and Jack, she thought, protesting inwardly. Was there? Last night was just a moment, and Brian didn't know about that anyway. It didn't matter, though; Brian's jealousy had little to do with reality or her and everything to do with the rivalry between the brothers and his need to come out on top. He would not be dissuaded from going to Salzburg.

She looked over at the conference table then. Herr Dykmans watched the two brothers debate, a glint of something at the corner of his eyes. Her irritation flared. Was he amused by this tussle among the team members trying to save his life? Then his eyes caught hers, held. No, it was

217

something else. Empathy. I've been part of a love triangle too, his gaze seemed to suggest.

She wanted to tell him the situation wasn't like that, not at all the same as his had been. But whatever this was, being caught in the power struggle between the two brothers was not a position she relished.

'All right,' she said, clearing her throat. It was time to take charge of the situation. 'Let's book the tickets. The three of us,' she did not meet Roger's gaze, 'are going to Salzburg.'

'I took care of your client,' Brian said to Charlotte as they boarded the train an hour later, steps ahead of Jack. They'd left Roger at the prison and headed directly to the station, no one speaking during the short car ride. Now, as they located an empty compartment, three seats facing forward and three to the rear, Brian showed no trace of the bluster he'd shown earlier. He was subdued, almost contrite, a little boy chastised. She'd always been able to bring him to this place, Charlotte reflected, simply by waiting out whatever storm seemed to be blowing through him. 'Kate Dolgenos is in Philadelphia right now.'

She nodded. 'I know.' But his fulfillment of that one promise in no way made up for the rest of it, the pain he'd caused years earlier, his failure to show up at the airport as promised a few days ago.

Brian sat down in the seat closest to the aisle, facing forward, and Jack dropped into the rear-facing seat farthest from his brother by the window. Charlotte hesitated. Her choice of where to sit seemed somehow symbolic – as if she were

218

picking between them. Ridiculous, given that they were all on the same side, at least in the legal sense. 'I'm going for coffee,' she said, choosing neither. 'Do either of you want anything?'

Jack opened his mouth as if to speak but no sound came out. Brian simply shot her a look of helpless abandonment, begging her not to leave. It was the first time the brothers had seen each other in years, she realized, and they did not want to be alone with each other.

But that was not, she decided a few minutes later as she settled in at a table in the café car, her problem. She was an attorney, not a therapist. She stirred her cappuccino and opened the copy of the *International Herald Tribune* she had purchased at the station, scanning the headlines, eager for distraction. A moment later she looked up again idly. The train had left the Munich city center and its residential surroundings, and in the distance the rolling green hills of southern Bavaria unfurled before her.

She sighed, feeling surprisingly relaxed. There had always been a kind of freedom and anonymity here, a simplicity that she'd lost somewhere along the way back home. I could just keep going, she thought suddenly. Leave all of the drama of Brian and Jack behind, hop one train and then another and see where I wind up. The boldness of the notion almost made her dizzy. She already lived alone, a life devoid of any ties. Why not enjoy some of the benefits of that solitude?

But even as she contemplated the idea, practical considerations rained down: she had a life in Philadelphia, a house, clients who were counting on her. And then there was Roger. Despite his cold demeanor and cryptic refusal to cooperate, there was something about him that she found strangely compelling. Not that he was sympathetic exactly, but he had a quiet resignation to which she could relate. Anyway, whether she liked him or not was irrelevant. She had taken on the case and he was her client now, and she would represent him to the end with the same dedication that she gave Marquan or any of the other kids she defended back home.

And that meant continuing to work with Jack, she thought, as his face appeared in her mind. She was seized by a sudden image of last night, Jack moving above her. What had happened? The whole thing was so surreal, it was as if it had been a dream. But an unmistakable heat rose within her, confirming that the encounter had indeed occurred, leaving her to wonder what it all meant. It's the stress, she decided. Two lonely people, working long hours together, caught up in the moment.

Still, she could not shake her sense of unease. It wasn't like her; she could have stopped him or said no. There had been others, of course, in the years between Brian and now, casual encounters that after a few dates had left her feeling more empty than anything else. But this had been different. It was as if a tiny crack, a fissure in the protective armor she had spent years putting up around herself, had been opened, leaving her feeling naked and exposed.

Irrelevant, she concluded finally, finishing her coffee. It had happened and it was over and now, with Brian here, it would not be an issue again. She stood, throwing her cup in the trash and refolding her newspaper before starting back toward the compartment.

Just then her BlackBerry vibrated against her side, signaling a message. She looked down, surprised. Contact with the outside world seemed so foreign now. She pulled out the device, clicked over to the Internet function, and logged into her Gmail account. The Web page loaded slowly, hampered, she was sure, by the lack of a strong signal in the mountainous terrain.

A new message, from Alicja Recka. Charlotte's heart seemed to skip a beat as she clicked on the e-mail and scrolled down. She had not expected to receive a response so quickly. *Lovely to hear from you,* it read. *I checked our records and regret to say it appears that Magda Dykmans died in the gas chamber at Belzec in 1943. Best, Alicja.*

Charlotte's stomach dropped. Suddenly it was as if she had known Magda, and the loss was hers as well as Roger's. Well, what had she expected, a happy ending after all these years?

Reluctantly, she headed back to the compartment to tell Jack and Brian the news. As she neared the door, she stopped, hearing voices. The brothers were actually talking to each other, which was a pleasant surprise. Perhaps they had managed to break the ice after all. She waited, not wanting to interrupt the possible reconciliation. But the volume of their conversation was rising now. She leaned in, listening more closely. Though she couldn't make out what they were saying, it was clear from their heated tones that it was not an amicable conversation.

I should walk away, she thought. Whatever is going on between them is none of my business. But her curiosity grew: What was it that was still such a bone of contention between them? Unable to resist, she leaned in closer.

'Leave her alone, Brian,' she heard Jack warn in a terse voice.

They're talking about me, Charlotte realized. She slipped back farther behind the doorframe.

'Why do you care, anyway?' Brian demanded. 'Is there something going on between the two of you?'

'Not at all,' Jack replied quickly, as though the question was a ridiculous one. Charlotte stifled a gasp, stung by his dismissive tone. 'I'm just saying that you shouldn't be toying with her like this. Dragging her into the case and then–'

Brian's voice rose in protest. 'I'm not–'

Charlotte stepped back, her eyes burning. It was more than just Jack's denial of what had taken place between them that hurt; she thought that they had become equals these past few days, that they worked well together. But to hear him now, he thought her unworthy of his brother's time – or his own.

Jack spoke again, 'And now, with Danielle pregnant...'

A rock slammed into Charlotte's chest. Though she'd known about Brian and Danielle's marriage for nearly a decade, the idea of a child legitimizing it all was more than she could bear. She spun and sped back down the corridor of the train, banging her elbow against a half-open compartment door but scarcely feeling the throb. She ran as fast as she could, dodging passengers and suitcases, as though she were outdoors back home and burning off some steam after a particularly grueling day in court by running the eight-mile loop on Kelly Drive.

A minute later Charlotte reached the café at the end of the moving train once more. She slowed, walking to the cracked window at the back of the car, watching the hills retreat. She stood motionless for several minutes, still breathing hard. What am I doing here, she wondered? Suddenly the full magnitude of it all slammed down upon her. Europe, Brian, these were feelings she had tucked away nearly a decade ago, and the pain, while still there, had at least scarred over, muted by time. How could she have been so foolish as to let them in again?

The tears flowed now in a way they hadn't for years, maybe not ever, even when Winnie died and she stood at the edge of the desolate cemetery, realizing for the first time how alone in the world she really was. Then she had gone into a functioning mode: there was the house to sell, a job to be secured. Afterward, when things had settled down and there might have been time to mourn, she had simply not chosen to reopen that door and let the feelings in. They were irrelevant, like a textbook for a course she had taken and would never use again. But now the grief burst forth and she wept openly, not caring who heard, her sobs echoing around the empty café car.

What was it about the Warringtons anyway? The fabric of her life was rich, filled with people and places and experiences. Yet she had let Brian – and now Jack – get under her skin, affect her in ways that no one else quite had.

'Hey.' Charlotte spun around. Brian stood behind her, juggling two cups of coffee. She stared at him, as if she had forgotten for a moment that he was here or had not expected him to find her on the train. He held one out to her wordlessly and she took it, sinking to the seat at one of the tables he indicated. He had not, she realized gratefully, asked if she was all right. Had he seen her outside the compartment when she fled?

'I'm sorry,' she said, fumbling with a sudden need to explain. 'It's just that–'

'Being here, after so many years,' he finished for her. 'It brings back a lot of memories, doesn't it?'

She hesitated, caught off guard by his seeming comprehension. This was the man she had forgotten about, stripped of all his bravado, empathetic and real. This was Brian at his most dangerous. 'I overheard you and Jack talking,' she confessed. She studied his expression, but if he was angry he gave no indication. 'Congratulations, about the baby and all.'

His face brightened. 'Thanks so much. I'm thrilled.'

She noticed he did not say *we*. 'Danielle must be excited, too.'

A flicker of something passed over his face. 'She is, I think. It's just the timing.'

Charlotte nodded, understanding. Danielle, already an income partner, would be up for the more senior equity partnership at her firm about now and maternity leave, time away from client development and billable hours, would surely hurt her chances. 'I'm not sure she's ready,' Brian added, 'to put someone else first.'

From anyone else, Charlotte reflected, the confession about his wife's lack of maternal instinct, made to an ex-girlfriend, might have sounded disloyal. But Brian's tone was nonjudgmental, matter of fact. He was not conveying regret, or suggesting that he would have preferred Charlotte in his wife's place, but rather reporting on the status quo as it now existed. 'It's a lifestyle change for sure,' she agreed. 'Do you know what you're having?'

'Not yet, and I'm not sure we're finding out. Danielle wants to know so we can decorate the nursery. But I think it's one of life's true mysteries. I wouldn't mind a daughter, though.'

Charlotte looked at him, surprised. She would have thought for sure that Brian wanted a son, for the football games and such. Suddenly she was aware of the strangeness of the conversation, not just the fact that she was sitting here with her ex-boyfriend, discussing his child with the woman he left her for – but the fact that it didn't seem to bother her that much at all. Her mind reeled back to the earlier exchange she'd heard between the two brothers. It wasn't the idea of Danielle and Brian having a child together that had upset her so much as the fact that Jack seemed to regard her as irrelevant.

The sky had grown dark; thick clouds clustered around the mountaintops. 'Did you want to go back?' she asked. 'I mean, it was good of you to come after me, but I'm sure you have work to do.'

'Nah,' he said, smiling. 'Jack's probably sleeping by now. There's no way to work through that kind of snoring anyway.'

She faltered, unsure how to react to the comment, which was amusing and true, but at the same time a bit too intimate for comfort. You actually snore far worse than he does, she wanted to tell Brian. Jack's was more of a gentle whistling, the wind through a narrow passageway, not the freight train his brother seemed to channel.

'I'm sorry,' Brian said abruptly. Something hard slammed into her stomach. It was the first time she heard Brian apologize for anything. Maybe if he had said as much a decade ago, things would have been easier to take.

'For what?' she asked, wondering if she shouldn't ask, if her assumptions about his apology were better than anything he might actually have to say.

'About the way things ended between us back then.' No, he wasn't sorry for what he had done, or for hurting her so. It was the messiness he regretted, the inconvenience of leaving behind a situation he couldn't feel good about. 'That we couldn't have been like you and Jack are now,' he added.

Charlotte's heart seemed to stop. Did Brian know what had transpired between her and his brother? Had Jack said something to him? 'Friends, I mean,' he added.

She exhaled silently, relieved. Brian was envious that his brother had gotten close to Charlotte in a way that he could not, but he didn't suspect more. Not that it mattered anyway. It was clear from the comments she had overheard that Jack did not regard her as significant.

We couldn't have stayed friends, she thought, because we never really were in the first place. 'Friends,' she said finally. 'I don't know if Jack would agree.'

'My brother's a hard guy to get to know,' Brian observed. 'He's just so melancholy.'

Charlotte was surprised by the remark. Years earlier, she might have agreed. But now she saw Jack as something else, not sad, but pensive and deep where Brian was not. The comment about his brother seemed unfair, and she wanted to remind him of the admonition they'd received in law school – personal attacks on your opponent undermine your credibility with the court.

They stared out the window, neither speaking, as the snowcapped peaks of the Obersalzberg unfolded before them in the mist and raindrops began to fall. 'Do you remember the Jefferson at night?' Brian asked, pulling her from her thoughts.

Charlotte nodded, the memory instantly coming into focus. It was a trip they had taken to Washington in late winter, an attempt on his part to take her mind off her dying mother, back when he still cared, before things went bad. Late at night after the Georgetown bars they'd caroused had closed, he roused her from half sleep, coaxing her from their hotel room. 'Where are we going?' she asked as he led her through the frigid night air, around Washington Harbor and the Kennedy Center toward the Mall, their breath rising in puffs above them. The streets were eerily silent and she worried that perhaps it was not safe to be out walking. They climbed the steps of the Lincoln Memorial, staring up in awed silence. Then they'd pressed on. She had no idea how much time had passed, and if the long walk seemed tiring she never noticed as they strolled along the reflecting pool to the Jefferson Memorial and the Tidal Basin, which seemed illuminated under the pale gray night sky.

The memory, one she had not allowed herself for years, was as vivid as though it had just happened. But why was he bringing it up now?

'That's what it reminds me of here,' he said. She opened her mouth to tell him that the bustling Washington metropolis, even at night, was the furthest thing from this alpine haven. Then she decided against it. Brian was, in his own clumsy way, trying to connect the two moments of solitude and retreat. And this was, she realized, the closest they might ever come to friendship. She wasn't going to ruin it by correcting him.

'It's hard, isn't it, to imagine the war here,' she offered instead. The snow-capped mountains looked tranquil, as though undisturbed for a thousand years. It was almost impossible to picture the tanks and other machinery of war that had rolled through here, causing such unbearable suffering just sixty-odd years ago.

Jack appeared in the door of the café car then. 'We're almost there,' he announced abruptly. Charlotte peered out the window, unable to discern any signs of civilization among the unbroken hills. But it was less than a few hundred kilometers between the two cities and he spoke with the confidence of a man who had traveled this route many times. Sure enough, a few minutes later, a church steeple came into view, nestled between two of the peaks, and then the mountains broke to reveal a sea of spires and red rooftops below.

Charlotte turned away. She could still feel the puffy redness around her eyes, giving away the fact that she had been crying. Jack did not seem to notice, but looked from the window to his watch, then back again with impatience. As she remembered his tone when he disavowed to Brian that there was anything between them, her anger grew. The man she had glimpsed last night at the hotel, gentle and open, was nowhere to be found. Had it been an act or had something changed afterward?

A few minutes later when the train had screeched to a halt, they stepped off onto the platform and made their way to the front of the station. The e-mail from Alicja, she remembered suddenly. She felt as though she should have said something earlier, but it had not felt right to tell Brian without Jack. 'Um, wait a second,' she said. They turned and looked at her expectantly. 'I have some news. After Roger told us about Magda, I did some checking with one of my contacts from years ago when I was researching in Poland.' She glanced up at Jack's face to see if he was angry that she'd done this without telling him. But his expression remained impassive. 'I just received an e-mail: it turns out that Magda died in the camps in 1943.'

'That's pretty much what we expected, isn't it?' Brian asked. 'That Magda died, I mean.'

She nodded. 'But knowing – well, I think that's going to be harder on Roger than anything.'

'If we tell him,' Jack interjected.

'If?' she repeated in disbelief. 'How can we not?'

'I'm just saying that the timing isn't great. Maybe we wait.' She opened her mouth to protest. Wasn't knowing always better? But he raised his hand. 'We can argue about that on the way back. Right now, we need to get to the clock shop.'

Outside the storm had stopped, leaving behind small puddles at the curb. They navigated around the bike racks and a short queue of waiting taxis, walked in the direction of the city center without speaking. As they reached the heart of the baroque Old Town, a light rain began to fall once more. Brian produced an umbrella and opened it over her.

They paused for a moment near the Salzburger Dom, huddling in the shadow of the cathedral as Jack consulted a map, then walked to a nearby shop to ask directions. Charlotte gazed from the now-vacant outdoor cafés up to the Hohensalzburg Castle, a massive fortress sitting on a hilltop overlooking the town. On her few earlier visits, she had always been indifferent to Salzburg. It seemed, like the rest of Austria, too perfect, a movie-set idea of what Europe was supposed to look like. And the pristine, untroubled environs gave no hint of the barbarism that had taken place there just over half a century ago.

She looked back down again. Across the Street she saw Jack, watching her through the shop window. She expected him to once again look away, but he caught her gaze, held it. A shiver passed through her. In that moment, she knew that the feelings were not hers alone. But then she remembered his comments about her to Brian on the train. How could she reconcile the man who seemed so dismissive when discussing her with his brother with the one who gazed at her with such longing now?

Jack returned a moment later and led them wordlessly from the square. They turned off the main thoroughfare into a narrow cobblestone alley. 'This should be it,' he said, stopping in front of a window cluttered with cheaply made cuckoo clocks.

An unseen bell jangled faintly as they opened the door. The shop was equally unimpressive inside. Rows of nearly identical cuckoo clocks intended for the tourists mingled indiscriminately with porcelain figurines clad in traditional Austrian garb. On the wall a faded poster advertised the *Sound of Music* tour in English. The shop was covered with a fine coat of dust, Charlotte noticed, as though nothing had been disturbed – or sold – in years. How could one possibly make a living with a business such as this?

She looked up, exchanging uncertain glances with Jack. But Brian pressed forward, undeterred. 'Hello,' he called loudly at the counter, his American bluster a cliché. Charlotte cringed.

From a doorway behind the counter, a man appeared. Wizened and bald, he had to be close to ninety. Almost the same age as Roger, Charlotte calculated, though the man looked twenty years older than their client. He blinked, as though surprised to actually have visitors in the store. 'Can I help you?' His English, while broken, was comprehensible, a baseline knowledge of the language

231

that she guessed was necessitated by his tourist clientele.

'We're here about a clock,' Brian announced abruptly.

'Of course. If you don't see anything you like here on the floor, I have some lovely larger cuckoos I can show you.'

'Excuse me,' Jack said, stepping forward. 'I'm afraid we may have misspoken.' Even without looking, Charlotte could feel the daggers Brian was shooting at his brother, furious at being corrected. She bit her lip, praying he would not say anything to interrupt what Jack was trying to do. 'We're looking for a very specific clock. Are you Herr Beamer?' Charlotte did not recall Roger giving them the clockmaker's name, but the man nodded slightly. 'We were sent by Roger Dykmans.'

The clockmaker hesitated, a strange look crossing his face. Clearly he had heard of Roger, but how much did he know, or care, about the case? It would have been impossible to avoid unless one had no source of news, no contact with the outside world. 'You know Herr Dykmans?' Jack prompted.

The clockmaker did not answer but led them with a gesture through a second doorway at the back of the shop. Suddenly, it was as if they were transported to another world, a century earlier perhaps, far removed from the bustle of the touristy thoroughfare. It was a workshop, simply lit, the smell of sawdust and turpentine thick in the air. Clocks of every size and description covered the walls, the workbench, and the counter, in

232

various states of composition and repair. From all around came the ticking of the endlessly moving timepieces.

The man cleared a space on one of the benches and indicated that it was for Charlotte. She started to sit down, then leapt up again, suppressing a yelp. There on the bench lay a dead bird, stiff and motionless. The man reached down and picked it up. It was then that she noticed it was not dead but fake, as he returned it to its place inside one of the clocks on the table. It had only looked real.

She perched awkwardly on the edge of the bench, scanning the room. There were clocks of every shape and size, but none resembled the one in the photo. 'So about Herr Dykmans,' she tried again.

The old man wrinkled his brow. 'I've never met Herr Dykmans personally, but he contacted me a few months ago about a matter.' The man spoke cryptically as though he were guarding state secrets and not an inquiry about a timepiece. 'I haven't heard from him again, though.'

'He was, um, unexpectedly detained,' Charlotte replied, glad that the man had not linked Roger with the accused war criminal in the headlines. Though perhaps, she thought cynically, he would not have minded. Austria had sided readily with the Nazis and had seemed to do little to atone for the war in the years since. 'But we're here on his behalf. Do you have the clock he was looking for?'

Herr Beamer eyed them warily, as though unsure whether they could be trusted. Then he walked to the shelf and rummaged among the clocks, packed so tightly she was not sure how he could tell one from the next. But he reached to the back and pulled out a burlap bag. He carried it over and set it on the table, gingerly removing the covering to reveal a small tabletop clock set under a dome of glass.

'This is it,' he said, and there was a glint in his eye that signaled the presence of something particularly rare and special in his trade. 'Are you acquainted with this type of clock?'

None of them responded. 'This is called an anniversary or four-hundred-day clock,' the shopkeeper continued. 'It is so named because it was made so that it only needed to be wound once a year.' Charlotte studied the clock, able to see it now in closer detail than had been possible in the photograph. There were four curved brass prongs suspended beneath the porcelain face, circular pendulums that she suspected would rotate in one direction and then the other if the clock was working and wound.

'The design was actually pioneered in America,' the old man continued, and Charlotte looked up at him, surprised. The timepiece seemed innately European, so at home here in this world of clocks. 'But a traveler brought the clock design to Germany at the turn of the century and it really took off here. So much so that American soldiers purchased them as souvenirs and took them back home in great numbers when the war was over.'

'It's not a particularly scarce clock, then?' Jack asked.

The man shook his head. 'Not at all.'

Charlotte's spirits fell. If this type of clock was

so common, what had made Roger think this was the one he was looking for?

'But the clock your friend inquired about was unique,' Herr Beamer added, seeming to read her thoughts. 'It was the first known anniversary clock made in Europe, designed at the turn of the century by a Bavarian farmer. Later the clocks were produced in the factories, but I researched this one and it is handmade and quite distinctive.' He pointed to a mark on the front of the clock. At first glance it appeared to be a chip, a place where the clock had been dropped or bumped. But upon closer examination, Charlotte could see that it was actually the initials *JRR* engraved in the base. 'This insignia sets the clock apart.'

'May I see it?' she asked. The man nodded. She picked the clock up. It was much smaller than she had imagined from the pictures, not even a foot high, though the brass base gave it a certain heft. The details were more intimate than the photograph had shown, the legs that supported the face elegant twists of gold. The pendulums did not move, she noted, but sat fixed in time, as did the hands of the clock, set at ten minutes to six. When had the clock last worked, she wondered? Had it simply run out and not been rewound or had something caused it to suddenly stop?

'Can you tell us where you got it?' Charlotte asked.

Herr Beamer bit his lip. There was a certain sensitivity, she knew, among those who bought and sold artifacts from the war, even if they had been honestly procured, a kind of guilt about

235

benefiting from the belongings of the dead. The shopkeeper went to a file drawer that looked like something from an old library and pulled out a card. 'This clock came to us from Heidelberg. It was sold to us by someone who had bought it off a young girl on the black market many years ago. She said it belonged to a Jewish family in Berlin before the war and she'd found it left behind.'

'Berlin,' Jack interrupted. 'That can't be right. The Dykmans clock was in Breslau through the war.'

The shopkeeper shrugged. 'The records are often unreliable.'

Jack stepped closer, pointed to a small, round mark on the back of the clock. 'What do you make of this?'

Charlotte ran her hand expertly over the strange, uneven hole. She wasn't a firearms expert but she had seen enough in her line of work to recognize the shape. 'A bullet,' she replied authoritatively. 'It must have grazed the clock but not gone through.'

'Quite a lucky break for whoever the shot was intended for,' Jack mused.

'And for the clock,' the shopkeeper added. 'If the bullet had hit the glass, the whole thing would have been destroyed.'

Jack walked over to the table and pulled the clock closer to him. He was just inches away from her now, and despite everything that had happened, it was all Charlotte could do not to shiver. He picked it up and turned it over gently.

'I'm sorry but the timepiece is very valuable,' Herr Beamer said. 'I'm afraid I must ask–'

'I won't hurt it,' Jack promised, sounding as

though he was talking about a living creature. On the bottom was a piece of brown cloth. Jack pried it back to reveal a brass base. Reaching out for a file that was on the workbench, he worked to separate the base from the clock.

'Carefully...' Herr Beamer implored under his breath.

It was a fake bottom, she realized. The actual base, now revealed, contained a small door. The compartment containing the information.

The clockmaker gasped. 'I had no idea. How did you know?'

Jack did not answer but worked at the small door. The room was completely silent except for the clocks that chirped like a flock of birds around them. There was a quiet pop and the door gave way. Jack reached inside, prying around with his finger, then shook his head, grimacing.

'Can you?' he asked Charlotte. 'Your fingers are smaller.' He held out the clock to her and she reached inside the compartment, feeling around the small box. Then she removed her hand, holding up her empty palm for the others to see.

'There's nothing in it,' she said. The compartment that supposedly contained the truth about what Roger had done was empty.

Ten

BRESLAU, 1943

Roger opened his eyes. He had slept a bit longer than usual after Magda's predawn departure and bright morning sunlight now streamed through the curtains. He stood, then walked to the window and opened it a crack. The air, though still brisk, carried a hint of spring. Birds called to one another from the eaves above.

He felt a strange sensation, an emotion so long forgotten he had trouble identifying it. Optimism, he recognized finally. His change in mood was a marked contrast to recent weeks, when he had awoken with a sense of dread that made him want to pull the duvet up and hide. Looking down at the empty courtyard of the synagogue below, it was not hard to understand why he had been so morose. Things had gotten undeniably worse in the winter months. Lectures at the university had been suspended without explanation for the rest of the semester. Rations had become tighter and the sirens sounded continuously at night.

But in the past few weeks the downward spiral seemed, if not to actually have reversed itself, at least to have reached a plateau. There was a kind of quiet and the Gestapo was less prevalent on the street. He'd heard whispers, also, that the Soviets were advancing, and that all available Germans were being redirected to the front. Rumors were that the deportations had died down too, though perhaps that was because the Nazis had simply concluded that there were no more Jews to be taken.

Almost none. Roger's stomach tightened as Magda appeared in his mind. A year had passed since the Nazis had visited the house, yet his heart still seemed to stop each time a car rumbled down their street, not beating again until the sound of the engine faded in the distance. Though she seemed to have escaped detection for now, nothing, save the Reich's defeat, would ease his fears. Of course the end of the war would likely signal Hans's permanent return and it seemed a cruel irony that the very thing that could ensure Magda's safety would surely end their affair as well.

He washed and dressed, then made his way downstairs. Magda stood in the doorway to the kitchen, already wearing her coat. She crouched to adjust the baby's hat low and snug around her brow.

'Darling, surely you aren't going out?' he asked. It was a familiar refrain – him begging her to stay home because it was too dangerous on the street, her insisting that if she allowed them to stop her then they had already won. But even with lectures canceled he usually departed for the library to work on his thesis before she started her day and he could tell by her guilty expression now that she more often than not refused to respect his wishes. He was reminded once again that there was a part of her he did not know, that in some ways she would always remain a stranger to him.

'I have to go to market,' she replied. 'Frau Hess said there's milk to be had.' She was going for the child. Magda would not pass up an opportunity to find nourishment for Anna. Her own milk had dried up just a few months after Anna was born, owing, he suspected, to the limited food that was available, as well as the slight nature of her build. They weren't starving, but more and more often their meal consisted mainly of a watery *eintopf stew*, intended to stretch whatever beans or potatoes could be had.

'Let me go for you,' he suggested.

She shook her head. 'I always go. You would only raise suspicion.'

'But it's too—'

'I'll not be a prisoner in my own home,' she retorted, cutting him off. Her eyes widened angrily. There was something in her determination that bespoke a darker side of her past, a place to which she would not be returned. He wanted to ask what had happened but he knew it was not the time, and that she would not answer.

There was a moment of stubborn silence as they stared at each other, neither backing down. Magda adjusted her cuffs. 'All right,' she said, relenting unexpectedly. There were circles under her eyes that betrayed a lack of sleep. It wasn't the child, he reflected, who was keeping her up nights. Born in the era of the bombing raid, Anna had quickly grown into a sound sleeper, not roused even as the house shook. No, it was worry that disturbed Magda's sleep, though whether for herself and Anna, or Hans, or all of them he did not know.

'Thank you, *Liebchen*,' he said.

There was a scuffling by his feet. *'Lee chen.'* Anna raised her tattered rag doll, imitating him. *'Lee chen.'* Roger looked from the child to her mother, then back again, and he could not help but chuckle at the child's attempt. Magda joined him and soon they were both laughing so much harder than the moment seemed to warrant, a grateful respite from the heaviness around them. For if they could still find a moment's lightness, he reflected, perhaps things weren't so bad after all.

Anna watched, wide-eyed and earnest, puzzled to have generated such a reaction. She held out her arms and Roger picked her up, his laughter subsiding. He exchanged uneasy glances with Magda. They would have to be more careful, now that seventeen-month-old Anna saw and re-peated so much. He handed the child to Magda, fighting the urge to kiss her as he did so. Then he turned and walked from the house.

He returned that night a bit later than usual, detained at the library by a conversation with one of his professors. He hesitated at the front door, still feeling that he should knock as he had the day he arrived. The perennial guest. Inside the foyer, he paused. The air seemed different and for a moment he wondered if Hans had come home unexpectedly. But it was not that kind of change; instead of seeming supercharged, the house felt hollow.

'Hello,' he called. He did not use Magda's

name, not wanting to sound overly familiar in case his instincts were mistaken and Hans had in fact returned. There was no response. Roger's skin prickled. Magda was always home this time of day, feeding Anna and preparing dinner. He walked through the kitchen but the countertops were scrubbed clean, the dishes that lay drying in the rack this morning now put away.

Willing himself to breathe calmly, he continued swiftly to the dining room. Nothing here seemed amiss, a thought that gave him fleeting comfort. Then he noticed Anna's milk cup lying sideways on the table, its precious contents spilled onto the placemat in a pool. The subtle message gripped his throat with an icy hand. Magda never would have permitted the child to be so careless, or allowed the spill to remain there. Something wasn't right.

He went back to the foyer, took the stairs two at a time. 'Magda,' he called now, not caring who heard him. He checked each room, including the water closet, but they were all empty. Then he raced back to the bedroom and pulled back the armoire. 'Magda,' he called into the dark gaping hole in the wall.

He returned downstairs, sinking to the bottom step in disbelief. Magda was gone, and Anna too. Had the Gestapo come again? He tried to tell himself to be calm. She could have gone visiting. But Magda did not have any friends, at least none that he knew of, and surely she would have left a note. No, a voice down deep said, full of certainty and foreboding. She had been taken by the Nazis, he was sure of it.

But if the Nazis had arrested Magda, surely there would have been signs of a struggle. Even as he thought this, though, he knew that Magda would not have fought in front of Anna and risked frightening the child or worse. With no time to flee or hide, she would have cooperated because it was the safest thing to do, ensuring their well-being, at least in the short run. Because she understood, despite being married to Hans, that resistance under such circumstances was futile.

What had brought the Gestapo this time? If it had been simple questions again, Magda and Anna would still be here. Had someone learned of Magda's background and tipped them off? It could have been one of the neighbors, like the family down the street who flew the large flag with the swastika from their second-floor balcony. Or perhaps an enemy of Hans – though it was hard to imagine anyone bearing ill will toward his charismatic brother, surely Hans had angered someone along the way in his work.

Roger's mind flashed back to the conversation he and Magda had that morning, the debate over whether it was too dangerous for her to go to market, her acquiescing to his request that she remain home. Now, looking around the empty kitchen, he cursed his own stubbornness. He had thought he knew best. But if Magda had gone out as she usually did, she and Anna might not have been here when the Nazis came. He had, in fact, caused her to be arrested.

I should have been here, Roger berated himself. But to do what, exactly? If Hans's contacts and influence hadn't been enough to protect Magda, there was little Roger could have done. He wished more than anything, though, that he had taken the chance and risked that one final embrace.

Enough, he thought. Regrets will not help Magda and Anna now. Breathe. Think.

Hans appeared in his mind. Surely his brother, with all of his connections, would be able to help. And he could not refuse, now that the worst had happened. He needed to find Hans. But how?

He ran back upstairs to Hans's office and opened the drawer his brother had indicated during their last conversation. Then he stopped short. The drawer was filled with money, neatly bound stacks of reichsmarks, dollars, and pounds. Why would one leave such a sum in a place where it could so easily be found? Because, he realized, it was intended to distract whoever found it from what lay beneath. Roger removed the money from the drawer, pried up the bottom. There were papers, undoubtedly related to Hans's work. He thumbed through, searching for Hans's contact information.

A minute later he found it, a paper listing addresses in Berlin, Warsaw, Prague. Where was Hans now? Berlin, he thought, recalling a vague reference his brother had made before his departure. Roger grabbed it and started from the office.

On the street he stopped again. He would send the telegram to Hans, of course, but there was no telling whether his brother was actually at the address now, or how long it would take to reach him if he was not. Magda might not have that kind of time. There had to be something else he could do.

244

He looked at the house to the right of theirs. It was occupied by the Baders, the elderly couple Magda had once mentioned. His breath caught. He did not dare to hope that Magda had gone to them, that they had been able to help before the Gestapo came. But perhaps they had seen something.

He walked to their door and rapped on it loudly, fighting the urge to knock a second time immediately. Frau Bader opened the door a crack and he could see that she was wearing an apron. 'Excuse me,' he began, 'I'm sorry to interrupt at dinnertime. But I was wondering, that is, my brother's wife and child, they seem to be gone. Perhaps you saw something...'

The woman eyed him warily, then shook her head. Today's dragnet had just missed her house and she would not risk its return by helping him.

Wordlessly, Frau Bader closed the door, leaving Roger standing on the front step alone. He considered knocking again, demanding answers. Then he decided against it – he didn't want to cause a fuss and he sensed from the old woman's steely demeanor that she would not be swayed. But the fear in her eyes told him all that he needed to know about what had happened to Magda and Anna that day.

Magda. His anxiety grew as her face appeared in his mind. Suddenly, he heard his brother's voice, as vividly as though he were standing beside him: *Take care of Magda if anything happens.* Roger's guilt rose to full boil. Of course, when Hans said that, he had anticipated something happening to himself; despite the concerns Roger had voiced,

Hans had never imagined it might be Magda whom something bad befell.

What would Hans do if he was here? He would go to Nazi headquarters, Roger decided, and ask – no, demand – information about his wife. So that was what Roger had to do now. He started into the street, then stopped again. How could he possibly manage it? Hans was important, and he had a way about him that made people bend to his will. But Roger was, well, just Roger. There was no other choice, he decided. He had to try.

Ten minutes later he reached the edge of the market square, *der Ring,* as the Germans called it. It was lined by tall row houses, their brightly colored facades now faded and covered with soot. He raced across the square toward the tur-reted Rathaus, which sat at the center. The gothic town hall had been expropriated by the Nazis as their headquarters and a large swastika flag now marred the ornate front of the red brick building. The air seemed to have grown suddenly colder and a sharp breeze blew, sending old newspapers and other debris dancing along the pavement.

In the doorway he stopped, scanning the names of the officials. Gauleiter Koch, he read, his eyes stopping on a nameplate halfway down the wall. Hans had referenced the official once as some-one with whom he had to deal. 'A total ass,' he said, 'but perhaps a bit less of a Nazi than some of them.'

Roger walked inside, looking straight ahead as he passed the guards' desk, trying not to run. A moment later he stepped off the lift at the second floor. Koch's office occupied a corner suite that had once belonged to the deputy mayor.

'Dykmans,' he said by way of introduction to the receptionist, who seemed to be packing her belongings for the day. The woman, blond and too heavily made up, raised an eyebrow. Roger took a deep breath. 'Hans Dykmans.'

'Is Gauleiter Koch expecting you? It's rather late.'

'Yes,' he lied again. As the receptionist disappeared through a door behind her desk, Roger tapped his foot impatiently, trying not to pace. In the corner, a grandfather clock ticked noisily. Watching it, Roger felt his anxiety rise – each second that passed put Magda farther away, lessening his chances of getting to her.

The office door swung open and a short, thick man walked out wearing his overcoat. *'Guten–'* Koch stopped his hearty greeting in mid-sentence, caught off guard by a visitor other than the one he had expected.

'I'm Roger Dykmans, Hans's brother,' Roger said, stepping forward quickly and shaking his hand. Struggling to keep his voice calm, he continued before the man could protest the fraudulent introduction. 'I'm sorry to call unannounced, but it is a very urgent matter. It will only take a moment.'

'Come in,' Koch said reluctantly. The office was adorned with Nazi paraphernalia, and photos of Koch and various people whom Roger assumed were important in the Reich. Behind the desk, wide windows offered a panorama of the city below, steeples etched against the late-day sky as the sun sank low to the rooftops. 'What is it?'

'My brother's wife, Magda, has disappeared.'
He swallowed. 'Their daughter, too. I came home
to find them gone.'

Roger could tell from Koch's expression that
the news did not come as a surprise. 'They are
Jews.' It was not a question.

Roger hesitated. 'I don't know,' he lied. 'She
may have some Jewish blood. But my brother, as
you know, does not.'

Koch sat down in his chair, exhaled impatiently.
'The orders have been to round up all the Jews
now, even partial Jews or those who intermarried.'

'Surely you can make an exception for Hans,
find out where she has gone.' He could hear his
voice rise with urgency in spite of himself. 'The
press coverage of a diplomat's wife being imprisoned would not be favorable.'

Koch paused, seeming to consider the point. 'I
have no idea if this woman was arrested or not.'

'You could make inquiries,' Roger pressed.

Koch whistled through his teeth. 'And I should
do that why?' Before Roger could answer, he continued. 'Perhaps I could help. That is, if you
could do something for me.'

Roger stared at the man, puzzled. What could
he possibly do that would be of use to the
German? 'Of course, if I can be of assistance–' he
managed.

'I want information on your brother's operations.'

Roger swayed as the floor seemed to drop out
beneath him. 'I don't understand.'

'Don't bother trying to deny it,' Koch said
bluntly as he played with the humidor that sat at

the edge of his desk. 'We've long suspected that Hans Dykmans is involved with resistance activities, but we haven't been able to prove it.'

Roger blinked. 'I'm sure I don't know what you're talking about.'

But Koch continued as though Roger had not spoken. 'And because your brother is so well-known he's been somewhat, let's say, untouchable. But if I could produce some evidence...'

It would, Roger finished silently for him, make his career. Inwardly he seethed. This man was trying to barter Magda's and Anna's lives for a promotion.

'My brother has never shared with me any information about his work,' Roger managed, concentrating on sounding earnest. It was not entirely a lie.

Koch shrugged. 'Okay. It makes no difference to me whether the woman and her child are freed or sent to the camps.'

An image flashed through Roger's mind then of the Jews who were rounded up in the synagogue courtyard, the man he'd seen beaten. Bile rose in his throat. 'What is it you want?'

'Information about your brother's operations that would demonstrate that he is involved. Something that would allow us to catch him in action.'

A hand seemed to clutch Roger's chest, making it impossible to breathe. 'I don't know...'

Koch turned his chair so he was facing away from Roger, who stifled the urge to leap across the desk and throttle the man's fat neck. 'It's up to you.' Koch gestured out the window. 'But I would act quickly, as the transport to the camps leaves tomorrow at dawn. You can contact me at my residence this evening with your decision.' He handed Roger a card. 'Think about what your brother would want.'

A minute later, Roger stood on the street shaking. His mind reeled. Koch was insisting that he give up information that would implicate Hans. Even if he had access to those kinds of things, how could he do it? His existing transgressions notwithstanding, Hans was still his brother and the notion of such a betrayal was unthinkable. But at the same time, he could not lose Magda and Anna.

As he started back toward the house, Koch's last words reverberated through his mind: What would Hans want him to do? The question was more complex than the German had known. Hans was, as Magda had once said, married to his work, and it was unlikely that he would give up a valuable operation, even to save his wife and child.

But Hans was not here, Roger concluded. This was not his call. And it was not, in point of fact, his child.

What would Magda say? he wondered, as he reached the front door, still ajar from his earlier flight. She, like Hans, would say not to do it, that her life was not worth compromising operations that could help many. At least that was what she would have said if it were just her life at stake. But with their child, whom she loved above all else, surely it would be a different story.

Roger saw Anna as she had looked that morning, arms outstretched upward to him, and he knew that he had no choice. In the foyer, he paused uncertainly. What could he give Koch that would be of value? Then he remembered the papers he had seen. He raced to the study and opened the drawer. He picked up some of the money, momentarily considering going back to Koch with a bribe. But he could tell even from his brief interaction with the man that his greed was not of the pecuniary kind. Only the information that could make his career would suffice.

Roger set aside the cash and pulled out the papers. As he scanned them, his jaw dropped. He had known instinctively that his brother was somehow part of the resistance. But he had no idea of the scope of his work. How was it possible that his brother, just a few years older than he, had been able to do so much? Hans, it seemed, had engineered the rescue of thousands of Jews, producing documents to allow them to emigrate from Poland and Germany and several other countries. But the documents all related to operations that had already taken place; those would be of no interest to Koch.

He continued further down the stack. Between the yellowed sheets was a letter detailing the visit of a delegation to a camp in Czechoslovakia – Theresienstadt, it was called. The plan seemed to involve helping some people leave the camp under pretense of an exchange. The documents were dated just two weeks earlier, and they appeared to reference events that had not yet taken place. Was this what Koch had in mind? He searched the rest of the drawer and found nothing else of interest. It would have to do.

As he started to leave the study he paused by the window, looking down at the courtyard of the synagogue below. The people Hans was trying to save in that camp were just like the Jews that had been taken before his eyes. If he turned over the plan, they would surely never be free. Could he risk the lives of so many strangers to protect the two people he loved most in the world?

Still deliberating, he folded the document and started to put it in his coat pocket. As he did, his hand brushed against something thick and woolen. He pulled out the mitten that Magda had knitted for him and held it aloft, fingering the rough material. He had to find a way to save her and Anna, but to do so without casting aside the lives of the others and becoming a man she would despise.

A telegram, he decided finally. He would give the documents to Koch, then as soon as he had Magda and Anna he would send Hans an urgent message letting him know that the operation had been compromised, allowing his brother time to regroup. Surely Hans had a contingency plan he could implement. Then everything would be fine. Satisfied, he tucked the documents away once more and hurried from the room.

Eleven

MUNICH, 2009

'Charley,' Jack said in a low voice as they walked from the car to the prison. 'Are you okay? You've been acting really strange.'

'I'm fine,' she replied coldly, not looking up, fighting the urge to confront him about his conversation with Brian. To deny that anything had taken place between them, that was one thing, but how dare he speak so condescendingly of her after all that they had been through together? She wanted to ask him if the other night had arisen out of some sort of pity too. But there was no time – Brian was rushing up behind them, pushing toward the conference room and Roger.

They hesitated at the door, none of them wanting to go first. 'We're confronting Roger about the truth,' she remarked. 'Again.'

'It's beginning to feel a bit familiar,' Jack conceded. 'Kinda makes you wonder why we're working so hard to help someone who we can't trust.'

'Not exactly,' she replied, before Brian could protest. 'It makes me wonder why he can't trust us. What has him so scared?'

Jack did not answer, but strode into the conference room. 'You lied to us,' he blurted out as Roger started to rise, with a lack of control more

253

reminiscent of his brother's demeanor than his own.

Roger looked as though he had been slapped. 'I beg your pardon–'

'Easy,' Brian hissed as he brushed past Charlotte, putting himself between his client and Jack. 'I think what my brother means to say–'

'Is that the clock was empty,' Jack finished, interrupting. 'There was nothing inside.'

Roger's eyes widened. 'I don't understand. You found the compartment?'

'On the bottom, yes. It was empty.'

Roger stared at Jack, not responding. His confusion appeared to be real, Charlotte observed with an appraising eye she usually reserved for witnesses. He genuinely seemed to believe that the clock should have contained the answers.

'It's been so many years,' Brian offered. 'Perhaps someone removed whatever it was that you were looking for.'

Roger shook his head. 'Impossible.'

Possible, Charlotte corrected silently, but unlikely. The compartment was so well hidden, it would have been almost undetectable unless one knew it was there.

'Herr Dykmans,' Jack said, his voice softer now. 'Why don't you just tell us what you expected the clock to hold?'

The old man sat back, his hands trembling as he reached for the cup of tea Brian slid in his direction. His shoulders slumped. 'There should have been a document showing that I never intended to go through with it.'

'Through with what?' Charlotte said, dreading

the answer even before her question was complete.

'The plan to sell out my brother to the Nazis.'

The room was silent. So he had done it after all, Charlotte thought, the full realization creeping up on her. She recalled a photograph she had seen in one of the case files of the children from the camp, the ones who had perished because of what he had done. Then she looked across the table at Roger's hands, which now seemed covered with blood.

'So you did it?' Brian asked bluntly, no longer remembering his own admonition to be delicate. Jack and Charlotte exchanged cringing looks, bracing themselves for the one answer that, as Roger's criminal defense team, they did not want to know. Charlotte considered telling him not to answer, then decided against it. It was too late to hide these things anymore.

'Yes ... I mean, no, that is, in a sense.' Roger swallowed. 'Let me explain. I've already told you about Magda, no?' Charlotte nodded, wondering if his memory was failing him or he was simply stalling for time. 'One day, I came home and found Magda and Anna gone.'

'Anna?' Charlotte interrupted.

Roger nodded. 'Magda's child.' Charlotte was surprised at this, the first mention of a child. But Roger did not, she noticed, say whether the child was Hans's or his own.

'It was my worst nightmare come true. Almost all of the other Jews had already been taken from Breslau to the camps. But few people knew that Magda was Jewish, and so we hoped because of that and the fact that she was Hans's wife, she might be spared.'

He lowered his head, running his hands through his hair as he continued. 'When Magda and her daughter disappeared, I was frantic. I searched the house, even the secret hiding place where I thought they might have gone. I knew I couldn't reach my brother in time, so I went to one of the senior Gestapo officials for our city, a man called Koch. I thought that because he was acquainted with Hans he might help me find out where Magda had been taken, perhaps even secure her release. Koch claimed he could help me get her out. But then he said something that stunned me – that the Nazis knew about Hans's work for the resistance. I always thought he had been so careful. Koch told me that the only way he would help me was if I provided concrete information about Hans's operations.'

'So you agreed? 'Jack asked.

Roger nodded. 'I agreed.'

'But you said Hans always kept you out of his work,' Charlotte interjected.

'He did. Once, though, right before the end, he showed me a drawer where he kept some money and information on how to make contact with him in case of an emergency. I knew that there were papers in that drawer, so I searched there for something I could give Koch that would satisfy him. I found documents referring to an operation in Czechoslovakia, a plan to get some people out of a camp under the pretext of an exchange program.'

Children, Charlotte thought, a lump forming in

her throat. Roger had to know, as she had from the documents in the case file, that it was a youth exchange and that children were the collateral damage of his actions. 'And you gave them to Koch?'

'Yes. But my intention was that as soon as I found Magda and Anna, I would send Hans a telegram through his contacts, telling him that his plan had been compromised so that he could change it. I thought I could give the information to Koch but still get to my brother in time. That way I would save Magda and our, I mean, her daughter.'

So the child was his after all, Charlotte thought. Roger continued, 'That way, no one would be hurt.' He paused to rub his eyes.

'But it didn't work,' Jack said, prompting him.

'No. Koch took the information, then claimed that Magda had already been removed from the city, that she was at a transit camp outside Munich. I raced there, but it was a lie, or too late. Magda was gone.'

Charlotte swallowed. 'And Hans?'

Roger shook his head. 'Arrested. He and his associates, and all of the people...' He still could not bring himself to call them children. 'All of the people that Hans was trying to save were killed.'

'So you never sent the telegram,' Jack said flatly.

'I tried,' Roger replied in a tone that suggested he had tried to convince himself of the fact many times over the years. 'Before I left to find Magda, I wrote a telegram to Hans, telling him the plan was compromised. I intended to send it as soon as I returned.'

'And you hid the telegram in the clock?' Charlotte asked.

'Yes, and I hid the clock in a hole in the wall that Magda had made as a possible hiding place. I knew that if the Nazis came to the house again, they wouldn't look there. And if I couldn't get back, I could get someone to find the telegram and send it for me.'

'Who?' Jack asked.

'There were neighbors next door, the Baders, who were known to be sympathetic to the Jewish plight. I left them a note asking them to please send the telegram for me if I didn't return in two days' time.' His shoulders sagged. 'But I guess they never did.'

'What happened after that?'

'After I made inquiries at the transit camp, I was detained by the Gestapo. They wanted to know why I was nosing around, and they thought I had more information about Hans's work. Eventually they realized that I didn't know anything and let me go. But by then it was too late.'

Too late, Charlotte thought. If only Roger had taken the time to send the telegram before racing off after Magda, things might have been so different.

'As I told you the other day,' Roger continued, 'I searched and searched for Magda, and my brother too, of course, though we soon learned the truth about his fate.'

'But you never found out what happened to Magda?'

'No, though at one of the deportation camps, I heard a story about a girl escaping and I thought...' His voice trailed off.

A rumor, Charlotte thought, so vague it could have been about anybody. Yet it had fueled Roger's hope for all of these years. She and Jack exchanged uneasy looks over Roger's head. They now had the very piece of information Roger had sought for decades. 'I'm sorry,' she said, 'but we learned that isn't what happened.'

'Oh?' Roger's voice trembled.

'Yes. I'm afraid that Magda died in the camps.'

Roger's face turned stony. 'How?'

She hesitated. But even as she dreaded telling the old man the gruesome truth about his one love, she knew that he needed to hear it in order to believe that it was true. 'The gas,' she said simply.

Roger's jaw slackened slightly, his expression turning from shock to disbelief as he digested the news and the truth replaced the hopes and assumptions he'd carried with him for so long. He leaned forward, dropping his head to his hands. Then he sank to the floor so swiftly that Charlotte wondered for a second if he might have passed out. But then he began heaving with great sobs.

Charlotte watched helplessly as Brian and Jack helped the old man back into the chair. The trips to Poland, the search for the clock. For Roger, it had always been about learning the truth about Magda. Surely he could not have thought after all of these years that the result might have been anything but this.

But at the same time she understood. Against reason, part of Roger had stubbornly clung to the belief that the answer might have been somehow different. That Magda had escaped and lived, even briefly. Now he was faced with the undeniable truth that the desperate measures he took to try to save Magda, which resulted in the deaths of so many, had all been in vain. Everything else he had been able to take over the years, but this was the breaking point.

Jack walked to the intercom to summon the guards, waving Charlotte and Brian away. 'How could you?' Brian demanded of Charlotte as they stepped out into the hall.

'He had the right to know the truth.'

'You've taken away everything he had to fight for.'

'No,' she protested, eyes flaring, unwilling to back down. 'Now that he knows the truth about Magda, he can concentrate on fighting for his freedom.' But inwardly she cringed, hearing the weakness in her own argument. Had she made a fatal mistake by telling him?

A few minutes later, when the guards had come and gone again, they walked back in the room. Roger sat slumped to one side, calmer now, eyes glassy from a sedative of some sort. 'Excuse me,' he said, as though apologizing to guests for being late.

'It's all right,' she said. 'I'm sorry the news was such a shock.'

'I suppose I always knew.' He dipped his chin at the admission. 'Still, part of me thought...' He did not finish the sentence.

Charlotte nodded. Despite its vast improbability, Roger had held fast to that one shred of hope that perhaps Magda had somehow survived, might even be alive today. It was the thing that had kept him going, enabled him to live with his ghosts and demons for all of these years. With that now gone, his entire world had crumbled.

'Herr Dykmans,' Jack began more softly than she had heard him speak. He stepped forward. 'I know that this is an incredibly painful time for you, but we must think about the trial. We only have a week–'

Charlotte looked up, surprised. Surely he didn't mean to tell Roger about the possibility of the case being elevated now, on top of everything else. Jack cleared his throat. 'That is, we simply don't have the evidence we need.' But Roger turned to the wall. The news about Magda had taken away his will to live, any reason he might have had to fight.

'Dammit,' Brian swore half an hour later, running a finger along the rim of his glass. Roger had sat stone-faced, unwilling or unable to respond to their entreaties for additional information that might help his case. When it was clear they would get no further, they had left the prison and now sat on stools clustered around a high table in the hotel bar. 'Three countries and we've got nothing.' She held her breath, waiting for him to berate her again for sharing with Roger the news about Magda, but he did not.

'I think,' Jack spoke slowly, 'we need to consider a plea deal.'

Charlotte watched him uneasily. Brian had returned from the bar a few minutes earlier with three vodka tonics. He did not, she realized, know the story of his brother's recent drinking problem, his need for abstinence. Jack had lifted the glass once, almost reflexively, and she had held her breath, waiting for him to take a sip and bring a wrecking ball to the thin wall of sobriety he'd rebuilt. But then he set the glass down and did not pick it up again.

'Hell no!' Brian exploded so loudly that a couple of women at the next table looked up to stare. He dealt in the world of high-stakes litigation, going for the big wins. He hadn't learned to swim in the murky waters of compromise, where sometimes meeting in the middle was the closest thing to a victory you got.

'We have less than a week,' Jack pressed, making his case. 'If we lose, it's life in prison without possibility of parole.'

'And if we plead, he's still going to get five or ten years at least,' Brian replied. 'That's a life sentence when you're Roger's age.'

Brian had a point, Charlotte reflected. Jack, however, was not convinced. 'But we have to try to do something,' he persisted. 'If we walk into court with nothing, they're going to eat him alive. The Germans have been under a lot of international pressure and they're looking for a big case with which to make a statement and show the world they're serious about chasing down the war criminals. They want to make an example of Roger.'

Charlotte took a large sip of her own drink, savoring the sting. She tuned out the debate between the two brothers, which played itself out like an old record. Always on opposite sides of the fence, vying for control.

What were they fighting for, anyway? Roger had

admitted to doing the very thing he'd been accused of and he was willing to accept his punishment. Maybe we should just make a deal and get him the most lenient sentence possible, she thought. Not because going to trial would be risky, as Jack feared, but because it was what Roger wanted.

Charlotte thought back to her cases over the years. She had defended some of the most broken kids society had to offer, kids who had hurt others seemingly without any remorse. Yet she had always found a shred of redemption, a shred of humanity she could cling to in order to push forward with their defense. Here, there was no doubt Roger had acted out of his love for Magda and Anna, his desire to save them. But the futility of his actions and the magnitude of the tragedy that had resulted from them were simply too great, and there was part of her that was tapped out, unwilling to go any further.

'So you just want to quit?' Brian demanded of his brother.

'I'm not saying that,' Jack replied. 'But sometimes you have to cut your losses.'

Brian did not respond, but stood and stormed from the bar. 'He just doesn't understand how these criminal matters work,' Jack lamented. 'And I don't want to approach the prosecutor until we're all on the same page. Because if she picks up on any sign of weakness and smells blood–' He stopped as she turned away. 'Charley, what's wrong?'

'I'm sick of it. This goddamned game between you and Brian. Always being caught in the middle. Like the thing that no one wants but can't take the trouble to give away.'

He stared at her blankly. 'What–?'

'I heard you on the train, telling Brian not to bother with me.'

'What? Oh God no, you've got it all wrong.' He stood up, running his hand through his hair as he paced. 'I was telling Brian not to be an asshole and hurt you all over again.'

She slammed down her glass. 'Brian and I are none of your concern. I'm a big girl, I can take care of myself.'

'No, that's not it either. I'm really fucking this up, aren't I?' She was surprised. Profanity was Brian's style, not Jack's. 'Charley, do you remember the day we met?'

Her mind reeled back to a barbecue at the Warringtons' beach house in the early autumn. Weary from the endless introductions and inane conversation, she had escaped down the back terrace to a dock overlooking the bay. 'You were standing by the edge of the water,' he continued. 'Your skirt was pink and you had some sort of flower in your hair, iris, maybe.'

'Aster,' she said, the image crystallizing in her mind. She had turned, expecting to see Brian approaching. Instead, there had been this thinner version of him, watching her from a distance.

'You were the most beautiful woman I had ever seen. And then when we spoke, I thought I was dreaming.' There was more emotion to his voice than Charlotte had ever heard before. 'Our conversation, our interests, your sense of humor, everything was perfect. Then Brian walked up and I realized you were his. I wanted to die.'

Charlotte's breath caught. Was it possible that Jack liked her back then? She had never imagined he might, had always taken his aloofness for distaste. 'I thought maybe you would see me too,' he added. 'But you were so wrapped up in Brian the Great, you never even noticed.'

That's not true, she wanted to say. Well, partially it was – she had been young and consumed with Brian. And Jack had terrified her in a way she could only understand now, with experience and the passage of years, that had in fact been born out of raw attraction. But remembering, it seemed so clear – how her throat seemed to seize whenever he entered a room, making it difficult to speak or breathe, the way she'd found it unbearable to be alone with him.

Later that night she'd been unable to sleep and had slipped from the guest room out onto the terrace into the cool evening air. It was a clear night and the sky, unmarred by the city lights, was a carpet of stars, dancing above the water. She craned her neck upward, so engrossed that it was several minutes before she heard a scratching sound and realized that she was not alone. Jack sat in a lawn chair a few feet away, also gazing upward.

'Oh!' she said, and his eyes dropped, meeting hers. Bathed in moonlight, he seemed almost mythic. Neither spoke for what seemed like an eternity. Finally, unable to bear it any longer, she had turned and fled back into the house, heart pounding.

He continued, drawing her from her memories. 'And now you turn up here out of the blue after all these years, and I think, maybe it's fate, or at least it could be if I believed in fate. But you still look at him like that.' She wanted to protest, but found that she could not. 'Not that I deserve anything good in my life after the mistakes I've made and the things I've done.' He cleared his throat. 'But I won't stand here and watch him hurt you again.'

She understood even more clearly then why Jack had been so aloof all those years ago and why he'd been so prickly since she'd arrived, even going so far as to deny his feelings for her. He'd been destroyed once by the baroness and Charlotte was the one person who could hurt him again – if he let her get that close.

'Jack–' She wanted to tell him it wasn't like that, that she knew the kind of pain he'd suffered and the fear of letting it happen again, that her feelings for Brian were all in the past and that she would not hurt him if given the chance.

But before she could continue, Brian reappeared at the table. 'Another round?' he asked, as if he and Jack had not clashed, his bravado amplified by the liquor.

She shook her head, overwhelmed by it all. 'I'm going to turn in.'

'Then I guess I will too.' Brian summoned the waiter and signed the check. Charlotte looked at Jack but he stared at his glass, seemingly miles away. She did not want to risk leaving him here alone, fearful he might take a sip of the now-watery drink. But a moment later he stood and followed them back out the hotel lobby.

At the elevator bank, they paused. Jack's eyes

met hers and despite all that had happened, she could not help but wonder if he wanted to come up again. But with Brian here there was no possibility of a repeat encounter. The elevator doors opened and Brian stood aside expectantly, waiting for her to enter. She could feel Jack's gaze, sense his resentment, as she stepped inside. She turned back. It's not like that, she wanted to tell him. She and Brian were just sharing an elevator, going to their separate floors. But the doors began to close.

'G'night, Charlotte,' Brian said fuzzily a minute later as the door opened at his floor. He stepped off, oblivious to what had just taken place.

She made her way to her room and closed the door, still stunned by Jack's revelation. What would have happened if she had met Jack first? Would they have been drawn together or would the timing have been just as wrong then as it was now? It was impossible to roll back the clock, to imagine not having fallen for Brian. That blinding, all-encompassing first love and the heartbreak that followed had become part of who she was, so inextricably linked to her identity and the story of her life that she could not disentangle them and get a clear picture of what might have been. No, she simply would not have been ready for Jack then, and he had the baroness and his own heartbreak to weather to make him who he was today.

And now? She turned the question over in her mind, considering. If she and Jack had been reunited under different circumstances, would it have worked? The question was a moot one. There was Brian and their history and this case, not to mention the fact that they lived on two separate continents, so their feelings, as undeniable as they were, would have to remain untapped, a great what-if in their lives. Perhaps that was better than trying it on and seeing that it really wasn't what she thought.

As she undressed, she still wondered if there might be a knock at the door, Jack venturing up to see her. But he would not, she realized as she climbed into bed, push his way in where he feared he might not be wanted. She couldn't help but listen for footsteps in the hallway, though, hoping until she fell asleep.

Sometime later, there was a pounding at the door. Jack, she thought, sitting up. Had he decided to come see her after all? Charlotte leapt to her feet, nearly stumbling, her head still fuzzy from the liquor.

She hurried to the door, opened it a crack. 'Brian,' she said, wondering with a sense of déjà vu if it was morning and she had overslept. But this time he wasn't dressed in his usual suit. Instead he wore sweatpants and a T-shirt and sported an unshaven jawline, images from almost a decade ago that had no place here. 'What is it?' she asked. 'What's wrong?'

He pushed past her into the room. 'Wait, I'm not–' she began.

But Brian burst in like an oversized puppy, unable to contain his energy. 'We got a call,' he announced breathlessly. 'It's from a woman in Italy and she claims to have proof that Roger is innocent.'

Twelve

EAST BERLIN, 1961

Anneke looked up from the beer stein she was drying. Across the bar, a group of students clustered around a table in the corner, laughing boisterously. One of the men lifted his head from the gathering. His eyes caught Anneke's and for a second she thought he might smile, but he turned away quickly.

She had first seen him nearly two months earlier when he came in with his friends, and he had returned nightly with the group ever since. He was about twenty-two or so, she guessed, with shaggy black hair that curled at the collar and pale skin that reminded her of the porcelain tea set that sat on the Stossels' mantelpiece. For weeks she had watched him when she was sure no one was looking, shivering when she got close to clear the table where he sat.

Anneke had taken the job at the bar the previous spring as a way to supplement her income and earn a few extra marks to help her mother pay the rent. It was little more than a ground-floor shop that had been converted, worn wooden tables and crude benches scattered throughout the room, a deer's head mounted above the fireplace. The job was a welcome break from her position at the Stossels', cleaning floors and polishing silver with only her mother and the dour-faced cook Inge for company. Not that the actual work here, clearing tables and washing dishes, was so much better. But the crowd, a mix of bohemian artists and students from the nearby university who willingly consumed the *Schwarz bier* or whatever liquor was available without complaint, was livelier than any she had ever seen. The occasional snippet of political debate or gossip she overheard as she picked up the glasses almost made up for the fact that the clientele were notoriously bad tippers.

When it was almost eleven and the crowd had thinned, Anneke went reluctantly into the kitchen to collect the garbage. It was always the least favorite part of her night, not so much for the drudgery of the task itself, but because it meant the bar would soon close and she would have to return home.

As she carried the trash out into the darkness of the alleyway behind the bar, she heard a rustling sound. 'Oh!' she exclaimed. Fearing a rat or worse, she jumped, dropping the bags. One opened as it hit the ground, scraps of food and soiled paper scattering across the pavement.

'Easy,' someone said through the darkness, a puff of smoke rising in the glow of the streetlight. A tiny shiver ran through her as she recognized the voice of the dark-haired young man from the conversations she had overheard in the bar. 'I didn't mean to startle you.'

What was he doing out here, she wondered? Patrons smoked freely inside. 'I wanted to get some air,' he added, answering her unspoken question.

Then better out front and not in the alley, which smelled of old food and urine, she wanted to say. He moved closer with the swiftness of a cat. 'Let me help you.' He bent to pick up the spilled garbage she had nearly forgotten was there. The tip of his cigarette gave off an acrid smell as he knelt and refilled the bag without any sign of hesitation or distaste. She dropped down, working beside him in silence.

'I'm Henryk,' he said when they finished, straightening in unison.

'Anneke.' They shook hands somewhat formally, and she was surprised that his fingers were as soft as the kid gloves Frau Stossel wore.

From the entrance to the bar there came a clattering and the portly silhouette of Herr Ders, the proprietor, filled the doorway. 'I've got to go,' she whispered, and Henryk seemed to vanish before she could finish the sentence, a lingering hint of smoke the only indication that he had been there at all.

She walked back inside with a sinking feeling, certain that Henryk's foray into the stench-filled alley had been a mistake and that the experience of helping her pick up garbage would ensure that he would never return. But the next night, as she stepped outside, she smelled the now-familiar perfume of his cigarette once more.

He held the pack out to her, an offering. Anneke shook her head. She had seen the way that smoking had drawn her mother's once-beautiful mouth into a tight pucker, caused her voice to go raspy. 'Are you a student at the university?' she ventured.

He nodded. 'Yes. That is, I'm on sabbatical this semester.' She didn't know what that was, but it sounded terribly intriguing. 'Are you in school?'

She smiled inwardly, brushing her hair, which was a color she'd seen described in magazines as dishwater blond, from her face. People always took her for much younger than twenty. 'I graduated two years ago.' She had managed to finish, fighting her mother's insistence that she drop out at fifteen to earn a living, instead working nights and weekends to bring in money. 'I would have loved to study at the university.' Of course that had been out of the question. It was almost impossible for a woman from her background to become eligible for higher education under the state system.

'Someday you'll be able to. Things will be different here,' Henryk declared. Anneke looked at him. He was talking of political change, throwing off the rulers and institutions that kept them in this God-awful state of economic depression while their fellow Berliners flourished just miles away on the other side of the newly constructed Wall.

But people in Anneke's world did not dare to speak of such things. She had heard bits of conversation in the café, bold political statements made by Henryk's friends or others like them. The remarks were always made with a touch of humor, though, just to make sure anyone who overheard – especially the Stasi agents and their spies, who were rumored to be everywhere – wouldn't think they were serious. She generally attributed such talk to the beer and the bravado brought on by the anonymity of a large noisy room.

Henryk wasn't joking now though, and he didn't seem the slightest bit drunk. He spoke clearly, breaking the silence of the darkened alleyway with his words.

'What do you mean?' she ventured. Even the question felt daring, and it seemed as if the police might come and take them away at any second.

'It hasn't always been this way,' he said. 'All of this,' he waved his hands around his head, as though swatting at flies, 'is just a phase. Governments change all the time and sometimes even for the better.'

Anneke paused to consider this. Though the present administration was all that she had ever known, she was aware on some level, of course, that there was a time before. When she had gone to school, the teachers made veiled references to the war and the previous regime from which the Red Army had liberated them. But despite the colorful picture painted by the textbooks, it always seemed to Anneke that bad was replaced by worse – in the past fifty years they had gone from losing a war to the Nazis to another defeat to the Communists. 'How?' she asked.

'The people have to make it happen,' he replied confidently. 'We have to demand change.' A shiver passed through Anneke. People who spoke up like that wound up disappearing to who-knows-where, hushed whispers about their departure the only evidence they had been here at all. She had seen it with a printer whose name she had forgotten. Once when she had been at his shop picking up something for the Stossels, she had noticed him producing something else, a newspaper of some sort. She asked her mother about it later that night.

'Best to mind our own business,' Bronia had said. And she was right, because two months later the printer was gone.

A wave of admiration swept over her then. Henryk was so brave. She wanted to ask what the people had to do to bring about these changes. Surely sitting in bars talking wasn't going to make things happen. But before she could speak, he ground out his cigarette. 'I've got to go.' And he disappeared from the alley, leaving her to wonder if she had said something wrong, or if he had simply been bored.

That night she trudged home to the apartment she shared with her mother. The housing estate where they lived had been one of the earliest rebuilding projects of the new government in the years after the war, and the twenty thousand units were quickly filled by Berliners weary of sharing cramped quarters with relatives in the housing shortages that plagued the city following the devastation of the bombing raids. The original plans had touted parks and playgrounds and other amenities. But the development had stagnated and the further improvements never came, and the land between the buildings remained barren and unpaved.

Anneke navigated the wooden planks that formed a bridge over the thick sea of muddy earth, still thinking about her conversation with Henryk, recalling what he had said about things changing, the opportunity for a better life. She had contemplated such things herself, of course. She wanted more than a few odd jobs pasted together, enough money to make it until the next time she got paid. But when she tried to picture what that might look like, the image was murky and indiscernible. In her wildest dreams, she did something working with books, in a library or perhaps a shop. In truth, there was little prospect for someone with her limited background and nonexistent resources. The most she'd been raised to expect was marriage to someone practical, like a pipe fitter or factory worker, who earned a passable living. She'd seen enough, though, to know that raising a bunch of kids and waiting for a man who came home drunk or angry or not at all was not for her. She'd rather carry on as she was, alone.

The next day Anneke awoke to another gray winter morning. Bronia snored loudly from the other room, having passed out on the sofa yet again. The two-room flat, its air heavy with stale cigarette smoke, seemed bleaker than ever. She looked out the cracked window at the endless sea of nondescript buildings in their apartment block, laundry hanging from the balconies like flags of all nations. A thin coating of snow, already gray and dirty, had fallen during the night. In the distance, a steel factory belched thick plumes of black smoke upward.

As she passed through the living room on her way to the water closet, Anneke took in her sleeping mother, still dressed in a too-tight skirt from the previous night. She considered trying to wake her for work, then decided against it, knowing it would be impossible. Sadness rose in her. Bronia had not always been like this. Anneke remembered a time when her petite blonde mother was vivacious and pretty, with a soft voice and laugh that seemed to draw people to her, especially men. When Anneke was eight there had been one man, Peter, with a kind smile and handlebar mustache, who made her mother laugh often. He had taken them for picnics in the park each Sunday, giving Anneke bread to feed the ducks and showing her how to fly a kite. He had stayed longer than the others, almost a year. Bronia had said in a hushed voice that there might be a little brother or sister for her the following winter. But then Peter was gone, as quickly as he had come, and her mother never spoke of the baby again.

There were others after that, men who shared vodka and watched television with her mother in the living room for a few weeks or months before disappearing. Most recently it had been a sinewy little man in a cheap suit who purported to work for some government agency. He could help them get a better flat, Bronia had bragged, if things went well. She always had such high hopes for the men she dated, even though they unfailingly broke her heart. Anneke disliked this one even more than most. She had not even bothered to learn his name.

Anneke arrived at work early that morning, busying herself with the floors, dreading Frau Stossel's inevitable questions about her mother's tardiness. Today Frau Stossel did not even seem to notice, though, instead brushing by without speaking on her way out. She was always occupied by some luncheon or other social duty related to her husband's position as a mid-ranking government official, or shuttling her twin sons, Karl and Klaus, to one of their young Communist pioneer meetings. Frau Stossel took her obligations seriously, pursuing them with an almost fervent zeal, more enthusiastically, it seemed, than her husband himself, who appeared content with the role of a rank-and-file bureaucrat.

'I'm off to the queues,' Inge announced, stepping around Anneke as she knelt cleaning the floor to the entranceway.

Anneke nodded. She had seen the lines outside the shops on Oranienburger Strasse on her way to work. They seemed to grow longer each day, people of various ages and backgrounds, women mostly, waiting to purchase whatever the stores had to offer. Whether they were hoping to procure meat or milk or a piece or two of fresh fruit, she did not know – and likely neither did they. If there were people in a queue, conventional wisdom held, then there was likely something worth waiting for on the other end, and one just hoped to get to the front before whatever it was ran out.

When Inge had gone, Anneke paused to look around the foyer. The Stossels lived in a two-story row house, wider than those adjacent to it, with a wrought-iron balcony off the back of the second floor overlooking a small garden. It was situated on the edge of what had once been the Jewish quarter, now a fragment of its former self. The large synagogue around the corner still bore the scars of the war, the shattered glass and burned walls, its gutted insides untouched from more than two decades ago. Because who had the money to fix a building like that when no one was going to use it?

Of course, people seldom spoke openly about what had happened. The teachers and textbooks that mentioned the war said nothing of the Jews – that Anneke had learned in hushed whispers from her mother and other grown-ups she over-heard when no one thought she was listening. Even if they hadn't said anything, the past would have been impossible to ignore. The ghosts of the Jews were everywhere – in the shells of the syna-gogues, and the faint Hebrew writing that could still be seen above the stores that had once been kosher butcher shops and groceries.

Some Jews remained in the city, but no one knew quite how many. A number of them had returned here from the camps, whether by choice or for lack of better options. Others, like Anneke's mother, Bronia, had managed to hide and escape the Nazi dragnet. Anneke wasn't sure how her mother had survived the war, and she'd learned long ago not to press for details. Even now, one did not publicize the fact that one was Jewish, the memories of what had happened still too fresh, the fear of losing one's job or being otherwise penal-ized all too real. Only a small group of Orthodox Jews was still visible – they could be seen walking silently to and from the small room at the back of Becker's hardware store that doubled as the shul, heads low, dutifully persistent in their observance. Anneke could not help but marvel that they had come back, in light of all that had happened.

Wasn't once in a lifetime enough?

The Stossels' house had once belonged to Jews, Anneke could tell by the faint impression that still remained in the doorway where the prayer box had once hung. She wondered who they were, what had become of them. Had they been able to escape? And once, when she was putting away clothes for Frau Stossel, she had found a gold chain bearing a Hebrew letter taped to the bottom of one of the dresser drawers. This surprised her – she had not imagined that the Stossels had the Jewish family's furniture as well. Perhaps the previous owners had left in a hurry, unable to take anything with them at all. She looked around the bedroom as if seeing everything for the first time. Had Frau Stossel's fur coat, indeed the very clothes on her back, once belonged to someone else? Anneke had tucked the necklace in her pocket. It wasn't stealing from the Stossels, she'd reasoned. They had already taken enough.

When the floors had been polished, Anneke retreated to the study under pretense of dusting. It was her favorite room in the Stossels' house, dark wood bookshelves wrapping around the walls and climbing to the ceiling. She wiped the lower shelves with a cloth, studying the works of Lenin and Marx that any good party official should have. Then she looked longingly at the overflowing upper shelves where the real treasures lay. The first time she had climbed the stepladder to clean the dusty tomes, she was amazed to discover a trove of Western literature, Twain and Hemingway and Faulkner, books now considered risky to have in one's possession. Studying their worn covers, she felt certain they had belonged to the previous occupants, read a hundred times each before being reluctantly left behind. Sometimes when she was sure that Frau Stossel would not be home for several hours, Anneke would pull one of the books from the shelf, holding the dustrag aloft as she read in case anyone walked into the room.

When five o'clock came that day, Anneke left the Stossels' and set out directly for the bar without stopping home. Outside the air was damp, a sign that more snow was imminent. She drew her coat more tightly around her, feeling the thin spots at the elbows. There wouldn't be money to get another, even a secondhand one like this, from the Saturday market until next year.

A lone goose honked overhead. Anneke peered upward in the semidarkness. Had the bird been left behind by the flock somehow or purposely gone its own way, resisting the mandate to migrate south for the winter?

That night, Henryk appeared in the alley behind the bar once more. 'Would you like to see a film?' he asked casually, as though ordering another beer inside. 'When you aren't working, I mean?'

Anneke hesitated, left nearly speechless by the invitation. 'Y-yes. Tomorrow is my day off.'

They met in front of the bar the following evening, and as they navigated from pavement to street between a row of tightly parked Wartburgs and Trabants, Henryk took her hand and tucked it under his arm. Anneke felt a surge of excitement, not minding that it was too soon for him to be taking such liberties, or that he should have at least asked first. She hoped he could not feel the knots where she'd stitched over the holes in her gloves.

The movie was a long Russian film with subtitles that had too many characters and subplots for Anneke to follow. Shortly after the opening credits rolled, Henryk kissed her, his cheek rough against her own, and she responded as well as she knew how. She shivered as Henryk's hand stroked her shoulder, then dropped lower. The grope, her first, seemed harmless enough. But when his hand traveled from her knee to her skirt, she pushed it away. She had seen enough from her mother to learn the consequences of headstrong love, and that having a child with no more than this was a recipe for poverty and a dead-end life. She wanted something better.

Anneke wondered if Henryk would avoid her after she rebuffed his advances, but he appeared again in the alley the next night as though nothing had happened. He told her that he lived in Köpenick, a district Anneke had seen through the window of the train on one of the few occasions when she and her mother had ventured out of the city. She vaguely recalled seeing a neighborhood of solid, slightly better than middle-class houses and a park with children that looked like it would have been a fun place to play.

'Not that I'm staying there much longer.' Her eyes widened. Did he mean to move out of his parents' house? Apartments were scarce these days and it was almost impossible to get approved for a flat unless you were married and had a family. 'I'm going to get out of Berlin,' he added.

An overwhelming sense of loss slammed into her stomach like a rock. Though they had known each other for only a short time, Henryk had quickly become part of the fabric of her life, their meetings the one bright spot in her dreary days.

'Where will you go?' she asked, managing to keep her tone neutral.

He shrugged. 'Paris, most likely.' Her breath caught. When he spoke of leaving, she'd imagined Dresden or one of the other cities in the east. In her wildest dreams, she had never conceived of escaping this godforsaken country altogether. Paris was epic. 'I can pursue my writing there,' he added.

What kept him from writing here? 'When?' she asked instead.

'In a few weeks, as soon as I can make arrangements.'

Marvel mixed with envy as Anneke considered his plan. The notion of leaving Berlin seemed unfathomable. Once it had been relatively easy to cross over the border. She'd had a classmate, Ruta, whose brother had done it and promised to bring her over and get her a job as soon as she graduated. But then a few months ago the Wall had begun to go up, and suddenly it was as if the western side of the city was another planet. Anneke pictured the dense barbed wire, the thick blocks of concrete that were being erected with alarming speed. How could Henryk possibly hope to get across?

'If I can get through the Wall to the south of the city, I know people who can help,' he said, seeming to read her thoughts. 'But it has to be soon.'

She nodded. The fortifications were growing day by day, permanent cement slabs replacing temporary wire, and she had heard talk that there would soon be not just the physical barrier but a wide swath of guarded land between east and west in order to deter anyone who might try to sneak across.

She wanted to ask what had happened to changing things here, the people forcing their government to reform. Surely he couldn't do that from Paris.

'Anneke,' Herr Ders called from inside, interrupting their conversation. She turned and walked back into the bar, trying to breathe over the lump in her chest. A few minutes later, Henryk came back in through the front door of the café, but she did not look up or meet his eyes, certain that he would be able to see her dismay.

Later that night, she lay awake in the flat, trying not to hear her mother snore off the half bottle of vodka she'd consumed earlier. Other than occasionally being late for work, Bronia was a functional drunk. She seldom became angry or morose – liquor was just part of her diet, like coffee for other people.

Anneke rolled onto her side, facing the wall. So Henryk was leaving, just like all of the men her mother knew. Well, what had she expected? Not a future together – an evening at the movies and a quick grope hardly bespoke that kind of commitment. But she'd pictured Henryk as a constant somehow, his nightly presence the promise of something better.

Henryk did not return to the café the next

evening or the one after and a deep pit formed low in Anneke's stomach as she wondered if he had already gone. But then on the third night he appeared again, looking the same as ever. He even ventured a slight smile in her direction, and when he stepped outside to smoke she found an excuse to return to the alley.

He made no attempt to explain his absence. 'You haven't told anyone, have you?' he asked straightaway, and she knew he was talking about Paris.

She shook her head. 'Of course not. I thought you might have left,' she confessed.

'Not yet. But the plans have come together sooner than I expected. I'm going in two days' time.' So her instincts about a more imminent departure had not been wrong. Her heart sank.

'Meet me later?' he asked. There was a deeper meaning to his words and she could tell that this time he meant not just for a movie.

She hesitated. A night, even with a boy as wonderful as Henryk, who was about to leave, was a great risk. But this could be their one night together, their last and only chance. 'Okay,' she conceded.

'Wait for me at the corner when you get off work.' As she cleared tables, her pulse raced. She wondered where they would go, what her first time would be like.

This time there was no pretense of a date, just a wordless trip to a one-room flat by the train station. She hadn't bothered to ask who it belonged to, where he had gotten the key. Afterward, as they lay in silence, she tried to ignore the stale, unfamiliar odor of the bedclothes. She didn't know what she had expected. It was neither exciting nor disappointing exactly, but somehow different from both. Henryk, despite all of his bravado, had been surprisingly awkward. He seemed to know enough to suggest that it probably wasn't his first time, but it didn't seem that there had been many others, a thought that was somehow comforting.

He lay on his back, hands clasped under his head. She kept herself confined to the space beside him, not sure if they were supposed to touch or not. He did not speak and she worried that he had been disappointed by the tryst.

'What are you thinking?' she ventured finally.

He looked over, as if he'd forgotten that she was still there. 'About leaving,' he replied, and the cold reality of his departure clamped down like a vise. 'I've got to pack, try to get some more money.'

'Take me with you,' Anneke said, not believing that the words were hers. She had not even dared to contemplate the idea before. But as soon as she spoke, it became her dearest and only wish. A picture evolved immediately in her head – a life together in Paris, a new start. She could study at the university, find work in a bookstore.

'Anneke,' he said gently, and she could tell he was going to refuse. 'Traveling with another person would be more difficult.'

'People are much more predisposed to help a couple than they are a single man,' she pointed out, gaining steam. 'I could get a job in a café there, earn enough to keep us going while you write.' He pursed his lips, seemingly unconvinced. 'And I can get money for our trip.'

His face brightened and he turned toward her. 'Really?'

She nodded, though in truth she didn't know how. Bronia lived from payday to payday, drinking whatever extra there was, and the few coins that Anneke stashed away from her work at the café wouldn't go far.

But he did not pursue the matter further. 'We should go,' he said instead, and their night ended abruptly on the street corner with an awkward kiss on the cheek that did not suggest the promise of anything further.

The next night Henryk and his friends appeared at the bar as always. Anneke was relieved – she had half expected that he might have already left. But there was something different, she quickly noticed. They were not only late but louder too, with a kind of cheer she hadn't seen previously, a boisterousness unheard of in these head-low-and-eyes-down times that suggested the bar was not their first stop that evening. And there was someone new with them – a girl. She sat down too close to Henryk. Anneke took in her shining eyes and the rich dark curls that she tossed as she spoke. Who was she?

Anneke looked down, concentrating on the beer she was pouring. Her eyes stung. Had she really thought that she and Henryk might be exclusive? Still, bringing another girl here of all places, so soon after they had been together, seemed particularly cruel. It served her right, Anneke thought miserably. Like Bronia always said, if you reach too high, you'll only fall on your face.

Anneke avoided Henryk's corner of the bar as long as she possibly could, but eventually Herr Ders remarked that they were low on glasses and the table needed to be cleared. She cringed as she drew close, not meeting Henryk's gaze.

Anneke did not bother to go to the alley, knowing that Henryk would remain at the table as long as the girl was there. But later, after the café closed and she swept the dirt from the kitchen floor, she was surprised to smell his familiar cigarette smoke through the open window.

Eventually, when she could put it off no longer, she carried the trash to the alley. 'You're still here,' she remarked, not looking up.

'*Ja.*'

She kicked at the pavement with her heel. 'And your friends?'

'Gone. I'm sorry I couldn't come out earlier.'

'No, of course not.' She fought to keep her voice neutral. 'You had company.'

'She's no one,' he protested earnestly. 'The sister of my friend Rolf.'

'I know,' Anneke replied, though in fact she did not. She had not seen the girl talking to anyone else.

'So you said you can get money...?'

She looked up. Was he seriously considering allowing her to join him or was he just attempting to assuage her hurt feelings over the girl? 'Yes.'

'We can leave tomorrow night. Do you know the old munitions factory in Friedrichshain?' She nodded, too stunned to speak. She had passed through the district, just south of the central

Mitte area where the bar was located, a number of times. 'Meet me at the front gate there tomorrow at midnight.' He did not wait for her to respond, but turned and walked from the alley.

She stood, watching in disbelief as he retreated. Did he really mean to take her along? His interest was hardly sentimental, she knew. It was about the promise of money. But that didn't matter. He would get her to Paris and then he would realize how much he liked her. And if he didn't, well, at least she would be out of here.

Out of here. She leaned against the alley wall as the magnitude of the plan crashed down upon her. Escaping Berlin seemed impossible, let alone making it all the way to Paris. Henryk was so sure of himself, though, and even though they'd known each other a short time, she sensed that she could trust him. Best to leave the details to him and just concentrate on getting the money she'd promised. But how? The Stossels, she decided, were her best possible source.

Her mind was still racing as she reached the Stossel house the next day, studying the furnishings with an appraising eye as she cleaned. They didn't keep cash around the house, at least not that she had seen. And Frau Stossel seemed to wear all of the jewelry she owned. Anneke thought of the simple Jewish necklace she had taken. It didn't seem likely to be worth much.

As she dusted the Stossels' living room, Anneke stopped, examining the domed clock on the mantelpiece, which she had passed a thousand times, as if seeing it anew. It looked valuable, nicer than the ones she had seen in the shop windows. And at just under a foot high, it was one of the few pieces among their artwork and other belongings that was small enough to take.

'Nice, isn't it?' a voice said behind her.

She jumped, then spun around to see Inge standing in the doorway to the foyer, holding a half-empty sack of onions and potatoes. 'I suppose,' she replied, trying to sound uninterested. 'I wonder if it was here before the war.'

But Inge shook her head. 'Not that one. Came in a box left at the door some time after the war ended, addressed to the previous owners, no return address. I remember because the mail wasn't running regularly again yet, but someone had managed to have it delivered, and had gone to a great deal of trouble to pack it safely.' She turned and plodded to the kitchen, leaving Anneke to wonder: Had the clock been intended as a gift, or something else? Whoever sent it surely didn't know that its intended recipients were gone.

Later that afternoon, as she was about to leave, she walked to the clock, then hesitated, suddenly feeling guilty. It wasn't that she felt badly for the Stossels; they had clearly done some taking themselves. But taking the clock seemed riskier than ever, especially since Inge had seen her eyeing it. And she couldn't help worrying about Bronia. When Anneke was gone, her mother would be left to fend for herself – what if the Stossels held her responsible for the theft?

She pushed her guilt back down. It wasn't as if she had a choice. Inhaling, she picked up the clock and started to put it in her bag. There was a shuffling sound behind her. She froze, and lifted the clock back to its previous place. Then she turned, prepared to offer her explanation of dusting. But there was no one there.

Once she was several blocks away from the Stossels' house, Anneke stopped, looking down uncertainly at her bulging rucksack, strained nearly to the breaking point by the clock. Taking the clock had seemed like a good idea at the time, but what to do with it now? There was an antique store she recalled seeing on her way to and from work. Perhaps she could sell the clock. She boarded the tram and as it made its way through the city with painstaking slowness, she held her breath, fearful that she would be stopped at any second by the police, who would ask what she was doing with such a piece.

Twenty minutes later, she reached the antique shop. 'I'd like to sell this clock,' she said to the owner, a fat man with a fringe of greasy hair ringing his nearly bald head.

She held her breath as he appraised the clock in a cursory manner, not bothering to ask where she had gotten it. 'Sixty marks,' he said without interest.

'But...' Sixty marks was more than she made in months, but it was nowhere near the kind of money she and Henryk would need for the trip. 'Surely such a treasure–'

The man shrugged. 'Who can afford luxuries these days? People only want to pay for food and heat. Of course, there's always room to negotiate,' he added, leering at the spot where the hem of Anneke's skirt touched her knee. Inwardly, she recoiled. For a fleeting second, she considered exploring the man's interest, negotiating any way she had to with the man to get the money she needed. Then her spine stiffened. She was not that desperate. She turned and walked from the store.

It was her night off from working at the bar, so she returned to the flat and waited in bed fully clothed, listening to the trains roll by below. She and Henryk were leaving, together. Anneke could scarcely believe it. A thousand questions raced through her mind: What would they do when they reached the other side of the Wall? How would they get to Paris? And what would happen once they were there? She drew her arms closer around herself. There were so many things she didn't know. But Henryk, she felt certain, would take care of them.

Her thoughts were interrupted by the sound of Bronia coming through the front door, followed by a second voice, indicating that she was not alone. Anneke groaned inwardly. She had hoped her mother might have an early night, pass out quickly so that she could slip from the flat undetected.

The conversation grew lower and muffled and Anneke tried to tune it out, bracing for the sounds she did not want to hear. But then the voices in the living room rose unexpectedly. Anneke tensed. A fight of some sort. There was a scuffling sound and Bronia let out a high-pitched yelp. Reluctantly, Anneke stood and raced into the tiny kitchen to find her mother cowering by the stove, the little man from the government raising his fist, ready to strike again.

Anger flared white hot inside Anneke. She reached for the first object she could find, a large pot. 'Get away from her!' she yelled, swinging the pot at the man's head when he did not respond. It grazed his temple, hard enough to daze him but not knock him out. The man turned, focusing his wrath on Anneke. Quickly she reached behind her and grabbed a knife, brandishing it. *'Raus!'*

This seemed to give the man pause. He stepped away, shaking his head. Then, without speaking, he walked out the front door of the flat. 'No, no!' Bronia called, starting after him. 'Wait–'

'Nein, Mutter,' Anneke said, restraining her mother and smelling the vodka that seeped from her skin and breath.

But the older woman pulled away. 'It's your fault! You've ruined everything for me. I never should have taken you.' She turned and ran into the living room and Anneke could hear the sound of another drink being poured.

Anneke considered going after her, then decided against it. There was nothing she could do to help Bronia. As she returned to the bedroom, her guilt rose. After she left, her mother truly would be all alone. But that was not enough to change Anneke's decision. This was her chance to get out and not become – as she feared would happen if she stayed behind – someone like Bronia herself.

She soon heard the familiar sound of snoring. It was eleven-thirty, Anneke noted, standing up. She reached behind the bed for the clock and as she did her hand brushed against a book. She pulled it out, running her hand over the cover.

Gone with the Wind. She hadn't meant to take it from the Stossels' library. She had stumbled upon it unexpectedly last spring when dusting the upper shelves, where it was hidden behind a history of the Red Army. She'd been instantly taken with the elegant woman in a flowing gown on the cover. She'd begun reading it, a few pages at a time when she could slip away, and had become engrossed in the story of Scarlett, a young woman living in a divided country like her own.

She had been reading it furtively one day when Herr Stossel walked into the study unexpectedly. Alarmed, she had dropped the book into her bag and forgotten about it until she came home that night. She would read a chapter and then return it the next day, she decided. Instead, she stayed awake long into the night, captivated by the story. And by that point she was so far along, another day before returning it couldn't possibly hurt, could it? A week later, she finished the book, then started reading it again. Each day she meant to return it but something always seemed to get in the way. It was so nice to have a book, the only thing to read in the flat except for some old women's magazines that Bronia kept in her nightstand.

Anneke turned the book over in her hand. She felt bad about taking it, in a way that she hadn't with the necklace or even the clock. And she really had meant to return it, only now she wouldn't have the chance. Bringing it with her to Paris seemed foolish when she needed the little space she had for other, more practical things. But she could not bear to leave it behind.

She reached down again and pulled out the clock. The unwieldy antique was not ideal for a swift getaway and she hoped Henryk would not be annoyed. But he had said they needed money and surely they could get a better price for it in the West. She picked it up and put it back in her bag, then tiptoed through the living room.

As she reached the front door, there was a noise behind her. She turned to find Bronia in her half-open housecoat, wavering unsteadily from the vodka. Her unfocused eyes traveled from Anneke's face to the rucksack, where the clock jutted out, then back again.

'Everything is fine, *Mutter*,' Anneke said, trying to sound soothing. 'Go back to sleep.' Anneke watched Bronia's face as she tried to process what her daughter was saying. Anneke faltered – there were so many things she wanted to tell her mother, who had done her best, though it was in fact not a very good job at all. She wanted to say thank-you and good-bye and that she would send money and perhaps even arrange for Bronia herself to leave when she was able. But her mother could not be trusted with the truth. 'Go to sleep,' Anneke repeated, and Bronia eyed her warily before turning and shuffling away.

Anneke made her way through the darkened streets, moving as swiftly as she could until she reached the munitions factory. Deserted since the end of the war, it was a hulking shell, crumbling stovepipes pointing forlornly upward, gaping holes where the windows had once been. She approached the main gate as Henryk had indicated, but there was no sign of him. She was a few minutes late, but surely Henryk would have waited. Perhaps he had been delayed as well.

She kept close to the munitions factory, trying to stay hidden in the shadows. Then she looked across at the mass of barbed wire and steel that now separated East from West. She shivered, taking in the makeshift tower that had been erected, bright lights shining down on the work site below.

At the corner, she glimpsed a police car, creeping slowly. She kept moving, circling the block so as not to arouse suspicion. As she walked, she recalled her conversation with her mother. It was a familiar one, Bronia blaming Anneke for ruining her life. But something she had said tonight was different: 'I never should have taken you.' What had she meant by that? Anneke shrugged off the question. Bronia was drunk, talking nonsense as always.

She returned to the specified meeting spot. Half an hour had passed at least and Henryk was still not there. She wondered if he was all right, whether someone had learned of his plan to flee. She started down the street, then stopped again. Where was she going? It was too late to go to the bar and ask Henryk's friends about his whereabouts. She did not know where Henryk lived, and she would not dare to go there even if she did. She thought of the flat where they had spent their lone night together. There was no reason to think he would necessarily be there, but she had to try something.

Twenty minutes later she reached the apartment block by the station. As she climbed the stairs to the flat, the dank odor brought back a wave of memories of the night they had shared. She reached the door and raised her hand to knock, then stopped. From inside came Henryk's low voice, then the familiar tinkling laugh of the girl from the café.

An icy hand seemed to grip her by the throat. Henryk had betrayed her. Of course he had never promised her anything, but their plans to leave together, the dream that they shared, suggested more. She stood motionless, uncertain what to do. Every instinct in her being told her to go inside and confront him, to demand the truth.

Paris, she thought, and suddenly the images of her new life began to slip from her mind. She pulled them back again. Over the past few days the dream had grown to be about something more than Henryk, something bigger. It had become her own, the first that she'd ever dared to have. If she confronted him now and they parted badly, he would leave her behind.

Go with him anyway, a voice inside her urged. Her other self protested: to say nothing about his betrayal and act as if she didn't know would be to live a lie. But once he had gotten her to Paris, she would no longer need him. She could set out on her own and make a life there. Quietly she started back down the stairs, feeling about ten years older than she had a few minutes earlier.

On the last step she stumbled, and the banging of her shoes as she recovered echoed through the stairway. Above a door opened and she heard footsteps. 'Anneke,' Henryk said breathlessly, appearing on the landing above.

The top three buttons of his shirt were undone, she noticed as he walked down the stairs toward her. She bit her lip, fighting the urge to demand answers about the girl. 'I went to the Wall, but you didn't show,' she said. 'So I came looking for you here.' Why did she feel the need to justify her actions after what he had done?

'I was running late,' he replied, and the explanation was so inadequate she almost laughed aloud.

'We should go,' she said, focusing on Paris and all of the things that lay ahead. 'Are you ready now?'

He looked away. 'Anneke,' he repeated and his breathing was calmer now, his tone solemn.

'What is it?'

'I can't.'

Her feet seemed to slip from beneath her and she leaned against the wall so as not topple. 'My father, he found out and he's stopping me—'

'In a few weeks then, maybe,' she said stubbornly. 'After he's no longer watching.' But even as she spoke she knew that there was more to it than that.

'It's not just that. My friend,' she could tell instantly from the catch in his voice that he was not talking about one of the other boys from the café but of the dark-haired girl in the flat. 'My friend thinks I should return to the university and my father has offered to pay my living expenses if I start this term.'

He continued speaking, but she could barely hear him over the buzzing in her ears. 'I'm sorry, Anneke.' She watched in disbelief as he turned and started to climb the stairs. She wondered what would have happened if she hadn't made her way to the flat. Would he have even bothered to leave the company of the dark-haired girl to come and tell Anneke he wasn't going, or would she still be standing alone on the darkened street corner waiting?

What now? She could dump the clock and go home and act as though nothing had happened. But it was too late for that. She found herself thinking of Scarlett O'Hara – what would her favorite heroine have done in this situation?

Go anyway, a voice not her own seemed to say. She hesitated, taken aback by the idea. Well, why not? She could make her way to the break in the Wall. She didn't have Henryk's contacts on the other side, but she would manage somehow.

'Wait,' she called after him. He turned back reluctantly. 'How – I mean, if one was going to go?'

A look of disbelief crossed his face and for a moment she thought he might refuse to give her the information. But then his expression turned to resignation. 'Down the street from the munitions factory, about a quarter mile south across from a butcher shop there's a gap in the Wall. If you can get over, there's a van that passes by that can take you out of the city for a price.'

'But the area by the munitions factory is a huge construction site. There are lights, hundreds of workers.'

'It's nearly impossible,' he conceded with a detachment that confirmed the mission was no longer his own. 'But perhaps farther down it won't be so conspicuous.' She glimpsed fear in his eyes then and knew that his decision not to go had nothing to do with returning to the university.

This time, she did not wait for him to turn away. 'Good-bye, Henryk,' she said, taking in his shrunken form. The breath beneath her words seemed to extinguish the last tiny flicker of what she had felt for him.

She walked from the building and started down the street, moving as swiftly as she could while carrying the rucksack. She didn't know what time the van would pass by, but she had surely been delayed from Henryk's original timetable by the detour to the flat. She looked over her shoulder, wondering if she should go back and ask. But there was no time and this was her journey now.

When she reached the Wall, she continued down the street, finding the butcher shop he had referenced. She looked at the Wall across from it but it appeared solid. Her heart sank. Had Henryk been misinformed?

Then a few feet down the road she saw it, a gap in the Wall where the concrete was missing – whether it had been broken or was not filled in yet she did not know – and a tangle of thick barbed wire was all that remained. She hurried to it. Closer now, she could see that it was hardly the break Henryk had been promised – a notch, cut out of the top of the Wall, not more than ten inches wide. It was several feet off the ground, and she had to find a foothold to reach it. How much easier it would have been if there had been two of them, one hoisted over first who could then reach back to help the other. A pang of regret shot through her. But there was no time to think about that now.

Taking a deep breath, she reached up and secured one foot in a small niche in the Wall. She looked at her rucksack, hesitating. It would be hard enough to climb over with two hands, much less with one tied up holding the bag. But she did not dare throw it over for fear of damaging the clock. She climbed up into the crevice, sliding one leg over the Wall, grimacing as she felt her tights rip. On the other side, there was a wide chasm, separating east from west. In that moment, she understood for the first time the distance she had to travel, the difficulty of the road ahead.

A light shone up at her suddenly. 'Halt!' The police, she panicked. How had they found her so quickly? Had Henryk told? No, there would have been nothing in it for him. Perhaps he had shared his plan with the girl at the flat, or maybe Bronia had become suspicious and summoned her government friend.

She struggled without success to pull her other leg over but she was stuck in the crevice, unable to move. A shot rang out and a bullet whizzed past, missing her shoulder by inches. They really meant to stop her at any cost. Desperately, she tugged herself loose, hurling herself toward the other side. There was another shot and something struck her, sending her lurching forward. I'm hit, she realized, though she felt no pain. She gave another tug and, still clutching the bag, fell into the darkness below.

Thirteen

LAKE COMO, 2009

'So she's a nun?' Charlotte asked a few hours later as the car raced south toward the Swiss–Italian border. She tried not to watch the road or notice the speed with which Brian pushed the rented Fiat around the terrifying alpine curves.

Brian nodded, not taking his eyes from the road. 'Her name is Anastasia Darien, and she's at a convent just south of Lake Como.'

'Did she say what she knew?' Charlotte pressed, for what seemed like the tenth time.

'No, like I told you, just that she had information that might help with Roger's defense.'

'And she wouldn't discuss it over the phone?' Jack asked from the backseat.

Brian raised an eyebrow in the rearview mirror. 'Would we be driving all night if she had?'

'True,' Jack relented. At the sound of his voice, conflict washed over Charlotte. She half wished she was sitting in the back with him, watching his profile, close enough to feel his warmth. Partly, though, she was relieved – their last conversation, interrupted by Brian, had not ended well. She didn't want to see a different look in his eyes than the one that had given her butterflies every time he had glanced her way for the past several days.

'Of course, she could just be a complete fraud,'

Jack added grimly. After Brian had come to Charlotte excitedly with the news, they'd called Jack, who returned quickly to the hotel. Despite the late hour, he had on the same clothes he was wearing earlier and Charlotte had wondered if he'd ever gone to bed. At the door to her room, he'd hesitated and she knew he was thinking of their night together.

Jack had been the most skeptical of the three about making the trek to Italy, and Charlotte had braced herself for a repeat of the debate over whether to travel to Salzburg. But things were different now – with Roger defeated by the news of Magda's death, there were few other leads to pursue, so Jack had quickly acquiesced to the trip. But now his cynicism seemed to return. 'We get phone calls like that all the time, false tips.'

Brian shifted gears as they descended a hill. 'To what end?'

Charlotte could hear the shrug in Jack's voice. 'Attention seekers, mostly. People read about a high-profile case in the paper and they want to be part of it. Or they think there's some sort of money involved, like a reward.'

'Well, we'll find out soon enough,' Brian replied, as they neared the border crossing. A guard stuck his head out of a small building and waved them through. On the other side, the terrain became steeper and the sky paled slightly behind them in a way that suggested morning was near.

They traveled in silence for some time, the predawn hush broken only by the whirring of the engine. Finally, they climbed another peak and as they cleared a cluster of trees, daylight broke, revealing a valley below. 'That's it,' Brian announced, pointing.

Even shrouded in dimness, the view was breathtaking. Kaletni Monastery sat nestled in a bluff covered with brightly colored autumn leaves, overlooking a massive expanse of water. It was a large medieval structure, a red-roofed chapel surrounded by a series of smaller buildings with arched windows hewn crudely from sandstone.

The road wound downward, depositing them at the monastery gates. There was no intercom or guard and Charlotte wondered how anyone might know they had arrived. But a moment later a nun shuffled toward them.

Brian rolled down the window. 'We're here to see Sister Anastasia.' Charlotte held her breath, half expecting the nun to deny them entrance. The woman seemed neither surprised nor troubled by the unannounced visitors before dawn, though, opening the gate and waving them inside. Brian pulled onto the patch of gravel she indicated.

Charlotte stepped out of the car, breathing the crisp morning air as she took in the panorama below once more. A breeze blew gently, sending the waters lapping against the rocks. There was little time to marvel, though – Jack and Brian were already following the nun down a path made of smooth, flat stones toward the high entrance to the monastery. It was Sunday morning, Charlotte noted, trying to get her bearings in relation to the days that had passed since leaving home. But the convent was quiet and still. They passed through a courtyard with a magnificently tended flower garden in the center, its pinks and blues a sharp contrast to the otherwise colorless surroundings.

The nun led them wordlessly down a corridor into a room that Charlotte took to be a dining hall, with long wooden tables pushed to either side. The ancient walls and floor gave off a damp smell.

The woman walked from the room, closing the door behind her, and the three of them stood in awkward silence. In the distance, a bell began to chime. Charlotte gazed out the window at a bird that swooped low over the rolling olive groves on the far side of the lake. What would it be like to live here, to wake up each day in such tranquil surroundings?

Suddenly aware of someone watching her, Charlotte lifted her head, her eyes meeting Jack's. She expected him to look away, but his gaze met hers, held. Her breath caught. Her mind spun back to the story Jack recounted of seeing her for the first time years ago. If she had looked up and noticed him, would it have been like this?

She shivered involuntarily, then wrapped her arms around herself against the chill. 'Here,' Jack said, coming up beside her and draping his jacket around her shoulders.

She hesitated, caught off guard by the intimate, unexpected gesture. 'Thanks. It's colder in here than outside.'

Behind her, Charlotte heard a scuffling noise and the three of them spun toward it in unison. There was someone else in the room, she noticed then, a woman wearing a plain gray dress that blended into the granite wall behind her, which had made her almost undetectable when she had been motionless. She stood facing away from them, looking out the window. Her hair was covered in matching gray cloth, a simpler version of the habit that the nun who escorted them in had worn.

'Hello?' Charlotte said uncertainly. The woman turned toward them and as her face became illuminated in the pale light, Charlotte gasped. She knew then exactly who the woman was and why she would indeed be able to help Roger, if anyone could. For though the habit obscured her hair and her face was lined with age, the features were unmistakable.

She studied the woman with disbelief, as though seeing a ghost. 'Magda?'

The woman shook her head slightly, her faint smile almost imperceptible. No, of course she wasn't. Magda had died in the camps. And Magda would have been Roger's age, even a few years older maybe. The statuesque woman who stood before them, beautiful even in nun's clothing, could not have been much more than sixty-five. But the wide cheeks and dark eyes were almost an exact replica of the images she had seen of Magda. Except for the dimpled chin, which was pure Roger.

'Anna?' Charlotte tried again, taking a step forward. 'Anna Dykmans?'

The woman blanched slightly, as though stung by the name. 'Yes, I was once called Anna. I go by Anastasia now.'

Charlotte's mind raced. Magda and Anna had died in Belzec. So how was it possible that she

305

was standing here before them?

No, she realized. Anna had not died. Magda had died in Belzec and the presumption had been that a child as young as Anna would have perished along with her mother. She remembered Roger's account of a rumor that a girl had escaped. Roger had assumed through his haze of desperation and hope that by 'girl' they had meant a young woman, and he had spent the intervening years searching for Magda. But perhaps the witness really had meant a small child, now the woman standing before them.

'Anastasia,' Charlotte said aloud, processing it. The name bore a hint of Anna, the girl that she had once been. But it was different enough that no one would have linked her to her former life. And the choice was ironic too, Charlotte reflected. Anastasia had been the youngest daughter of the Russian czar Nicholas, and the legend persisted that she had escaped the execution of the royal family by the Bolsheviks and was living somewhere under an assumed identity. Risen from the ashes, as the woman standing before them seemed to be. 'But you were Anna Dykmans?'

'Yes. Darien is my married surname.'

Married, Charlotte reflected. So the woman hadn't been in the convent her entire life. What would prompt one to give up the outside world and retreat here? Charlotte thought of her own flight to Philadelphia after the pain of her mother's death and Brian's betrayal. Perhaps vows of solitude weren't such a strange idea after all.

'You are wondering,' Anastasia said in broken English, 'how it is that I am alive? There are a

306

great many answers to that question: fate, luck, the goodwill of strangers, some of whom died as a result of their selflessness...' She drifted off, as though lost in her memories.

'How did you escape the camps?' Charlotte prompted gently.

The woman looked up at her, eyes clearing. 'Oh, I was never in the camps. When my mother heard the Nazis coming to our door, she somehow got me to our neighbors, the Baders. They were known as people who had helped Jews.'

Charlotte tried to process the information. The whole time Roger had been searching for Magda and Anna, the child had been so close by. In fact, when he had gone to the Baders to ask if they had seen anything, Anna would have been right there. Why hadn't they returned the child to him, or at least let him know that she was there? Were they doing what they thought best to protect Anna, or had they simply been too afraid?

So Magda had been able to spirit Anna away before her arrest. Of course, the Nazis would have known that Magda had a child, would have demanded her whereabouts. But Magda surely had not given up that information and she had paid with her life.

'The Baders were good people, but ultimately the Nazis grew wise to their ways and came back for them. We were all arrested and sent to a detention center.' The older woman shuddered 'From there we were put on a truck headed to one of the camps. But before we reached our destination, Frau Bader pushed me off the truck into the woods. I don't know how she expected me to survive. You can imagine the odds.' Charlotte nodded. A young child, alone in the forest. She might have starved or been picked up by the Nazis or someone sympathetic to them. 'A couple found me and hid me until after the war.'

She continued, 'It wasn't one of those fairy tales you hear about these days, the family adopting the little child and raising her as their own. They kept me in the cellar and when food was scarce, I was the one who went without. It was a nightmare and I sometimes wished I was in the camp with the Baders.' Anastasia's voice trailed off and Charlotte found herself curious and relieved in equal parts when the older woman did not say more about her experiences in hiding. 'After the war, they deposited me at a displaced persons camp. A woman in East Berlin took me in exchange for a modest government stipend that was being offered to anyone who would care for children.

'Of course, I never knew most of this. I was less than two years old when I lost my mother and my memories were hazy, soon obscured by time. The woman in Berlin who raised me, Bronia she was called, became the only mother I had ever known. Then, when I was older, I was able to escape over the Wall and flee to the West.'

'Have you been a nun ever since?' Brian interjected and Charlotte cringed inwardly, hoping his outburst would not stop Anastasia from speaking freely.

But she shook her head and continued. 'I married and lived in London for a time. But I never really felt at home in the outside world. So after my husband died, I made my way here. You must think it strange, my being in a convent when my birth mother was Jewish – my stepmother, Bronia, as well. But after I fled Berlin, I was taken in by some nuns in the south of France and it was there that for the first time I found peace. At the time, I didn't know that this would be my calling so I went out into the world.'

'How did you find out?' Charlotte asked. 'About your real family, I mean.'

'Right before I left Berlin, Bronia said something that made me wonder about my childhood. My curiosity grew over time, and years later, well after the Iron Curtain fell, I returned to the East to do some digging. I found Bronia's adoption file and the records from the displaced persons camp, and ultimately even the documents where the Nazis had registered me with the Baders at the time of our arrest.' Watching the woman's face, Charlotte could imagine her search for answers, finding the documents that chronicled her own history of tragedy and suffering. 'Finally, I was able to discover my real family in Breslau. There was nothing there anymore, of course; the house had long since been expropriated, first by the Nazis and later by the Communists. But I learned that my mother perished in the camps.'

'I'm sorry,' Jack said gently. 'And your father?'

Charlotte looked up. Was he referring to Roger or Hans? But Jack was being purposely vague, she could tell, unsure how much Anastasia knew.

'I've researched it,' the woman replied. 'And I learned that Hans Dykmans was killed by the Nazis shortly after his arrest.'

Charlotte stifled a gasp. Anastasia had no idea that her real father was Roger.

Your father is alive, Charlotte wanted to shout. But she did not. That information, on top of everything else, might upset Anastasia, keep her from telling them what they needed to know.

'You contacted us about some information?' Jack prompted.

'Yes, recently I learned about the Dykmans case. It's been in the news for some time, I know, but we have so little contact with the outside world here. A few weeks ago, a visitor to the convent left a newspaper behind and that's when I saw the story.'

'Did you know about your uncle?' Charlotte asked, the last word sticking in her throat.

Anastasia shook her head. 'I'd learned from my earlier research that my father had a brother and a sister, but I assumed they were long since gone. Then I saw the article and started digging – I was amazed to discover that Roger Dykmans was still alive. And that's when I remembered the clock.' She paused, swallowing. 'When I went back to Breslau, I mean Wroclaw, I knocked on the door of the neighbors who I learned had saved me, the Baders. They had perished in the camps, but the woman who lived in the house was an elderly cousin of theirs and she gave me a clock that she said had belonged to my family.

'At the time I was struck because the clock was exactly like one I had seen in Berlin years earlier, right down to the maker's insignia. One I had stolen, in fact, to finance my escape to the West.' Was it the same clock that they had seen in Salz-

310

burg, Charlotte wondered? What were the odds of two such unique timepieces existing and crossing the paths of this one woman in a lifetime?

'It wasn't until some time after I brought the clock back with me that I discovered the telegram,' Anastasia continued. Charlotte's breath caught and she willed herself to remain silent and let the older woman continue, rather than demanding to see the document. 'I wanted to know more about its significance, so I wrote to the Baders' cousin, but my letter was returned unopened – the woman had either moved on or died.'

Which explained, Charlotte thought, why Roger had come up empty when he had later returned to Wroclaw, looking for the clock. 'And then, when I heard about the charges against my uncle and realized that the telegram might somehow be relevant, I knew that I had to contact you.'

'Do you have it?' Brian asked. The woman reached behind her and produced a timepiece identical to the one they had seen in Salzburg.

Charlotte stepped forward and studied the clock. It could be a replica, she thought, willing herself to be calm. But the farmer's initials engraved in the bottom left little doubt. How was it possible? He must have made more than one, she realized.

'It's in the bottom,' Anastasia said in a low voice, reading Charlotte's unspoken thoughts. With trembling hands, Charlotte turned the clock over and opened the compartment. She pulled out the piece of yellowed paper and even before she unfolded it, she knew.

It was a telegram from Roger. She studied the German, then handed it to Jack to translate aloud:

My brother:

Magda arrested. Czech camp plan compromised. Make alternative plans at once. Roger.

Charlotte and Jack exchanged looks behind the older woman. So Roger had written the telegram after all. But why hadn't the Baders sent it for him as he had requested? Perhaps because the Nazis had arrested them before they had the chance. Or maybe they had simply been too scared. Things would have been so very different for everyone if they had – not just for Roger and Hans but also for the children who might not have died and the generations that might have come from them.

'Will this help?' Anastasia asked, gesturing to the paper. 'I mean, surely people can see that my uncle didn't mean to hurt my father at all.'

'It will,' Jack replied, but there was a hesitation in his voice, and Charlotte knew that he was picturing Roger, slumped over in the conference room, having learned the truth about Magda and lost his will to live. The telegram alone would not be enough without Roger's testimony. 'But there's one thing that would help even more.'

'Anna, I mean Anastasia,' Charlotte said tentatively, 'we need to ask you for something else. We need you to come to Munich with us.'

The older woman cocked her head, not understanding. 'Why?'

'We need all the help we can get with Roger's defense,' Jack replied. 'You see, the prosecutor is trying to elevate the case to a higher court, which

312

likely means a longer sentence if he's convicted. They want to make an example of him, and we only have a few more days to convince the court that the charges are unfounded.'

'But surely now if he testifies and explains–'

'He won't,' Jack said quietly, interrupting her. Anastasia tilted her head, brow wrinkling.

Charlotte jumped in to explain. 'Your–' she said, catching herself. 'Roger only recently learned of your mother's death and it devastated him. He's given up on defending himself.'

'I don't understand.'

Charlotte hesitated, realizing she needed to back up. 'Roger cared a great deal for your mother. That's why he gave the information about Hans's plans to the Nazis, trying to bargain for information to save your mother and you. So when he learned she had died after all, he was very upset.'

'But how would my coming to Munich possibly help?'

Charlotte swallowed. She could hide the truth from the older woman no longer. There had been enough secrets and lies these past sixty-plus years. Like Roger, Anastasia had the right to know the truth. 'I know this may come as a terrible shock,' she began.

'Charlotte–' Brian said behind her, his voice rising in warning.

But she had gone too far to turn back now. 'Roger is your father.'

Anastasia stared at her blankly. 'How could that possibly–?' The older woman sat down on one of the benches, shaking. 'Some water, please.' Charlotte rushed to her side, pouring a glass from the

313

clay pitcher that sat on the table and worrying that she had gone too far.

Jack sat down beside her. 'Roger and your mother had strong feelings for each other. Feelings they could not resist. He's your father, Anastasia.'

The woman opened her mouth as though to deny what she was being told. Then a flash of recognition crossed her face and Charlotte wondered if she had recalled a memory from earliest childhood, some image that confirmed the truth. 'Did my father, I mean, did Hans know?'

Jack shook his head. 'We don't think so. And I'm sure he loved you and your mother very much.'

Anastasia raised a trembling hand to her cheek. 'And Roger's alive?' She did not, Charlotte noticed, refer to him as her father.

'Yes, and seeing you, we think, might give him the will to fight for his freedom.'

Anastasia did not answer but looked slowly around the room, then out the window. She was contemplating the sanctuary that this place had given her for so long, the terror she must feel at the prospect of leaving. Much like Charlotte's own difficult decision to come out of the safety of her life back home and take on this case. 'I don't know,' Anastasia managed finally. 'I haven't left here often.'

Charlotte nodded, understanding. Anastasia had come to feel safe within these walls and she didn't want to leave the comfort of her surroundings. But at the same time, there was something that had made her go searching for the truth about her family, that had made her reach out with the information about Roger. To try to help.

314

It was a conflict she recognized within herself. She placed a hand on the older woman's shoulder. 'There are many kinds of callings,' she said softly.

'All right,' Anastasia said finally, swallowing. 'I'll go with you. When?'

'Right away,' Brian interjected, his voice shattering the tranquil atmosphere.

Jack stepped forward and Charlotte winced, waiting for him to rebuke Brian. But for once, the brothers were in complete agreement. 'We need to leave now. If we have any hope of saving your father, there isn't a moment to lose.'

Fourteen

FRANKFURT, 1911

Johann looked out the front window of the mercantile shop. The street was choked thick, as it seemed to be at every hour of the day or night, with horse-drawn wagons and men on foot and the occasional auto trying without success to navigate through the crowds. The noisy, chaotic city dwarfed the village near which he had spent almost his entire life, a sharp contrast to the bucolic countryside he had left behind. He felt a tug of longing as always when he thought of his home. It was midsummer now and the crops would be growing nearly waist high, waving in perfect unison in the wind.

Assuming, that is, there were crops anymore. More than eight years had passed since the morning when he came home and found Rebecca by the barn. After he had fallen to the ground beside her, Johann sat motionless, holding his wife and stroking her hair. A seemingly endless waterfall of tears coursed downward, mixing with the dirt and blood.

When his eyes had at long last run dry, he straightened. Whether minutes or hours had passed he did not know. Finally, with legs that seemed unable to hold him, he stood and lifted Rebecca. He carried her to the house and set her on the bed. Then he put on the kettle and filled the large basin tub they used each week, and bathed her like a child.

When he had dried her and placed her on the bed once more, he opened the wardrobe. The dresses, a tapestry of their days together, unleashed a torrent of images, and he grabbed one without looking, then closed the door quickly as if to silence the unbearable cacophony of memories. The dress dropped to the ground and he hastened to pick it up again with shaking hands. It was the pale yellow frock she had worn on their wedding day. He pulled the dress over her head, tugging the material taut across her belly, caressing the child that he would never know, now still within her womb.

An hour later, he stood by the cluster of trees behind the barn, looking down at the pile of stones marking Rebecca's burial spot. He should have called the rabbi to say a proper blessing, he thought, or at least notified her parents. They deserved the chance to say farewell to their only child. It was not only that he felt too cowardly and broken to face their wrath, the blame they would cast at him for somehow causing her demise. He did not want to dilute his grief, to share those last few minutes they had together with anyone.

He lifted his head, taking in the fields. Part of him wanted to stay, to linger in this place where Rebecca had drawn her last breath. The notion of severing his only remaining tie to her seemed unbearable. But he could not imagine living in the cold, empty house without her laughter and warmth. No, there was nothing left here for him now.

He then thought of the other clock, wrapped in muslin and buried beneath the floorboards in the cellar. He had made them at the same time, side by side, and the two looked nearly identical. Only a trained eye, examining closely, could see that the one he'd kept was a bit nicer, the details finer, the metal more lustrous. That one had been meant for Rebecca. It was a magnificent gift, worth more than most of their belongings combined. She would have scolded him, he knew, for wasting the materials and not selling the second clock as well. She was practical like that, always had been, long before the hardships of her life with him had required it. But he had wanted her to have this precious clock, the finest he had ever made or seen. She deserved it.

But now she would never know. If only he had given the clock to her sooner, shown it to her while he had the chance.

This realization seemed to compound his grief and he knew that if he did not keep moving now, he would never go. Johann walked to the workshop at the back of the barn and drew back the floorboards once more. There, buried so deeply that one might not have noticed it if not looking, was the second clock. He pulled it out with trembling hands, remembering how he planned to give it to Rebecca on the eve of their departure. But that would not happen now.

Johann wondered if the traveler was still at Hoffel's, whether he would be as enthusiastic about a second clock, pay the same sum over again. But even as he thought this, he knew he could never part with it. The clock was his last, best symbol of his love for his wife, even though she had not seen or touched it. No, he would keep the clock with him for as long as he was able, not sell it unless his life depended on it. He wrapped it in the cloth on which it had nestled and carried it from the barn.

'I'm sorry,' he said to the pile of stones. With great effort, he turned away and walked through the barn a final time before leaving his home forever.

More than eight years had passed since that day. Johann had left the farm intending to carry out their plan of moving to America. But the trip had proven disastrous – he'd gotten a ride with some unscrupulous men who had charged him a small fortune to transport him to the border and then robbed and abandoned him in Frankfurt.

As he stood helplessly on a city street bigger and busier than any he had ever known, Johann's grief had turned to despair. Not a fraction of the way into his journey and he could go no farther. He was almost glad that Rebecca was not here to see what a failure she had married. Then he looked desperately down at the clock, tucked into the bag. It would surely fetch enough of a sum to help him continue onward.

Farther down the street, he found a shop with all manner of items for sale in the front window. A bell tinkled as he walked inside. 'Yes?' the ginger-haired proprietor behind the counter said, looking at Johann over his glasses.

Johann hesitated. 'I was wondering...' But he

could not bring himself to propose selling the clock. He looked around the shop. A sign in the window caught his eye: HELP WANTED. 'I would like to inquire about the job.'

The man looked Johann over from head to toe, though not unkindly. 'Have you experience in a shop?'

'Yes,' Johann lied. 'I'm good at fixing things too, clocks and other small mechanical devices.'

And so he had stayed. The shopkeeper, Franz, let him sleep in the back storeroom. The first night, as he made himself a bed of burlap sacks on the floor, listening to the noise from the alehouse next door, his heart sank. This was the farthest thing from the life he had envisioned for himself and Rebecca and their child. It's only temporary, he told himself that night and each thereafter as he lay on the storeroom floor. *I will still go to America.* But the mantra grew fainter and by the time he had earned enough to pay for the one-room flat above the shop, he had stopped repeating it altogether.

Once or twice he fleetingly considered returning to the farm. But he could not bear to face the life he had left. And he knew instinctively the land was gone, taken over by some lucky person who happened upon the deserted homestead and petitioned the provincial government for ownership. Or perhaps Rebecca's parents had sold it.

It was almost eleven now, he thought, judging by the flow of traffic on the street. Hannah would be coming by soon to bring him lunch, as she did every day at this hour. He sighed. He had married Franz's plain, freckle-faced sister more than two years after arriving here. When he first met her, the notion of being with a woman other than Rebecca was unfathomable. But Hannah came by the shop patiently each day and he found that he enjoyed his conversations with her and later the warmth of her body.

A few minutes later, as if on cue, Hannah appeared around the corner, moving more slowly now with her growing girth. Hannah looked nothing like Rebecca had when she was carrying Johann's child, a fact that made the situation easier to bear. Whereas Rebecca had retained her figure but for the round swell of her belly, Hannah had grown big all around like a barrel and the pregnancy seemed to weigh on her rather than give her a glow. But perhaps all of that heft would serve her well – she had a sturdiness about her that suggested she would weather childbirth without issue.

Hannah entered the shop, dropping the bag that Johann knew would contain a sandwich of thick bread and cheese down on the counter as if it were heavier than it actually was. 'Busy this morning?' she asked.

'About the usual.' The colloquy was always the same.

'I'd best be on my way. Bring some milk home if you can.'

He managed a smile, which she returned. 'I shall.'

As Johann watched her retreat, a sense of sadness overcame him. The marriage was not an unhappy one. He and Hannah were amicable partners and had he not known the passion of his time with Rebecca, he might have never guessed that more was possible. But Hannah deserved better, he thought guiltily. If she suspected that there was something more to be had, though, she did not show it. Rather, she accepted the companionship he offered, never expressing dissatisfaction. And now that the child she had long wanted (fathering a child had once again proven difficult for Johann) was on the way, she seemed to notice or care even less if there was some part of himself that he could not give her.

The bell above the door tinkled, drawing Johann from his thoughts. A stout man with a thick gray beard walked in. There was something familiar about him, Johann noticed immediately. He ran through in his mind the catalog of regular customers who frequented the shop, but could not find the man among them. 'Can I help you?' he asked.

'Yes, I'm meant to see the proprietor, Herr Litt, about some of our hardware–' The man stopped in mid-sentence, his gaze rising to the shelf above Johann's head. It was the clock, Johann knew. For the first two years he had worked in the shop, he had kept the timepiece hidden among his few possessions, bringing it out each night only to polish the glass and run his finger over the fine mechanisms and remember. But then one day, as he prepared to move from the flat upstairs to the small house he and Hannah were to share, he studied it, considering what to do. It would not feel right to bring the clock, his last true memento of Rebecca, into his new house, where he would share a bed with Hannah. The memories were too great. So he dusted it off and put it on the shelf in the shop. The clock seemed to glow on display, as if glad to see daylight after being hidden for so long. Customers often remarked upon it, asking if it was for sale.

But the man who stood before him was staring at the timepiece even longer than was customary. He pulled at his beard, as though in deep thought. Johann realized then why the man looked familiar – it was the man from Herr Hoffel's *Gasthaus*, the traveler who had bought the other clock. The passage of time had altered his appearance significantly – his hair was almost entirely white and he seemed to have added a jowl at his chin for each year that had passed.

Johann held his breath. Would the man recognize him? But Johann himself had been of no significance that day so many years ago – it was only the clock that he remembered. 'That timepiece,' the traveler said finally, still stroking his beard. 'It's extraordinary. May I?'

Reluctantly, Johann lifted the clock from the shelf and set it down on the counter in front of the man. 'It's not for sale,' he said quickly, his voice more abrupt than he had intended.

'I have one like it,' the traveler replied, as if to clarify his intent. 'But I've long wanted to find the man who made it to see if more might be commissioned. Do you have any idea where I might find him?'

Johann shook his head. Though he had repaired a number of timepieces in his years at the shop, simple commercial clocks mostly, he had not made a single one. He had tried once, but the gift seemed to be gone. He could no longer remember the techniques his father had shown him and his fingers seemed clumsy and thick. In that way above all others, he had not been able to move on.

It was just as well, he reflected now. To make the anniversary clock over again would be to cheapen the memory and all it stood for. 'No,' he said finally. 'I'm afraid I don't know anyone who could make such a timepiece.'

'It's a shame really,' the traveler said, and there was a glint in his eye that made Johann wonder if the man recognized him after all. 'One could make a fortune with such skill.' Johann considered the notion briefly. He and Hannah could surely use the extra money with a child on the way. 'Enough to have anything he ever wanted,' the man added.

And what if, Johann wanted to ask, the very thing one wanted could not be bought? But before he could speak, there was a clattering and Franz appeared to usher the man into the back room. Johann replaced the clock up on the shelf and reached for the sandwich Hannah had brought him.

Fifteen

MUNICH, 2009

They stood in the waiting area of the prison, not speaking. It was odd, Charlotte mused, being detained here after days of breezing straight into the conference room to see Roger. Strange how she had come to feel at home here in such a short time. Maybe Philadelphia was not the only place she could be comfortable after all.

She looked at Brian, who paced the floor in his usual manner. 'Let me go and see about the delay,' Jack had said a few minutes earlier, slipping inside to find out why it was taking so long for them to be brought to Roger. Charlotte, too, found herself unable to sit still, leaping from one of the plastic chairs to a standing position, then back again. Her mind raced. What would Roger say when presented with the daughter he had thought dead for so many years? Would it give him the will to fight for his freedom?

Only Anna (Charlotte could not help thinking of her by her childhood name) did not seem nervous, she noted. The woman stood by the narrow window, clutching the clock. She gazed outside, as she had at the convent, motionless except for an occasional fiddling with her cuffs. She still wore her simple gray dress, but she had removed the headpiece, and her hair, an opulent silver, was tied at the back of her neck in a knot. Earlier, as they arrived, Charlotte had watched Anna's face as she took in the massive walled prison, wondering what she was feeling: trepidation at meeting the father she never knew existed, hope that the information she'd found in the clock might help to free him? It was a shame, Charlotte reflected, that they had to meet for the first time in such a setting.

Anna's eyes darted in Charlotte's direction and Charlotte looked away hurriedly, embarrassed to have been caught staring. They had spoken little on the ride from Italy and, despite the wealth of information about her past that Anna had revealed at the convent, there were so many things Charlotte wanted to ask her still, about how she had survived, not just the war but the years after. What had made her decide to retreat to a life of solitude, and more importantly, had it given her what she was looking for? And would that change now that she had found Roger and could get some of the answers that had been kept from her these many years?

But Anna had sat close to the door, her body turned away in a manner that did not seem to invite conversation. After a time, she opened a tattered book that Charlotte had not known she was carrying. 'What are you reading?' she could not help but ask. Anna held up the book and Charlotte looked over, expecting to see the Bible. *'Gone with the Wind?'* she asked, unable to contain her surprise.

'I've always loved it,' Anna had replied simply and Charlotte sensed a story she would likely never hear.

The waiting room door opened now and Jack's head appeared. 'Charley, can you come here for a second?' His face was pinched and pale, she noted as she followed him into the hallway. Her uneasiness rose. She and Jack had not been alone since their conversation in the hotel bar the previous evening; in fact, he seemed to be deliberately avoiding her. Surely he wasn't trying to address their personal issues here and now.

'Jack, what is it? What's wrong?'

He leaned into her so unexpectedly she almost fell beneath the weight, his entire body seeming to crumple. 'Roger's dead.'

Forty minutes later they stood in the prison infirmary, two on either side of the narrow bed. 'When?' Charlotte asked Jack in a low voice.

'They found him about an hour before we arrived. The guard said he thought Roger was just napping. Could have been his heart.'

Or not, Charlotte thought. She had seen Roger's medical records when she'd reviewed the case files. He had been as healthy as a man thirty years younger, no trace of heart disease or any other ailment. To her, a less clinical explanation seemed likely: Roger had been at such a point of despair when they left him yesterday, he had simply given up.

If only you'd managed to hang on for one more day, she wanted to tell him. But his face was calmer than she had ever seen it, all signs of the anguish he'd shown yesterday gone. No, this was what he wanted. The corners of his lips were even pressed upward in a faint smile, and she knew then that he had been thinking of Magda when he died.

We know now, she communicated with him silently. We found the telegram. You were telling the truth. You didn't mean to do it after all.

She studied Roger, trying to place the emotion she was feeling. Not grief, exactly; she hadn't known him well enough for that. But there was a kind of sadness in not having been able to help him before it was too late, like the kids back home who slipped through the cracks despite her best efforts to save them. With Roger, though, it was something more, a sense of a kindred spirit who had spent years caught in a past life he couldn't quite shed. Only now he had finally been set free.

Charlotte looked up then at the daughter whom Roger had not known was alive all these years, confronted now with the reality of his death. She expected to see anger on Anna's face at being denied a reunion with the father she had only just found, at missing her one chance to say farewell by just hours. But the woman's expression was beatific, filled with peace and love.

You and your mother were everything to him, Charlotte wanted to tell Anna. But it was not her place. 'I'm sorry you didn't get to meet your father,' she offered instead.

'Me too,' Anna replied. 'But I'm glad I found him.' It was more than the fact that she was a nun, Charlotte realized, that gave her this sense of calm. The woman had simply known so much pain and loss that she accepted the unexpected twists and turns in her life as they came.

'We should give you a minute,' Charlotte said, nudging Jack and Brian into the hallway. Through the glass she could see Anna, bending to kiss Roger's cheek. 'So what now?'

'Well, the case will be dropped, obviously,' Jack said. 'I'll take the telegram and make sure the record gets corrected so that Roger's name is cleared posthumously.'

Charlotte nodded. The vindication was not as good as it would have been while Roger was alive, but it would have to do. Glancing through the window, she could see the clock by Roger's bedside. The one treasure he had been seeking now seemed almost irrelevant.

There was a vibrating sound from Jack's pocket. 'Excuse me,' he said, pulling out his phone and stepping around the corner.

'Acquittal after he's gone,' Brian remarked dryly. 'It just feels so unsatisfactory.'

'Not to me,' Charlotte interjected.

He turned to her. 'That's considered a win in your line of work?'

'I suppose. Sometimes just being able to walk away is enough. To me a win is not seeing the same kids back in court. It's a hollow kind of victory – not like in the movies when the kid gets a second chance, turns his life around, and graduates at the head of his class from Princeton. It doesn't work that way – most of my clients are lucky to finish high school, or get to community college.' She was babbling, she realized now, as she watched Brian's eyes glaze over. He didn't understand, never would. But she didn't care. 'So many of them disappear into the void, though, and I don't hear from them again – I don't know if they turned their lives around or wound up pregnant or dead.'

'Pregnant or dead?' Brian's mouth twisted. 'Are those equivalent?'

'That's not what I meant. But pregnant at sixteen – yeah, I think your life is over.'

He did not reply and she knew he was thinking of Danielle, her ambivalence about having a family, and the baby that was coming regardless.

Anna stepped into the hall then and Charlotte walked toward her, grateful for the interruption. 'Thank you,' the older woman said, and whether she meant for the moment of privacy or bringing her here, or something altogether different, Charlotte didn't know. Anna turned to Jack as he reappeared. 'I'd like to make arrangements, that is, for his burial.'

Where, Charlotte wondered, would he go? Roger had spent the past sixty-plus years alone. And there was no grave for Magda, or even Hans, to bury him beside.

'There's a family plot in Wadowice,' Jack offered. 'I believe his parents are buried there.'

'Or perhaps I could take him back to the grave-yard at the convent,' Anna proposed tentatively. 'It would be nice to have him close.' So despite the answers that finding her father had brought, the older woman would be returning to her life of solitude. Perhaps, Charlotte thought uncomfortably, some habits, such as retreat, became so entrenched in a person that no amount of closure can change them.

The next morning, Brian and Charlotte stood at the gate in the Munich airport. Charlotte shifted awkwardly from one foot to the other. Their departure had been a hasty one, Brian announcing as they left the prison that he had to get back to New York to prepare for a big hearing the following week. When he'd offered to book Charlotte a direct flight to Philadelphia at the same time, she'd hesitated, looking toward Jack. After all of the time they'd spent working together in recent days, her departure seemed so abrupt. But Jack had turned away, not meeting her eyes, still embarrassed, perhaps, by their conversation the other night at the bar. Or maybe he had just moved on mentally to his next project, already returning to his insular lifestyle, as Anna had done after making arrangements for Roger's burial. No, the case was over and there was no reason for her to stay any longer.

There had been no suggestion of a farewell dinner – despite the acquittal, Roger's death left them with little to celebrate and so they'd parted hurriedly the previous evening. 'I'm sorry not to be coming to the airport with you,' Jack said to her when Brian had gone to confirm their flight reservations. 'There's just so much work to catch up on–'

'I understand.' In truth, she knew it was more than that – the awkwardness that had descended between them over the past few days had seemed to thicken and calcify, and she cursed the things that remained unsaid between them.

'Good luck,' he added quietly. 'I mean, with Marquan's case and all.'

'And to you,' she replied stiffly, not quite sure what she meant, or what his life would look like now that the all-consuming work of defending Roger had ended.

Brian stepped off the elevator then, interrupting them with a complaint about difficulty getting through to the airline. Jack and Charlotte stepped apart. Then the brothers shook hands and mumbled something about perhaps seeing one another over the holidays, the ice between them loosened but not quite thawed. Then Jack had turned and walked out of the hotel, shoulders hunched. Charlotte watched, the gnawing feeling in the pit of her stomach growing as she fought the urge to run after him. She looked back down the terminal now, wishing he would appear as if in the movies.

'It's too bad,' Brian said, interrupting her thoughts. She looked up at him, puzzled. 'About Jack, I mean.' Her breath caught. Could he possibly know? 'I guess the past few days helped a little, but it sucks being estranged from family.' For Brian, the statement qualified as profound. Charlotte relaxed slightly; he was not talking about her. 'It's just that he's so closed off from the world. Damaged goods.'

She opened her mouth to protest that nothing could be further from the truth. But there was no point. 'He liked you back then,' Brian added. 'Funny, huh?'

So Brian knew after all. 'He mentioned.' She swallowed. 'But it was no big deal.'

'No, I mean he was crazy about you. And when I broke up with you, he was furious.' Charlotte's mind whirled. For all the time she had spent with Jack in recent days and all that he had told her, she had not known, had never even suspected, that the rift between the brothers had actually been about her. But she'd known about their falling out prior to Brian's ending their relationship, so it couldn't have been the breakup that angered Jack. More likely he discovered that Brian was seeing Danielle behind her back and was infuriated by the betrayal.

She considered pointing out to Brian the half-truth still imbedded in his explanation, then decided it was not worth the effort. 'So he was mad at you about me?'

'Enough to not speak with me for almost a decade.' Suddenly the picture was clear. Jack hadn't disliked her, as she'd originally suspected – the opposite had, in fact, been true. He liked her too much but had kept his distance because anything more was unthinkable. And his aloofness all of those years ago was his attempt to stay away from her, to mask his feelings out of loyalty to his brother. But when Brian had callously cast her aside for Danielle, Jack had seen it as a personal betrayal and more than he could bear or forgive.

I should go back, she thought, suddenly seized with the impulse to run to Jack. But what would she say? It was all so long ago, and their case was over now. She had her own life and it was time for her to return to it. An announcement came over the loudspeaker then, calling her flight. 'I've got to go.' She picked up her bag.

'Thank you,' Brian said with more sincerity

than she had ever heard him speak.

For a moment she thought he might try to hug or kiss her and she was more relieved than disappointed when he did neither.

'Good luck,' she managed. 'I mean, with the baby and all.'

She turned, and this time did not look back.

Epilogue

PHILADELPHIA, 2009

Charlotte set her bags down in the entranceway. Instantly, Mitzi was at her feet, purring as she rubbed up against Charlotte's legs in equal parts recrimination and greeting. Charlotte picked her up. 'Yes, I missed you too,' she said in a soothing voice as she walked into the kitchen, noting with relief that the dry cat food was still half full and the water bowl the neighbor had changed remained unsoiled. She freshened the water and opened a can of wet food.

Leaving behind a satisfied Mitzi, she walked into the living room. As she looked around, a wave of warmth washed over her. The renovated row house, with its high ceilings and exposed beams and brick, had been a labor of love, a six-month project on which she spent every spare minute and dollar. The results had been well worth the effort: it was the perfect home, comfortable and airy, with sunlight dancing across the hardwood floors.

Charlotte sank into the overstuffed blue chair by the fireplace, curling her legs beneath her and picking up the pile of mail that had accumulated during her absence. Sadness welled up in her unexpectedly. Despite her love for the house, being back here felt, well, hollow somehow. There was much to be done, of course – laundry from the trip to be washed and groceries purchased, and tomorrow she would be in the office at the crack of dawn to make sure that Kate Dolgenos was doing everything she should to help Marquan. It seemed to pale, though, in comparison to Roger and Magda and the decades-old mystery they had solved, like something right out of a novel. But that had been a moment. And life couldn't be all moments, could it?

As if on cue, Jack appeared unbidden in her mind. What was he doing now? Was he still clearing up the aftermath of the Dykmans case or had he returned to other matters in his private practice? Was he bored too?

She took out the business card he had given her shortly after her arrival in Munich, considering. There was an e-mail address and she thought about dropping him a message saying hi and ... what exactly? They had not left things at a keep-in-touch kind of stage. She recalled the night they spent together, the looks they exchanged, and the quiet understanding they seemed to share. Yet a business card was all that remained, maybe because their lives had pulled them in two different directions or because things were too complex. No, a casual e-mail message would be too much and at the same time not enough.

Then she heard Brian's words, telling her that his brother had feelings for her years ago. Why hadn't Jack said anything? Well why, more to the point, hadn't she? In her mind she saw that moment in the hotel bar the other evening, when she could have owned up to how she felt. She wanted to blame it on the interruption, the fact that Brian had arrived before she had a chance. But there was always a way if one really wanted something. No, the truth was she simply hadn't been brave enough.

It's too late now, she decided, setting the mail aside. What's done is done. Standing, she pushed the thoughts from her mind and set about unpacking and fitting back into the life that she had chosen.

Charlotte stepped out of the Criminal Justice Center and walked to the corner. A sharp breeze gusted down the street, sending leaves and a piece of crumpled newspaper flying. She drew her coat more tightly around her midsection. It was early November now, more than a month since she had returned from Europe, and the air had an unmistakable feel of the impending winter.

She crossed Market Street and made her way toward the office, still thinking about the hearing she had had that morning for Laquanna, a fifteen-year-old accused of drug possession. The girl was undoubtedly guilty, but if there was only some way to get her a reduced sentence in some sort of rehabilitative program...

She walked into the office, still lost in thought. 'Whoa!' Doreen cried, as Charlotte collided with her, sending the stack of files she was carrying flying in all directions.

'Sorry,' Charlotte mumbled, stooping to pick up the scattered papers. 'I wasn't paying attention.'

'Shocking,' Doreen replied, a note of humor in her voice. Charlotte's absentmindedness when focusing on a case was legendary. She had once accidentally walked into a toilet and broken a toe while preparing for a closing argument in a trial.

Charlotte handed the papers to Doreen, who promptly passed them back again. 'I was just taking these to your mailbox,' she said.

Charlotte groaned. Her colleagues might have covered her cases while she was gone, but the mountain of paperwork they'd left behind for her was taking forever to clear. 'Thanks.' She started down the hall.

'Wait, there's–' Doreen began, but Charlotte continued on, lost in thought.

Charlotte stepped into her office and stopped short as a tall figure caught her eye. Someone was there. Her breath caught. A male visitor sat in the chair across from her desk once more. Only this time it wasn't Brian.

'Jack,' she gasped.

He stood up, unfolding himself in a way that was unmistakably familiar from his brother's earlier appearance. 'Hello, Charley.'

A strange sense of déjà vu came over her. It was more than just the reminders of Brian's earlier visit, she realized. She had seen this. She pulled the image from a haze of dreams, half buried in the jet lag of the days following her return. She didn't believe in prescience, but in the dream she had envisioned Jack sitting exactly like he was now. She had woken up shaken by the vividness of the image, telling herself that it couldn't happen. But now he was actually here, a fact that was almost unfathomable. What, she tried to recall from her dream, had he wanted?

'I don't understand,' she managed. 'What are

you doing here?'

'Just passing through because of a case,' he replied. His words echoed Brian's weeks earlier, but with Jack, the excuse seemed even more highly implausible. Was he serious?

No, of course not. Jack had no business that would bring him to Philadelphia. Her mind raced. Perhaps a personal matter had brought him back to the States. 'Is your family all right?'

'Everyone's fine.' She waited for him to offer an alternative explanation for his visit, but he remained silent, his gaze holding her own. No, he had come to see her. Her stomach tightened.

A wave of conflicting emotions washed over her then, surprise and confusion and curiosity mixing with the fact that she was, well, genuinely glad to see him. The tiny office space suddenly seemed too cramped to hold both of them and everything she was feeling. She didn't want to run away from him, as she had when Brian came looking for her. But she needed air.

'Is there somewhere we can get some coffee?' he asked, sensing her discomfort.

She nodded, setting the papers down on her desk and gesturing for him to follow. She could feel the curious stares of her coworkers as they walked through the office and they wondered about this tall, attractive man, the second such visitor to the normally solitary Charlotte in recent months. She stole a glance upward at Jack. His eyes were clearer and he seemed less haggard than she remembered, as if a weight had somehow been lifted. And the stubble that usually covered his cheeks and chin was gone as well. 'You've shaved,' she remarked abruptly.

He half smiled. 'I thought it was time for a change. How did Marquan's case go?'

'Really well,' she replied. 'Better than expected. Kate Dolgenos did a great job and Marquan got four years in a decent facility, followed by parole. They've got a vocational training program there so he should still be able to graduate high school on time if he really applies himself.' If. There were still a hundred roadblocks between Marquan and a happy ending.

'That's great, though you're being too modest. I'm sure you had a lot to do with the result.'

Neither spoke further as they stepped out onto the street, stopping at the hot dog vendor. As Jack handed her one of the Styrofoam cups, she couldn't help but contrast the dark bitter brew with the foamy lattes they had enjoyed in Munich weeks earlier. But he took a sip, not seeming to notice. 'Roger's name was cleared,' he said.

'I know. I saw the story in the press.' The article had been brief, just a mention that a document had been found exonerating Roger posthumously. It had seemed so inadequate – there was no reference to Magda or the clock or all of the passion and heartbreak that underscored the tale. A secret history left for only a few of them to know.

He raised his coffee cup once more. 'I helped to settle his affairs these past few weeks. Anna, I mean Anastasia, will get everything. Per Roger's wishes in his will, she's donating the house in Wadowice, which will become a museum dedicated to prewar life in the town, showing the relations between Jews and Poles.'

Charlotte nodded. Amidst the horrific legacy of the war, the backdrop of pogroms and hatred that had painted the centuries black, there was a quieter side of the story that almost no one ever heard, a tapestry woven from the simple fabric of everyday life, with Poles and Jews coexisting peacefully beside one another, interacting as customers and tradesmen, teachers and students, guests and friends. Even lovers, she thought, picturing Roger and Magda as a young couple. Anna's museum would pay tribute to both of her parents and their unspoken love by trying to illuminate a tiny piece of that tapestry so that visitors who stopped in when passing through the town could see more than just blood.

'So it's really over.'

'It is.'

'I appreciate your telling me.' She swallowed. 'Though you came an awfully long way to do it.' He looked away, not answering. 'I mean, I'm sure you've got a lot of work to catch up on at the firm, now that Roger's case has ended.'

'I quit.'

'Oh.' She studied his profile. What was he running away from this time?

'That is, I'm taking on a new project,' he said. 'I've been given a grant by the Ark Foundation to start up a new nonprofit. We're going to take on cases like Roger's, finding forensic and other evidence to protect those who may have been wrongfully accused. Kind of like an equal justice project, only on an international level.'

'You're changing teams,' she remarked. 'Crossing over to the dark side of defense work.'

'Well, Roger's case convinced me that things aren't always as black and white as they seem.' He cleared his throat. 'You had a lot to do with that too.' He paused. 'Come work with me, Charley.'

She stared at him, too surprised to speak. 'I-I don't understand,' she managed finally.

'We're going to need someone like you, who's good with the witnesses and the evidence.' He half smiled once more. 'Whose instinct to defend the accused and whose sense of justice are stronger than mine.'

He was serious. Just over a month ago he hadn't even wanted her working on Roger's case. You could have anyone, she wanted to say. The best investigators and criminal attorneys in Europe. 'I need your help,' he added.

The same thing that Brian had said, she mused. The request for help, someone always wanting what she had to give, or more. But what about her needs? She opened her mouth to tell him no thank you, that she had a life here and a job that she loved. But then she remembered the thrill of racing round Europe working on Roger's case. With Jack. The murmur of emotions in her head rose to a roar.

'Why didn't you just call?' she asked abruptly. Jack's eyes widened. 'Don't get me wrong. I'm glad to see you.' She could feel a faint blush begin to creep up from her collar. 'And I'm flattered really. But wouldn't it have been easier to phone, or even e-mail?'

'I suppose,' he admitted slowly, gazing down the street once more as though the answers lay in the traffic snarled at Broad and Chestnut. He rubbed his chin in the now-familiar way that meant he was choosing his next words with care. 'I certainly didn't plan on this. I mean, I considered you for the position right away and I was planning to reach out to you as soon as I got settled in at The Hague. I knew as soon as the grant came through that you were the right person. You just ... make things work so much better.'

Easy, she thought, as a lump formed in her throat. He could just be talking about the job. But his tone seemed to suggest something deeper.

He continued, 'Then yesterday morning, as I was wrapping things up at my office, some flowers arrived. They were from Anna – I mean, Anastasia – with a note expressing her appreciation for everything we had done for her family, especially Roger.'

'That was thoughtful,' Charlotte remarked, unsure how the information related to her or his job offer.

'The flowers...' he paused. 'They were asters.' He turned back, his eyes meeting hers squarely. 'Asters. What are the odds?'

They are a fall flower, she wanted to say, but did not. 'What a coincidence,' she remarked instead, managing to keep her voice even as his gaze held her own.

'It was more than that,' he insisted. 'Like a sign or something.'

Quite an admission, she reflected, from someone who purported not to believe in fate. 'Or another chance,' he added. She nodded, understanding. He'd taken it as another opportunity to tell her everything that he had left unsaid years ago, a second or maybe even a third chance, if you counted their missed connection years ago when she had been with Brian.

Of course even now, Jack had not said everything – his words, as always, fell shy of what he really meant. But she knew how much it had taken for him to go this far after everything he had been through – knew because it was that hard for her too. He had been brave enough to go where she had only wished to the other night in the hotel.

Still, the revelation of his feelings did not make it easier to confront the dilemma that his proposal, so dramatic and unexpected, posed for her. 'I don't know,' she said finally, swallowing. 'I mean, I need to think about it.'

A brief flicker crossed his face and he blinked. It was not surprise, she realized; he did not share Brian's sense of entitlement that the world would give him exactly what he wanted. Rather, he was disappointed. 'I'm flying back tonight,' he said. He had not, she calculated, been on the ground twenty-four hours. 'If you want to call me before then, that's great. Otherwise I'll be in Munich tomorrow, then on to the Netherlands to open our office.'

'That's quick,' she observed.

'There's a case involving a defendant at The Hague that's scheduled to go to trial in two months and we want to be up and running in order to jump in on that one before it's too late.' There was a gleam in his eyes as though a part of him, long dormant, had come back to life. 'It's a Bosnian doctor who's been accused of aiding in interrogations, but we really think that this is a case of mistaken identity–'

'Really?' It was still hard to imagine Jack switching sides after all of the work he had done at the Tribunal.

'Yes, and there's a chance we can get our hands on some DNA evidence–' Seeing her smile, he broke off in mid-sentence. 'What is it?'

'You just seem so idealistic is all.'

He laughed. 'And you seem more cynical. Kind of like we switched places somewhere along the way.'

Not exactly, Charlotte thought. Meeting Roger and learning the truth about what he had done, making the worst possible choice for all of the right reasons, had certainly challenged some of her long-held assumptions about guilt and inno-cence. It wasn't cynicism, though – just a more grounded perspective. But it wasn't something she could readily explain to Jack.

'So we've got to move quickly,' Jack continued. 'Of course, if you need more time, take it. I'll – I mean, we will be waiting.'

He lowered his head and before she could react, his lips were on hers, purposeful and firm. She gasped. Though it was not the passion they had known in the hotel or even the attic, the promise and intent were unmistakable.

Before she could respond, he broke away, straightening. He gave her one long last look and it seemed for a moment as though there was something else. 'Take care, Charley.' Then he was gone, striding toward Broad Street and hailing a cab.

Go after him, a voice not her own seemed to say. But she stood numbly, watching as he sped away, letting him leave again. A moment later, as she stood alone on the street, she wondered if she had imagined it. Had Jack actually been here? It had not been a dream this time, though. And he had asked her to do ... what exactly? To pack up her life again, not as Brian had asked, for a few weeks, but this time for good.

She walked back up to her office, looked around. How could she just up and leave? This was her whole world. She had a job helping the accused, but Jack was offering her the chance to do much the same work on a different scale. And beyond that, the office was just four walls. She had a house she could sell (or lease, if she wanted to keep it as a safety net), a cat she could take with her.

But for what? A job she didn't know anything about. She had no idea how much it paid (not that it would be hard to top her salary as a public defender) or how stable it would be. And what about working with Jack? Their interactions had been prickly at best on the Dykmans case, heated and confrontational as often as not. It was possible that they would hate each other, that it would be a disastrous working relationship.

I'm really considering it, she realized. A few months ago, the notion of picking up and leaving the safety of this world would have been unthinkable. But stepping away from it and working on the case with Jack had helped her to put some of the old ghosts to rest, and she could contemplate possibilities now that she hadn't known existed.

She saw Jack's eyes as she entered her office, the spark of hope and something more. He could have gotten anyone to work with him. He could have called or e-mailed. But he had come all the way to Philadelphia to ask her himself. No, this was about something more than a job.

A life in Europe, working together with Jack. Suddenly the potential unfurled before her. Now she was freed from all the baggage of the past, finally free to live her dreams.

She picked up her bag and started out, closing the door firmly behind her.

Acknowledgements

The inspiration for this book was a beautiful, antique timepiece, known as an anniversary clock, which my husband, Phillip, gave me for our first wedding anniversary. I was intrigued by the history of this unique type of clock and as I began to research it, I imagined the lives it had touched over the past century and *The Things We Cherished* began to unfold.

Of course any writer will tell you that the road from inspiration to finished book is long and I am grateful to the many people who have taken this journey with me. I'm indebted to my incredible agent, Scott Hoffman, and his team at Folio Literary and Film Management, and my gifted editors, Phyllis Grann and Jackeline Montalvo, and their team at Doubleday, for sharing my vision for this book and bringing it to life. I'd also like to recognize my UK editor, Rebecca Saunders, and her team at Sphere for their excellent work.

The Things We Cherished enabled me to return to the familiar and beloved terrain of Jewish life in Europe and I'm so grateful to the many people and places that have inspired and influenced my work. While the events and some of the places in the book are fictional, I have learned a great deal from certain historical works, including: *The Pity of It All: A Portrait of the German-Jewish Epoch 1743–1933* by Amos Elon and *A Community Under Siege: The Jews of Breslau Under Nazism* by Abraham Ascher. As usual, the mistakes are all mine.

Just to make it interesting, I wrote this book during the same period of time in which I was pregnant with and gave birth to my twin daughters, Charlotte and Elizabeth. Finishing the book while caring for three children under the age of two (including my wonderful son, Ben) was no easy feat and I owe deep thanks to an army of family and friends: my husband, Phillip, who is the most hands-on father I've ever seen or heard of; my parents, Gene and Marsha, who have stopped their lives to help care for my kids; my brother, Jay; my in-laws, Ann and Wayne; plus Joanne and Sarah and others too many to name. Without you, none of this would be possible or worthwhile.

The publishers hope that this book has given you enjoyable reading. Large Print Books are especially designed to be as easy to see and hold as possible. If you wish a complete list of our books please ask at your local library or write directly to:

Magna Large Print Books
Magna House, Long Preston,
Skipton, North Yorkshire.
BD23 4ND

This Large Print Book for the partially sighted, who cannot read normal print, is published under the auspices of

THE ULVERSCROFT FOUNDATION